Shooting Sean

Colin Bateman

W F HOWES LTD

This large print edition published in 2002 by
W F Howes Ltd
Units 6/7, Victoria Mills, Fowke Street
Rothley, Leicester LE7 7PJ

1 3 5 7 9 10 8 6 4 2

First published in 2001
by HarperCollins*Publishers*

A CIP catalogue record for this book is available
from the British Library

ISBN 1 84197 515 X

Typeset by Palimpsest Book Production Limited,
Polmont, Stirlingshire
Printed and bound in Great Britain
by Antony Rowe Ltd, Chippenham, Wilts.

For Andrea and Matthew

CHAPTER 1

Las Vegas is my kind of town.

Which is a pity because I was sitting in a gentrified bar on Great Victoria Street, Belfast's Golden Mile, or kilometre, and not that golden, waiting to meet the shitehawk who'd cheated me out of thousands.

It had been raining for thirteen days in a row. It wasn't quite a deluge of biblical proportions, but it felt like it. It thundered out of the sky, stinging. It wasn't even nice weather for ducks; they hid under bushes and dreamt about small children with mouldy bread. Or so I imagined. Summer was supposed to be just around the corner, which would have been fine in a square world, but it was round, and it felt like we could wait for ever.

I sat nursing a Diet Coke, my back to the window, wondering if they'd played the music as loud in my day, and then checked my reflection in the bar mirror in case I'd suddenly turned into Val Doonican.

The place was buzzing with students. They all looked perfectly normal and happy. Many sported little goatee beards. Some of the guys did as

1

well. They were young and enjoying themselves, although for all I knew they were out of their heads on Ecstasy or whatever drug was in vogue or *Cosmopolitan*. I was out of touch. I had not been in a bar in months.

This had been my local, once. And now I didn't know a soul. Not even a barman. The bouncer on the door had glanced at me on the way in and I'd nodded hello, but I think he was only wondering what an old git like me was doing hanging about in a student bar. I could have stopped and explained to him that it hadn't always been a trendy student bar, that it had once just been a spit-and-sawdust pub with peeling wallpaper and a dart board and piss-covered toilet floors and a cast of mouldy old men who smelt of pigeons, sweat and pigeon sweat, who studied the racing form in the *Daily Mirror* and complained about the loudness of the music from a jukebox which contained only singles by Smokie, Racing Cars and Abba. I could have told him all of this, but whoever tried explaining anything to a bouncer without getting thumped?

And then my arm was jostled and Sam Cameron was standing there grinning like the tooth fairy suddenly stumbled on a set of dentures.

'Dan,' he said, 'how are ya?' Before I managed to get my scowl in place he said: 'Jeez, this place has changed.' He lifted my glass and sniffed at it.

'Diet Coke,' I said.

'Ah. Right.' He raised an inquisitive eyebrow.

'I don't drink any more,' I said. A moment later I added, 'Or any less. I'm on duty.'

'Working?'

'Babysitting.'

Cameron looked about him for any sign of a baby.

'In about half an hour. So make it quick.'

'Dan, I detect a certain chilliness towards me.'

'You always were quick on the uptake.'

'I didn't think you'd be the type to bear a grudge.'

'And I didn't think you'd have the nerve to show your face north of the border after what you did to me.'

'*Dan*,' he said. He turned to the bar and ordered himself a Sprite. He glanced back, jangling the money for it in his hand for a moment. 'A Sprite and a Diet Coke. How the mighty have fallen, eh?'

'Right.'

He smiled and settled himself into a seat. He took a drink. He smiled. He took another drink. He smiled.

I said, 'What the fuck are you looking so happy about?'

He shrugged. 'Just full of the joys of spring.'

'Well, if you're so fucking happy, howse about giving me the sixty grand you owe me?'

'Dan. C'mon. I don't owe you that.'

'Yes, you do, you piggy-eyed, pudding-bowl-haircutted bastard. You floppy-mouthed, shite-stirring . . . bollocks, thing, stuff . . .'

3

I trailed off. I'd even lost the knack of . . . *that*.

'You've been preparing that one for a while,' he said.

'On the contrary, I've been trying not to think about you at all.'

It was a lie, of course. I'd thought about him a lot. And after discussing our situation with Patricia before coming to this meeting, we'd agreed maturely that either I got some financial satisfaction or I splattered what little brains he had over the footpath.

It went like this. Two years before, he had hired me to write a book about Fat Boy McMaster's unsuccessful challenge for the world heavyweight title, a doomed attempt to take Mike Tyson's crown at Madison Square Garden on St Patrick's Day. I'd realised before I was long into it that it didn't matter a twig that Fat Boy was hopelessly outclassed, what was important was the possibility that his manager Geordie McClean would make millions from it. Fat Boy was on funeral expenses. Anyway, it turned out to be more than just a fight. Fat Boy's sister got kidnapped by some renegade Sinn Feiners and he got blackmailed into calling for the British to get out of Ulster, as if they needed any encouragement. In some small way I helped to get her back. Fat Boy put up a good show in the ring, got flattened in the end, avoided hospital, became a national hero, wrote his own book, cut a couple of records, then landed his own television chat show.

The boy done well.

I was one of the first guests on his chat show. My own book on his illustrious career had sold extremely well, particularly in America, and I was in line to receive anywhere between sixty and a hundred thousand in royalties – Cameron had been too cheapskate to come up with anything much by way of advance. Two weeks before he was due to hand over the cheque, *he* got hit with a libel suit. Not me. Cameron had published a book about the music business; the author had carelessly named the head of a radio station as someone who wasn't beyond accepting cash in return for airplay, and the head had sued. A jury awarded him half a million in damages, and Cameron's company went down the tubes with my money. So Fat Boy invited me onto national television to discuss my poverty and have a good laugh.

He was a good guy, but, hey, this was television.

What you don't have, you don't miss.

That's the old saying.

But fuck it, I missed it.

What was worse was seeing Cameron bounce back a few weeks later with a brand-new company and hit number one in the bestseller lists with his first publication, *The Little Book of Panic*, a ridiculous farrago of homespun philosophy for the e-generation that earned him a million.

No wonder spring was in the fucking air.

'So at least you're in a position to pay me back.'

5

'No, I'm in a position to pay you to do something else.'

'I wouldn't work for you if you were the last person on earth.'

'Yes, you would, Dan. You're here.'

'I was curious.'

'More than that. You're short of cash.'

'I'm not short of cash.'

'Yes, you are. I haven't seen your by-line in a year.'

I shrugged. He had a point. Somehow, after having a bestseller, it gets difficult to go back to scrambling around for little stories about little people. Especially when some fucker owes you sixty grand.

'Dan, you have to let bygones be bygones.'

'That's what Mark Chapman said.'

'I'm not Mark Chapman.'

'That's a matter of opinion.'

'Dan, legally . . .'

'I don't give a fuck about *legally*. I give a fuck about what's right.'

He took a sip of his Sprite. 'Since when?'

I sighed. I got up off my seat. 'I have to go.'

He nodded. 'I didn't know you had a kid.'

'I'll sell you him for sixty grand. Ginger hair included.'

'Dan, don't be so hostile.'

He tapped his fingers on the bar. I sat again. It was raining hard against the window. The hip-hop crap on the jukebox was really getting on my wick.

6

'Did you ever finish that novel?'

'Yes.'

'I don't suppose you'd care to show . . .'

'Fuck off.'

'Do you go to the movies at all, Dan?'

'Are you asking me out?'

'No, I'm asking you if you go to the movies at all.'

'Some.'

'You'll know Sean O'Toole, then.'

'You don't have to go to the movies to know Sean O'Toole. Everybody knows Sean O'Toole. He's a fucking fixture in *Hello*. Lifestyles of the rich and vacant. Patricia reads it all the time. She loves the expensive houses she can't have because some cunt ripped sixty grand off of me.'

Cameron stood up. He took out his wallet and extracted a card. He wrote a number on the back of it, then placed it on my beer mat. My Diet Coke mat. 'Dan, I'm staying at the Europa. Give me a call if you calm down. Give my regards to Trish. And stop being such a wanker.'

He walked out of the bar.

Nobody calls me a wanker and gets away with it.

There were girls, students, student girls perhaps, looking at me. I shrugged. I ordered a pint of Harp.

No. Sorry. *Everybody* calls me a wanker and gets away with it.

CHAPTER 2

I spent another three hours in the bar. It was a re-familiarisation process. It wasn't exactly unpleasant. I didn't talk to anybody. I listened. I watched. I drank. It could all be counted as research, and therefore tax deductible. Or so I deluded myself. I didn't pay tax. How could you pay tax on fuck-all squared in a box? Patricia was earning twice as much as I was and only working three days a week in the civil service and the rest of the time looking after Little Stevie, and the government paid for that as well.

I was at a low ebb.

I needed a motivation class.

I had no job, and could barely manage my signature without getting writer's cramp. I was broke. I had a wife I loved and a child I mostly kind of loved, and my social life had gone to the wall.

No more nights out, no more parties, Jesus, almost no more friends. There are compensations to having a child, of course, just sometimes it's hard to put your finger on them. Particularly when it's not your child, although I tried not to think about that, or even mention it, unless I was drunk

8

and then I'd tell complete strangers even if they weren't the slightest bit interested and standing on the other side of the bar eating crisps.

I was a goldfish.

A hamster on a wheel.

It wasn't Patricia's fault. She didn't keep me on a tight leash. She'd say, go out, but then add *if you must.* In the old days I wouldn't have heard that last bit, or I'd ignore it, but now it was harder, harder with Little Stevie playing on the floor. He was a wee cutie. He loved me to bits.

He was born with ginger hair. Then for a brief, hopeful moment it faded. Then it grew back with a vengeance and I was depressed. I don't know why. There is nothing spectacularly bad about ginger hair. It's not as if Hitler was ginger. Or Neil Diamond. Indeed, one is inclined to speculate how much worse the world might have been if either of them had been born what we sarcastically refer to as strawberry blond, but in truth the problem would not have arisen. Nobody votes ginger, and recording contracts are not doled out to ginger baps. Think about it. Name one.

Simply Red.

Well, you can stick your Simply Red records up your hole.

By the time I left the bar the sun had finally begun to poke through the clouds. It hadn't quite stopped raining, but it was light enough to walk as far as a bus stop. We no longer had our terraced house in the Holy Land. Sold up, moved three or four miles up the road, still in Belfast, but out into the suburbs into a nice bungalow with an overgrown garden and a nice view of other nice bungalows. The estate should have been called *Nice Bungalows*, but it wasn't. It was called *Fairview*, and whoever named it must have had a keen sense of humour, or none at all.

When I finally arrived outside our nice bungalow I found Patricia standing in the garden crazy paving. She just looked at me, her hair sweated and little bits of cement on her face like the Gorgon with dandruff, and I walked past her into the house for a pee and all I had was a tut to accompany me.

When I had finished and downed a pint of water, I stood in the doorway watching her for several moments. There was a pile of broken flagstones she'd had delivered the week before, and there was sand and cement powder and buckets of water, and she was mixing it all up with an expertise I found frightening. I couldn't even mix drinks without falling over. Little Stevie was deftly mixing and moulding his own cement. I'm not sure exactly what he was making, but it seemed certain that it would soon harden into something that I would later break my toe on.

'You should take that up professionally,' I said to Patricia as she hammered another piece of flag-stone into place. She didn't look up. 'You could call it *Patricia's Crazy Paving*. Or just shorten it to *Patricia's Crazy*.'

She sighed and said, 'You're not funny, Dan.'

'I think you'll find my readers disagree.'

'You don't have any readers, Dan. That was then, this is now.'

'S.E. Hinton.'

'I'm sorry?'

'*That Was Then, This Is Now*. A novel by S.E. Hinton, she did *Rumblefish* and *The Outsiders*. Not Camus, the other one with the teen gangs and . . .'

'Will you stop parading your fucking literary shite and give me a hand?'

'Did I ever tell you that if you managed to clean up your language you could pass for Wilde himself?'

'Did I ever tell you, you were an arsehole?'

'Marty Wilde, of course.' I remained in the doorway. After a while I said, 'I don't garden, Trish.'

'Above it, are you?'

I thought about that for several moments, then nodded.

'For the last six months,' she said, 'you seem to have been above everything.'

'Except you.'

She looked at me.

'You may take something sexual out of that if you wish,' I said.

'Don't start, Dan.'

'What did you think this morning when you got up: either I'll have sex with my husband or I'll crazy pave the garden? Shit, I think I'll crazy pave the garden.'

'Don't be such a wanker, Dan.'

There comes a point when being called a wanker changes from being one person's abuse to being the consensus of opinion. I sighed. Little Stevie, having tired of art, came up and put a handful of wet cement on my groin.

My favourite trousers.

I shouted at him and he started crying.

I picked him up and he put his cement hands on my favourite shirt.

I didn't used to be like this about clothes. Maybe Trish was right. Maybe I was getting airs and graces.

'Did you talk to Sam?'

'Si.'

'Did you get the money.'

'Ni.'

'Did you kill him?'

'Nay.'

She sighed and hammered another broken flag into place. 'Do you want to tell me what happened?'

I shook my head. She looked at me. I said: 'He wants me to work for him again.'

'He didn't offer you the money?'

'No. Of course not. It's gone. We know that.'

'So what did you say?'

'I told him to fuck off.'

'Fair enough.'

'Fuck . . . off,' said Little Stevie.

'Oh, shit,' said Trish, dropping a flag and hurrying across to take Little Stevie Cement out of my arms.

12

'Shit,' said Little Stevie.

'Oh, fuck,' I said.

'Stop it, for fuck sake!' Trish shouted, turning away with Little Stevie in her arms and giggling at the same time. Then she launched into a long involved story about naughty words and what happens to little boys who use them. It was pretty tame stuff. What she really needed was a big stick with a nail in the end, but I guess times have changed.

I took him inside and put him down in front of the telly with the Cartoon Network. *Scooby-Doo* was on. Except it was some crappy modern version with a Scooby Junior and not so much acid. Still, he didn't seem to mind. I could already see cement prints forming up on the settee, but I let him be. Indoors, like outdoors, was Patricia's domain.

I took two cans of Harp from the fridge. They were the last two of a crate I'd bought at Christmas, and the fact that they were still unopened constituted some kind of sad personal best. They were exactly three months past their drink-by date. I had no idea what drinking expired alcohol could do to you beyond giving you a sore head in the morning, but I was prepared to take the risk. I'm that kind of guy. Living life on the edge, and formerly, beneath the hedge. I gave a can to Patricia and she nodded gratefully. She popped it. I popped mine. We didn't clink tins. There was no need to. We loved each other, we just had a funny way of showing it.

She said: 'What are you going to do?'

'About life in general, or general Sam?'

'General Sam.'

I shrugged. 'As you know, I don't have any opinions of my own, I come to you for that.'

'Well, is he offering to pay you for what he wants you to do?'

'We didn't get into it.'

'But he must be pretty keen on you doing this job, whatever it is, or he wouldn't have travelled up to meet you knowing what he did to you.'

'I suppose.'

'So whatever it is, he knows he's going to have to pay you well for it.'

'I suppose.'

'So why not take the job, get paid up front, and then tell him to fuck off.'

'Because then he'd sue me and then we'd be in even worse financial straits than we are now.'

'Okay. Good point.' She thought for a moment. 'Then do the job, but do it badly. Nobody can prove you did it badly. You'll still get paid.'

'But wouldn't that be rather cold and calculating?'

Patricia nodded. She looked rather beautiful standing there like a builder. She loved me dearly but didn't know what to do with me. And likewise. She took a first sip of her beer.

'This tastes odd,' she said.

'I know,' I said, 'but we must persevere.'

14

CHAPTER 3

We went to the Virgin cinema on the Dublin Road. Sam and I. He bought the tickets. I insisted on a large salted popcorn, a bag of Opal Fruits and a vat of Diet Coke. He smiled knowingly. We sat in a double seat. Others smiled knowingly. We ignored them. We weren't there to relax. We were there to work. It wasn't exactly working down a coal mine or ritually slaughtering cattle for the lucrative eastern markets, but it was doing something I didn't want to do and getting paid for it, and to my mind that was work.

The lights went down, the music went up. It was a modern cinema and the sound was deafening. I sat with my fingers in my ears. I could see Sam looking at me out of the corner of his eye. I knew what he was thinking. That I was going soft. That I, who had cranked out the Clash past the pain barrier, was cowering down because of a mere movie soundtrack. Perhaps he had a point. I was out of the loop. Music, drink, sex. Once you lose them, you lose them big. Only strong will and determination could get you back in. And I am nothing if not strong-willed. Although

15

I would settle for two out of the three at any one time, and in any combination.

The movie was called *Light Years from Home* and it was a science fiction effort starring Sean O'Toole. Our Sean. From just down the road, a hop, skip and a jump away. We tended to talk like that though we didn't know him from Adamski and he hadn't lived here since year dot. He had no training as such, just done a few stunts, a few walk-ons; he'd played a heavy in some local TV drama, nothing much more than a bit part, but he'd been spotted by a vacationing Hollywood casting director, and within a year he was a leading man in an action adventure which grossed $150 million, and he was made. Sean was, is, a big, attractive man girls swooned over, but the thing I liked about him was that he didn't come off with any of the usual wank about his art; he made it clear that he went to Hollywood for the money and the fact that out there 'it doesn't rain all the fucking time'. He seemed to enjoy a drink and the company of glamorous women, and I could relate to that. Patricia could be glamorous when she didn't have cement on her face.

We settled into the film. After fifteen minutes of alien insects exploding into green slime I whispered to Sam, 'Why are we watching this farrago of shite?'

'Sean O'Toole.'

'Yes, I gather that.'

'For purposes of comparison.'

'With what?'

16

'I'm just getting to that. Shall we adjourn to the bar?'

They were words lifted directly from my gravestone, but I wasn't giving him the satisfaction of knowing that. I stifled a smile and came out with something gruff and macho, although actually it was popcorn stuck in my throat. As we stood up he nodded down at the half-ton of popcorn and the Diet Coke and the Opal Fruits and he hissed, 'You're not leaving them, are you?'

'Of course not,' I said, and reached for them, deliberately kicking the popcorn over in the process, which in turn tumbled the Diet Coke. For good measure I accidentally slapped the Opal Fruit bag off the arm of the seat and they spilled out into the growing lake of Diet Coke on the carpet. 'Oops,' I said.

I can be a cruel man, when I try. Mind, at this rate it would take me thirty-four years to pay off the £60,000 he owed me.

We crossed the foyer silently and emerged back out on the Dublin Road. Morrisons was just across the road. It was a new bar made up to look old. The BBC building was opposite so there were a lot of familiar media faces sitting at the bar complaining about bureaucracy. We found a corner table and I looked at Sam expectantly for several moments until he got the hint and went to the bar. He didn't ask what I wanted, though he could probably tell that if he came back with a Diet Coke I would kill him.

17

He brought one pint of Harp for me and a bottle of Corona with a slice of lime wedged into the top.

'If that was ever fashionable, Sam, it certainly isn't now.'

'Who cares? I like it.'

'A commendable attitude.' It was an attitude that clearly extended also to his wardrobe and haircut. I have never been particularly fashionable myself, but I usually try to avoid flying in the face of it. Sam was a sartorial rebel, but I suspect he wasn't even aware of it. One also has to take into account the lack of stylistic judgement which goes hand in hand with Sam's country of origin, i.e. the twenty-six counties of Ireland which are not yet British.

'So,' I said, 'Sean O'Toole. You want a book on Sean O'Toole.'

He nodded.

'Surely there are already books on Sean O'Toole?'

He nodded.

'So what's the angle?'

He removed the slice of lime from the top of his bottle and took a slug. Then he set the bottle down and wiped his fingers deftly across his lips. He fixed me with a professional look and said: 'I want one to coincide with his funeral.'

'What is it?' I asked, familiar with the territory. 'Cancer?'

Sam shook his head.

'Heart? Aids? MS?'

'Bullet.'

'He's been shot?'

'No, but he will be.'

'You mean you're planning on having him shot?'

'No, of course not.'

'Then why so sure?'

'Because I've just read the script of his new movie. And people aren't going to be happy.'

'Who, exactly?'

'Well now.' He took another drink. I looked out of the window. It was starting to spit again. Patricia would be starting to curse. The crazy paving would never get finished. It would be like that house in *Petrocelli*. I took another drink. 'Sean is like most actors who earn a lot of money, he wants respect, but all Hollywood respects is box office. Sure, he gets pampered and paid an obscene amount of money, but you can only get so much and then it starts to become meaningless.'

'I can relate to that.'

'Don't start, Dan.'

I shrugged.

'The best most actors like Sean can hope for is an honorary Oscar if they manage to avoid dying before they're eighty.'

'So?'

'So if they're looking for respect they go down one of two routes. A, they appear in low-budget indie movies and hope to sneak an Oscar nod . . .'

'Like Bruce Willis in *Pulp Fiction* . . .'

'Yeah, or Stallone in *Copland* . . . and usually fall flat on their faces, or they direct. The history of Hollywood is littered with the carcasses of actors who thought they could direct. But occasionally a little gem turns up. Kevin Costner cleaned up with *Dances With Wolves* . . .'

'And had to give it all back with *The Postman* . . .'

'Warren Beatty did it with *Reds*.'

'And then apologised with *Love Affair* and *Dick Tracy*.'

Sam smiled. 'We know our movies. The lesson being . . .'

'Do it once, accept your award, get out while the going is good.'

'Exactly.'

'So Sean wants to direct.'

'No, Sean *is* directing.'

'Really? I hadn't heard.'

'He's raised the money independently of the studios, so there's been no real need to publicise it. He started shooting three weeks ago. It's called *The Brigadier*. Wrote the screenplay, stars, directs. Makes the fucking coffee for all I know.'

'So what's the problem, who wants to kill him?'

'*The Brigadier* is based on the life of Michael O'Ryan.'

'Oh! *Right*. I see.'

And I did see, and suddenly it was clear why Sam was interested in a biography of the soon-to-be late Sean O'Toole. Michael O'Ryan was one of the biggest mass killers known to patriotism. Since the peace deal had gone through he had been living in quiet retirement in Wicklow, but nobody doubted that he still had his fingers on the pulse or the throat of whatever went down in Northern Ireland.

'Wasn't Michael O'Ryan known as the Colonel?' I asked.

'He was. *The Brigadier* is an attempt to fool him into thinking it's about somebody else.'

'I see. Fooled me.' I lifted my drink again. 'I take it Sean's film isn't an affectionate pen portrait?'

Sam shook his head. If Sean O'Toole had the balls to make a film about Michael O'Ryan then fair play to him, and I would make sure my funeral pants were pressed.

CHAPTER 4

The Belfast–Dublin Express has this much in common with the Orient Express: it's a train.

It takes two and a half hours. It used to take four back in the days when you could break up the only rail link between the two countries by placing a bomb on the line, prompting immediate panic, mass evacuation and international condemnation. You pass through Newry, then cross the border – although the only indication of a frontier is the sadly vacant army watchtowers that straddle it – then stop briefly at the former IRA stronghold of Dundalk before passing over the beautiful Boyne River and on to Drogheda where Oliver Plunkett's head sits mouldering in the cathedral before finally pulling into Connolly Street Station in the centre of Dublin. Somewhere along the line you have to get your Queen's shillings changed into De Valera punts. To the international traveller there aren't many other differences. The accent is softer. You will have to keep your eye open for occasional signs in a dead language. And you have to watch you don't step on the beggar mothers with their black-faced children who sit cross-legged on the bridges over the Liffey. It can be lovely and ethereal, equally bleak and frightening. There is heroin and poverty on a scale not dreamt of in Belfast. But it's a town you can get pissed in without having to look over your shoulder. In Belfast you turn into Mr Paranoid. Ireland is filled with artists, musicians and writers. Not just because it's green and mystical, but because there are really good tax breaks for artists, musicians and writers. The most prosperous *artistes* live in splendid fortified mansions just along the coast from Dublin in and around the picturesque little village of Killiney. Rock stars like U2. Chris de Burgh. Even Damon Hill. (There is an art to driving a racing car.) And, of course, Sean O'Toole.

I took a taxi from the station to Jury's Hotel in Ballsbridge and checked in. They asked me how I would be paying and I told them that if past experience was anything to go by probably with my life and the thin girl with the thick spectacles reached deep into her soul for a smile and repeated the question. I said cash and she asked if she could take a swipe of my credit card anyway and I told her truthfully that I didn't have a credit card.

'You don't have a credit card?' She fixed me with the sort of glare that I usually reserved for gypsies and Christians.

'No,' I said.

'That's most unusual,' she said.

'I'm an unusual man,' I said, helpfully.

'Are you here on business?'

23

I nodded.

'But you don't have a credit card?'

'The judge said it wasn't safe to give me one. Not after the mix-up with the elephants.' She opened her mouth, but before anything could come out I said: 'Joke. If it's a problem I can pay a deposit.'

She looked me in the eye and said: 'No, Mr Starkey, that won't be a problem.'

I smiled gratefully and filled in the paperwork. She gave me an electronic key and told me my room was on the eighth floor. I thanked her and said I was expecting a call from Sean O'Toole. 'Aren't we all,' she said.

I barely had enough time to establish that there was no mini-bar in the room when the phone rang and the same receptionist said, 'Sean O'Toole for you, Mr Starkey.'

I thanked her. I would have expected her to say 'somebody claiming to be Sean O'Toole for you', but then I heard his voice and realised that there was no mistaking it. It was a voice that defied mimicry. Soft yet hard. Smooth yet tough. Ladies and gentlemen, but mostly ladies, Sean O'Toole.

I said: 'Sean, I've told you to stop bothering me.'

There was a pause, and I was about to jump in with an apology when there came a long low laugh, like a morning fog rolling over a peat bog, followed swiftly by: 'Dan Starkey. I used to read your column. Whatever happened to it? Bigger and better things, yeah?'

'Smaller and worse,' I said. I thanked him for calling. It was unusual for a star of his magnitude to call anybody directly. I had been expecting a flunky. Sam had said I would be contacted. It was a don't-call-us-we'll-call-you situation. Security around Sean was tight generally, because he was a STAR, and now doubly so because of the subject matter of his new movie. 'How's filming going?' I asked.

'Slowly,' he said. 'The bastard director doesn't know what he's doing.'

I laughed. 'How long have you known Sam?' I asked.

'Too long,' he said.

I was warming to him. 'So how come you've agreed to cooperate on this biography thing?'

'Because he offered me three quarters of a million pounds.'

'Do you *need* three quarters of a million pounds?'

'No, but *The Brigadier* does.'

'Brigadier the person or brigadier the movie?'

'The movie. We had a shortfall in the financing. Sam called at just the right time.'

'So Sam's financing the movie, but doesn't know it? Nice one.'

'It was either that or put my own money into it, and I'm not that bloody stupid.'

'So,' I said, 'when can I come and see you?'

'Come down to the set. Hang around. We'll play it by ear.'

'And is there anything you won't talk about?'

'My wives. My girlfriends. The drugs. The Jewish conspiracy in Hollywood.'

'Are you serious?'

'Rarely.'

We chatted for a couple more minutes. Sean – look, first-name terms already – said it would take a while to clear things with his security people, so I should come along to the set first thing in the morning.

When I put the phone down I lifted my travelling bag and set it on the bed. There were three shirts and four T-shirts inside, enough to do me six months, folded by her own fair hand and thus there was no need to unpack them. Keeping them flat was a Voyager II laptop computer.

I plugged it in, then found the phone socket and connected the modem. In seconds I was hooked into the Internet and typing Sean's name into the Yahoo search engine. I was instantly offered 35,000 documents to choose from. I logged into the newsgroups and found 335 sites dedicated to news and gossip about my friend Sean. It was so easy. It was so *not me* to be able to cope with it. I had withstood the march of progress for many years; calculators, light bulbs and electric toothbrushes had all outfoxed me in their time, but my portable computer was a delight. I loved the idea of being able to write on the hoof and then send a story down the line, although usually to the wrong person. I loved the idea of being able to research a complete book without leaving the sanctity of my

26

hotel room. If I wanted I could do it all from here. I could perform an electronic paste and scissors job on Sean and more than satisfy Patricia's criteria for accepting Sam's job: doing it badly.

There was only one thing stopping me. The lack of a mini-bar. And, I suppose, deep down, buried under great mountains of regrets, dishonesty and empty tins, my conscience.

I exited the web and shut down the computer. There was too much to take in at one sitting. It needed to be sifted through at leisure, and on some-body else's phone bill. It was a remarkable way to get information, and also vaguely unsatisfying. It was too easy. It was like being given the key to the sweetie shop, when the real joy lay in saving your money and buying that one special chocolate bar. It would have taken me a year to gather that much info on Sean in the real world, a year of investigation, subterfuge and sweat. But with this there was no sense of achievement. Perhaps journalism was dying in cyberspace. Or maybe it was just becoming something else.

I lay back on the bed and closed my eyes. I thought about Patricia for a while and how she'd stuck by me even though I was a wanker. We'd been through thick and thin together, but mostly thin. I'd had an affair and she'd had at least two in revenge. There was a child by one of those affairs, a child with ginger hair, Little Stevie. I'd only been gone a couple of hours and I missed him already.

I called her up. I didn't say anything smart. I just said, 'Hello.'

She said: 'What's wrong with you?'

'Nothing. I miss you.'

'You're sure nothing's wrong?'

'I just called to say I love you.'

'Listen, Stevie Wonder, what are you up to?'

'Can I not call and express my love without you accusing me of something?'

'I didn't accuse you of anything.' She paused for a moment. Then, 'I miss you too.'

'Are you sure?'

'Yes, I'm sure. Have you met him yet?'

'I spoke to him on the phone. He seems very nice.'

'He's gorgeous.'

'I'll reserve judgement on that. What're you doing now?'

'I finished the crazy paving. At last. I'm going to have a bath. With my boy.'

'I wish I was there.'

'Hey, you're in Dublin, you're in a hotel, some expenses paid. Relax.'

'I know. I should.'

'But be good.'

'I'm always good.'

'You know what I mean.'

'I know what you mean. Don't worry. I'm going to order some room service, watch some TV, get a good night's sleep. Give Little Stevie a kiss for me, okay? I'll call you in the morning.'

We made kissy noises and I put the phone down. Three minutes later I was downstairs in the bar.

She *told* me to relax.

CHAPTER 5

I was on pint three when a woman settled onto the stool beside me and purred to the barman, 'Calypso coffee, two sugars.'

He had one eye on the racing high up on the wall behind her. He reeled it back in, smiled and said, 'Certainly, madam,' but the look said thanks a bunch. He peeled a damp betting slip off the bar and toddled off to prepare her drink. There is a certain knack to calypso coffee, but it is more time-consuming than difficult. Tia Maria, sugar, hot water, cream, mixed with a final sprinkling of coffee. Best not drunk by the pint.

She was tall, maybe just under six feet. She'd short blonde hair and an asymmetrical Julie Christie kind of a face. She wore a skirt that was half an inch north of decent. Three-inch stiletto heels and a short white leather jacket. Just enough white teeth to suggest she would bite if cornered, or approached. I should have folded up my gratis newspaper and returned to my room, but when the drink's in the wit's out, as my old uncle once said, shortly before he was crushed by a piano. In my heyday three pints would have been a drop in the ocean, but I was so long out of practice, it *was* the ocean, or at least a reasonably unpolluted inland sea with a small but impressive tourist trade.

I smiled round at her. Why not? It was my first real opportunity to practise the lingo, to make sure I could blend seamlessly into my surroundings if the need arose. 'Top of the mornin' to ya,' I said in my finest *Quiet Man* brogue. She managed a short smile and an almost imperceptible nod. It was, of course, a come-on. But I wasn't coming on. I was just messing about. It's what I do. It rarely gets me into trouble. 'What's a fine filly like yerself doin' in a den of iniquity the like o' this?'

'Ordering a drink.'

'Aye, well, you're in the right place for that.' I leaned back in my chair and took a good look at her legs. 'You've a right set of pins on ya, girl, d'ye know that?'

Her eyes narrowed. 'I'm sorry,' she said coolly, 'are you on some sort of drugs?'

'No,' I said.

'Well, your accent's all over the place.'

The barman arrived back with her calypso coffee. 'Will I charge it to your room?'

'No, I'll pay cash.' She had a small leather purse tied about her midriff. No room for cigarettes or make-up. Not even a fork for stabbing obnoxious drunks.

Or money, it appeared. Her face reddened slightly as she tried to make a show of delving into the darkest corners of her purse.

'Let me,' I said magnanimously. She looked up. Gratefulness wasn't exactly etched on her face, but she was in a corner. 'Charge it to my room,' I said.

The barman looked to her for approval. She gave a short nod and a shorter smile and lifted the glass.

'Thanks,' she said.

'No problem. Are you, ahm, working here?'

'Excuse me?'

'I just thought, y'know, the short skirt . . .'

'Thanks for the drink,' she spat, 'now fuck off.' She turned sharply away. I rolled my eyes at the barman; he ignored me. I unfolded my paper and tried to make like it was water off a duck's back.

And then I was slammed off my seat and my lips were sucking the polished wooden floor. It smelt of Flash. *Flash cleans floors fast without scratching.* I rolled and looked groggily up at the woman looking angrily down.

'What gives you the fucking right to insult me like that? You fucking prick.'

'Wanker, actually,' I murmured.

'What?'

'Nothing. I'm sorry.' I pulled myself up to my knees. 'I was only raking. I overestimated your sense of humour.'

'It wasn't funny.'

'It would have been if you were sitting over there.' I pointed across the bar. She followed my finger. There were a couple of elderly ladies sitting at a table laughing at us. 'They run a street theatre company, I was auditioning for a part. My humblest apologies.'

I scrambled to my feet. She looked from me to the ladies, who looked away. I put my hand out.

'You are talking the biggest load of shite,' she said, her eyes no longer quite as angry.

'No, honest native American. They're two of the leading lights in Dublin street theatre.'

She shook her head once, then strode across to a small table a couple of yards behind me. She sat down and cupped her fingers around her hot drink. She glowered angrily across at the old women, who looked away. There was a framed photo of Brendan Behan above her head, one I hadn't seen before, and my eyes lingered on it. She thought I was watching her. So I did, and I gave her a little smile. She looked away again.

'Sorry,' I said.

She ignored me.

'You're from up north,' I said. 'Accent like that, you could cut butter with it.'

She shrugged.

'So am I.'

Her eyes snapped towards mine. 'So we should bond and face the world together?' she spat. 'Northerners are the *last* people who should meet up in other countries.'

'At least you're acknowledging it's another

33

country. We have that much in common. Northern Protestants against the black Irish hordes.'

'Get a life.'

I was on a bar stool. She was sitting down. I was perched at least three feet above her. I lifted my pint. I said, 'Do you mind if I come down to your level?' I nodded at the table.

'After what you said?'

'I was only joking. Misplaced. I'm sorry.'

She rolled her eyes, but she didn't object when I sat down. 'You pack a mean punch,' I said.

'You have to in my business.'

'Oh yeah. What's that?'

'Not what you think, anyway.'

'I apologised for that. Go on. What do you do?'

She let out a sigh. I nodded, raised my eyebrows. She sighed again. Finally she smiled impatiently and said: 'Guess.'

'Do you have to dress like that for your work?'

'No. But it helps. Sometimes.'

'But it's not essential?'

'No.'

There was a sudden shout and we both looked up. The barman was shaking his fist triumphantly at the television. 'Forty to one! Forty to fucking one!' He let out a raucous laugh then looked carefully about the bar. He said, quietly, 'The drinks are on me,' and I was up there like a shot.

'Pint of Harp,' I said, 'and . . .'

'Tequila, if you're asking,' my new friend said.

'Bit of luck on the gee-gees,' I said.

The barman smiled as he poured. 'First this year. You must be good luck.'

The old women, the only other drinkers in the bar, looked hopefully across, but the barman ignored them and they soon returned their attention to each other, neither of them willing to admit that they might be hard of hearing.

I took the drinks back to our table. As I sat I said: 'You're in public relations. It's kind of expected that you dress a bit sexily, but you've gone a little further than that, so you're connected to the entertainment business, any other branch and you'd be considered over the top. But you're obviously not the kind of dodo that just smiles and gives out free T-shirts, so you're an executive of some description. Probably you own your own company, you have some high-profile clients. Pop stars. Possibly they live here as tax exiles, maybe out at Killiney.' I took a sip. 'Close?'

She smiled properly for the first time. It was kind of cute, if you were in the market. 'Maybe. What about you?'

'You tell me.'

She looked as much of me up and down as she could with me sitting behind a table. A finger went to her lip, pulled slightly on the bottom one. She was absolutely beautiful.

'Drunk and lecherous,' she said. 'But I guess that's no way to earn a living. I'd say you were a reporter.'

'Jesus. Is it that obvious?'

35

She nodded. 'I work with a lot of reporters. What're you down for?'

I shrugged. 'This and that.'

'Northern Protestants don't travel down here for this and that. And they don't stay in Jury's and charge drinks for people they don't even know to their room. So you have an expense account.'

I held up my hands. 'Fair enough. I'm down to interview Sean O'Toole.'

'*Seriously*?'

'Seriously.'

I don't know. Was I trying to impress her? Dropping his name? I told myself not. If she worked in the PR business surely she wasn't going to be that thrilled by my meeting a movie star. Yet her eyes were suddenly wide and starry. She reached forward and lightly clutched my knee. 'What's he like?' she gasped.

'Don't know yet. Spoke to him on the phone. Seems okay.'

'God, what did he say?'

I shrugged. 'Nothing much.'

'God, where are you meeting him?'

'Not sure, he's to call back.'

'I *love* Sean O'Toole. Isn't he making a movie down here?'

'Yeah. I think so.'

'Do you know what it is?'

'Not really, no. Dare say I'll find out.'

'You don't give much away.' She took a long sip of her drink. She looked at the table. Then she turned her eyes on me, slightly narrowed now, dark and penetrating. Her lips seemed redder, fuller, the glint of bone-white teeth ever so slightly cannibalistic. 'I'd do anything to meet Sean O'Toole.'

I laughed. I took a drink. Beams of sunlight shone through the bar's single window. It was one of those old Irish pubs, all dark panelling and ancient artefacts. It had probably been knocked together by a specialist theme pub company and was about as authentic as the Turin shroud. It didn't matter to thick American tourists, and it didn't matter to me. What mattered to me was the beautiful girl opposite with her calculating eyes.

'I mean it,' she said.

'I'm sure you do.'

'My company's going through a rough time. If I had a client like Sean O'Toole, even just for his Irish stuff, I'd be made.'

'Well,' I said.

'Take me with you. To meet him.'

'Sorry,' I said. 'I can't.'

'Go on, please.'

'Really, I can't.'

'I'll pay you if you want.'

'Really, I can't.'

'A thousand quid. Just for an introduction. Just to get me onto the set.'

'Sorry,' I said.

'Please.'

'I can't.'

I took another drink. She had changed in a

minute from a gorgeous, intense, self-confident woman into a teenybopper.

She leant forward across the table. I felt an urgent need to check out the table. The fact that her small breasts were almost perfectly exposed by her new position was incidental. Or coincidental. Or occidental. Words were not easy to come by. She whispered. 'I can make it worth your while another way.'

I cleared my throat and held onto my pint for safety.

'I'll take you upstairs and give you the best fuck of your life.'

I smiled bashfully.

'Anything you want.'

The smile widened.

They were the hardest words I ever had to say. 'I'm sorry, no.'

She sat back, taking her perfectly formed breasts with her. Her lips pursed. 'You won't do this one little thing for me? What harm's it going to do?'

'None probably.'

'What about coke? Do you take coke?'

'Diet Coke,' I said.

'You're a fool,' she said. 'You have to cut the best deal you can in this world.'

'Maybe so. Maybe I am.'

'Is there *anything* I can do?'

'Do you have a complete collection of *Spiderman* comics? Not for me, you understand, but for my son. Especially the difficult to get . . .' I smiled as I trailed off. 'Sorry. If I could I would. But I can't. Sorry. That probably means you don't want another drink.'

She nodded once and stood up.

'Sorry,' I said again.

'Congratulations,' she said.

She opened her purse and the tips of her fine thin fingers crept in. I had noted before that there was no room for a fork or money, but it didn't preclude the possibility of there being a tiny pistol, an eye-piercing hat pin or a fingernail's worth of Semtex inside waiting for me. I tensed.

Instead she produced a small plastic card and set it on the table before me.

'This is your security clearance for the set. A car will pick you up at ten tomorrow morning. Sean sends his regards.' She picked up her drink and drained it. 'After a shaky start,' she purred, 'you pulled it back. Sean likes to be sure about these things. See you tomorrow, and thanks for the drink.'

And then she was gone.

CHAPTER 6

I showered, I shaved, I took six paracetamol. I had not remained in the bar a great deal longer. Paranoia and drink do not sit comfortably together, and I could not sit there comfortably thinking I was going to be tested again. When people spoke to me I ignored them, when I went to the gents I locked myself in a cubicle. They'd been sneaky and I didn't like it. I adjourned to my room and ordered half a dozen bottles of Becks on room service and drifted off to sleep watching fat black women punch each other on a cable re-run of *Jerry Springer*. On a cool, grey morning I phoned Patricia and told her more or less what had happened and she said, 'You poor lamb.'

'There's no need for sarcasm.'

'If you'd stayed in your room like you'd said, it wouldn't have happened.'

'*She* approached *me*.'

'Aye.'

'She offered me all sorts of sex and I turned it down. You should be congratulating me.'

'Dan. You're married. It should go without saying that you turned it down. You don't get a Blue Peter badge for that.'

'Put Little Stevie on, I'll get more sympathy from him.'

I didn't, of course. He asked what toys I was bringing him home. I explained to him that he didn't get a toy every time I went away and that he had hundreds of lovely toys already. He put the phone down.

I dabbed on some aftershave, purchased some Polos in the shop downstairs and then waited outside the hotel door for the stretch limo. It was three minutes before ten. Of course nobody had mentioned a stretch limo. I had just thought. Movies. Hollywood. Big star. So for a few moments I presumed that the small bearded guy sitting in the rusting Ford Fiesta was waving at somebody else. It was sitting about twenty yards away in a parking space. I ignored him and popped back inside to buy a newspaper. The *Irish Times*. When I came back outside the car was right outside the door and the bearded bloke was sitting on the bonnet.

He nodded at me, I nodded at him and rested back against the pillar and tried to find the sports section. When I lowered the paper he was staring at me. I said, 'You're not . . . ?'

'I am.'

I looked at the car. 'I expected . . .'

'You obviously haven't worked on a low-budget movie before.'

'I haven't worked on any movie before.'

He opened the door for me. I climbed in. There was a yellowing *Sun* sitting on the passenger seat. I pushed it off. I put my feet gingerly on the floor. It was thick with hairs, like a cat had been shaving.

He put his hand out. 'Davie. I'll be your driver.'

I put my hand out. 'Dan. I'll be your long-haired lover from Liverpool.'

He nodded. We drove out of Ballsbridge and back towards the centre of Dublin. 'I'm writing a book on Sean,' I said.

'Aye, I know.'

'Known him long?'

'About six weeks.'

'What's he like?'

'Don't really know. Nice enough.'

'Good director?'

'I'm just the driver, not Barry fucking Norman.'

'Fair enough.'

I concentrated on the *Irish Times*. I couldn't make head nor tail of the politics, so I started to leaf through the property section. There were no prices on the houses. But none of them looked like you'd get much change from a million quid. All were for sale by auction. They did things funny, south of the border. We did things serious, up north. We had peace, but they had prosperity. We had laid down our lives in the fight against Hitler and they'd never fired a shot in anger. They had the youngest population in Europe and we had Alex Hurricane Higgins. They had money, ambition, and political refugees, we had no money, little ambition and politicians we wished were refugees.

We had George Best, they had U2. It wasn't comparing like with like, and I wasn't quite sure who had the best deal.

We pulled into an industrial estate. Davie drove between broken bottles and shattered breezeblocks. We came to a large warehouse. It was surrounded by a high fence with barbed wire on top. There were two security guards on the gate. I flashed my pass. They told me to do it more slowly.

Davie drove round to the back of the warehouse, and it was like driving onto the Shankhill Road. They'd mocked up a section of Belfast's most notorious – or welcoming, depending on your point of view – Protestant enclave and were about to start shooting a gun battle. It was my first time on a movie set. There was a big camera, a crane, a lot of lights, and about fifty people. Most of them seemed to be just hanging around, but they probably all had something to do. Sean O'Toole, with baseball cap and jacket, sat in a director's chair staring at a video monitor. There was a drape being held over the top of the monitor to block out the glare of the sun. An assistant director was shouting at extras not to move from their positions. I stood with my arms folded and tried not to look impressed. Davie asked if I wanted a coffee and I said Diet Coke. He rolled his eyes and muttered something but went off to look for it nevertheless.

Nothing much seemed to be happening. Twice I was asked for my security clearance. Sean disappeared for several minutes and when he reappeared he was dressed in Belfast chic circa 1985, a purple-and-white shell suit. He was carrying a gun. As he spoke to the other actors he pulled a balaclava over his head. What little of his face that was visible was then touched up by a make-up girl. I resolved to speak to her. Make-up girls, legend had it, were the ones to talk to if you wanted the real lowdown on how the stars behaved. Then the assistant director warned everyone to cover their ears and shouted action. After a couple of moments Sean burst through the door of a mocked-up taxi office, shooting left and right. A policeman fell, wounded. Sean paused long enough to shoot him in the head where he lay, then ran off to the left. The AD shouted cut. Everybody clapped. Sean, still in balaclava, hurried across and watched a replay of the scene on the monitor, conferred quietly with the director of photography – the cameraman to you or me – and then called for another take.

I couldn't see a problem with the first one, but what did I know, besides the fact that Davie hadn't returned with my drink and the blonde from the bar was walking towards me, smiling.

'Hi,' she said quietly, 'I'm Alice.'

'Hi,' I said, 'I'm Dan.'

'Shhhh,' said the sound man. Alice raised her eyebrows and beckoned me towards a green double-decker bus which I'd somehow failed to notice sitting back against the rear wall of the warehouse. To judge from the trays of cutlery and tea dispensers sitting outside, it evidently doubled as a canteen.

'Upstairs or downstairs?' she asked as she stepped up onto the bus.

'Up,' I said.

'The troublemakers always go upstairs,' she said.

'Uhm,' I said, leading the way up the short spiral staircase. The upstairs had been converted into a little cafeteria. Davie sat at the nearest table as we emerged, reading a paper and drinking coffee. He didn't look up. There was an unopened can of Diet Coke warming on his table. 'Is this for me?' I said.

He grunted, I lifted it. I walked down to the front of the bus and slid in behind a table. Alice sat opposite me. If anything she looked even more beautiful in daylight. I started twisting my wedding ring. She looked at it for several moments. I stopped.

'Sean's inviting you for lunch,' she said.

I nodded. 'Here?'

'No,' she said, but looked as if she'd neglected to add the *of course not*. 'His caravan.'

I smiled. 'He doesn't mix with the plebs.'

'Yes, of course he does. But he can work in the caravan and eat at the same time. Have you any idea how absolutely all-consuming directing a film is?'

'No.'

'Well, take my word for it. It's two years out of your life. Twenty-four hours a day. A year to prepare. Ten weeks to shoot. Four months' editing, sound, all the post-production stuff, then you have

45

to go out and sell it to the distributors, and once they get it you have to go out on the road and sell it to the punters. It's total commitment. It's your life.'

I nodded appreciatively. 'So he doesn't mix with the plebs.'

She drummed her fingers on the table. 'Why you?'

'Why me what?'

'Why did Sam Cameron want *you* to write this book? There must be a thousand hacks out there ready to jump at the chance, a thousand who haven't a degree in sarcasm.'

I shrugged. 'Maybe he recognises talent. Maybe the fact that Sean and I come from the same place. Maybe he owes me a favour. Maybe he owes me a fortune. Maybe he knows I'll write a good book. Maybe he knows I won't kiss Sean's expensive arse. What does it matter, here I am, I'm here to do a job, Sean's agreed to it.' She looked a little taken aback. I tried the smile again. 'Maybe I could start by interviewing you,' I said softly. 'What exactly do you do for Sean?'

'You mean what's my job?' I nodded. 'I'm his personal assistant.'

'What's that, like a glorified PR or do you run his bath for him?'

She took a deep breath. She glanced at her watch. 'Sean will break for lunch in about half an hour.' She stood up. 'I'll see you then.'

'Why? I mean, no offence, but I'd prefer to talk

to him alone. Or do you have to cut his carrots up for him?'

Her eyes narrowed. One step too far, or thirty-nine. 'No, I just like to be on hand to make sure arseholes like you don't upset him.'

'Oh, right.'

She walked quickly towards the stairs. She glanced back once, her face heavy with a scowl, then clattered down the steps. I watched her cross towards the set, a mobile phone pressed to her ear. The sound guy shouted something I couldn't make out at her and she snapped something back; as far as I could make out the second word was *off*.

I had no idea why I was being so nasty towards her, except perhaps it was the only way I could think of preventing her from falling in love with me.

Or something like that.

CHAPTER 7

I'd been expecting something fancy, a caravan that was basically a bungalow on wheels, with a jacuzzi filled with bubbly young women and a chef standing by to serve poached vegetables and caviar, six bedrooms, water beds, a TV the size of a cow and enough cocaine to keep the nose rebuilders busy for months. What I got was a dumpy rusty wee thing like my parents used to take to Portrush every year. The kind you didn't get into with a key, you used a tin opener. There was one type of water, cold, and the onboard cuisine consisted of a tin of corned beef and a packet of Tayto cheese and onion. I looked at Sean O'Toole, his millions in the bank, his good looks, his charm, his halo and said: 'Nice place.'

He smiled and waved me in. He was still in his *Brigadier* gear. The make-up was thick on his face and hands. He was a movie star, but the closer I got the tireder he looked. It was in his eyes, mostly, and beneath them. 'I'm told directing a movie is a twenty-four-hour-a-day job,' I said.

'At least,' Sean replied. He cleared some newspapers off a seat. *The Sun. The Belfast Newsletter.*

As I sat down there came a brief knock on the door and Alice put her head round. I smiled keenly at her, but if she noticed she didn't react. Her eyes were on his. She appeared to have been running. She said, 'I should sit in on this, Sean,' and began to mount the couple of steps.

But he said: 'Nah, it's okay. Get some lunch. I can cope.'

She looked a little peeved. Exclusion from my company often gets them that way. 'But he's . . .'

'A journalist, I know. But he's working for me.'

'Actually,' I said, 'technically, I'm working for Sam.'

'But I have approval over what you write.'

'I doubt that.'

He looked at me, then at Alice. 'What's he talking about?'

Alice sighed. 'I told you. It was in the contract. I *told you*, Sean.'

He rolled his eyes. 'And I told you, I've a thousand and one people shouting in my ear every day, I can't remember everything. Tell me now.'

'It's too bloody late now, Sean.' She looked across at me. 'He's *allowed* an opinion, and that scares the balls off me.'

'That would just leave the two,' I said.

Sean turned blue eyes on me. 'He doesn't look that scary.'

'I'm a pussy cat,' I said.

'*Yeah*,' she said.

49

Sean laughed. 'Have you two gotten off on the wrong foot or something?'

'I bought her a drink at the hotel,' I said, 'and she punched my lights out. But don't worry, it's pretty much par for the course.'

'She can be a little temperamental.'

'Please don't talk about me as if I'm not here.'

'Did you hear something?' Sean asked, looking directly at me.

'Sean. Can I have a word outside?'

He rolled his eyes. 'Alice. I'm a big boy. I can look after myself.'

'No,' she said, 'you're a little boy and he'll play you like a' – she paused, searching for the right word – 'thing.'

'Maybe *you* should write it then,' I suggested, 'given your mastery of . . .'

Sean held up his hands. 'Girls. Please. Remember. I' – and he pointed at himself – 'that's me, I am the movie star. I am the director. Dan, you want to write a book about me; I am contractually obligated to provide material for it. Let's do that. Alice will provide me with a tape recorder so that I have a record of everything I say and can't be misquoted. Your take on everything is your own affair, but please be nice. Alice, I know you're a little paranoid because of this Colonel chap and you think the last thing we need is a motormouth on set stirring up trouble. But believe me, I can handle it. Just send somebody across with the tape recorder.' He turned her round and pushed her gently out of the door. She was in the act of saying 'But . . .' when he pulled the door firmly shut.

He turned, looked at me, shook his head and said: 'So, have you ever tried crack cocaine?'

A few moments later, after I'd just kind of shrugged and looked away, he said, 'No, neither have I. Would you like a cup of tea?'

Two pots in and we were getting on famously. We'd grown up in Belfast within a couple of hundred yards of each other, our experiences divided only by religion, a razor-wire-topped peace line and three hundred years of hatred. He was a bit of a joker at school, but not because he was bullied. He had some kind of a belt in judo. If he had the mind to he could have told people jokes and then beaten them up if they didn't chortle. But he'd given up the judo 'because it hurt'. Besides, he got bitten by the acting bug, or more precisely by Elaine Hunter, a teacher who ran the drama club at the neighbouring girls' school and who'd come into Sean's school looking for somebody to play the lead in a production of *Grease*. The John Travolta part. There had been plenty of summer lovin' after that, and pretty Elaine Hunter could have been arrested for it.

It was great stuff. He was fifteen, and now here we were sitting over Typhoo tea and he was giving me, literally, a blow-by-blow account of his first sexual relationship. Then there was a knock on the door and a girl's voice said, 'Five minutes, Sean, you'll need to get to make-up,' and a pained expression crossed his face and he said: 'Nobody ever calls me Mister round here.'

He poured another cup. When I raised an eyebrow he said, 'I'm the boss.' Then his eyes twinkled and he said: 'You'll be wanting to talk to Elaine Hunter, then.' I nodded. He said: 'She won't talk. None of them will. You see, Dan, I always leave my girls on good terms. I'm a restless soul, but I don't make enemies. I could call any of them up today for a natter and they'd have me round for a cup of tea. With their husbands and kids sitting there beside them and none the wiser.' He gave a short wistful little laugh. 'I suppose I used to be a bit of a charmer.'

'Used to?'

'Ah, look at me now,' and he pulled at the bags beneath his eyes I'd noticed on the way in. 'Gone to seed.'

'I think you'll find half the women in the world disagree.'

'Nice of you to say, but I'm losing it. Hence the directing. Hence the character parts. Still. I can hardly complain, the life I've had.'

'Sean, you're only forty-one.'

'But not in doggy years.'

He winked at me. I nodded and gave a conspiratorial smile, although I had no idea what he was on about. If I looked as good as he did when I reached forty-one, I'd have had a head transplant. 'Do you retain enough charm to work it on Michael O'Ryan?' I asked.

Sean put down his cup. He stood up. He said, 'Come with me. I want to show you something.'

We stepped out of the caravan. The make-up girl came towards him, but he waved her away. Fifty yards away across a short expanse of concrete the cast and crew of *The Brigadier* stood waiting for the star of the show, but he led me away from the set towards the catering bus and then on around the corner of the warehouse, the opposite side to the one Davie had driven me in that morning. As we walked, two guys in too-tight shirts and clicking heels fell into step behind us. As I glanced nervously back I noted that there were distinct bulges visible in their jackets that probably weren't autograph books. Sean didn't seem to notice our companions, although they were big enough to block out the sun.

As he walked, Sean said: 'I don't know how the fuck he got hold of the script. They're all numbered, they're all printed on red paper to prevent photocopying, they're all security tagged. Anybody tries to take one home alarms go off and they're sacked on the spot, if not executed.' He sighed as he walked. 'Maybe he hasn't even got one. But he knows what's in it. I suppose you can't stop people talking.'

'How do you know?' I asked. 'He's been in touch?'

'You might say that.'

He stopped. I stopped. He nodded forward.

It took me several moments to realise what it

was I was now looking at. A ton or more of blackened, twisted metal. There was a rectangular frame of sorts sitting on a set of wheels, but the rubber had long since been burned off them and both axles were knotted. Glass lay shattered on the ground along with charred pieces of furniture. The caravan might once have contained six bedrooms, a jacuzzi of nymphets and a television the size of a cow, but now it had the best air conditioning in Ireland.

Sean gave a low little laugh. 'That's why I'm slumming it in the sardine can. Michael O'Ryan came a-calling.'

CHAPTER 8

'Trish?'

'Dan. What's wrong?'

'Nothing's wrong. Is something wrong with you?'

'No, of course there isn't. I mean, why are you calling? What have you done?'

'I haven't done anything. Why must I have done something? I was bored, I just thought . . .'

'I do not exist purely to relieve you of boredom.'

'Thank goodness, you don't do a very good job . . .'

'Dan . . . what do you want?'

'You.'

'Oh. Right. It's that time of the day again. You've sex on the brain.'

'I'm trying to be romantic and you have to reduce everything to sex.'

'It's *me*. Patricia. Your wife. You're talking about sex. You are *obsessed* by sex.'

'Only because I'm not getting any.'

'You're getting plenty. Only last week . . .'

'Exactly! I'm a three-times-a-day man . . .'

'You were *never* a three-times-a-day man!'

'I never got the chance!'

'Dan, is there something I can do for you? I'm up to my eyes in dishes here.'

'Sorry. I was only asking for a minute of your time.'

'Which is about as long as the sex takes. Sorry. That was below the belt.'

'And an outright lie.'

'And an outright lie. Usually you manage . . .'

'Please put Little Stevie on before I drive home and divorce you.'

She put Little Stevie on. He said, 'Daddy, have you bought me my present yet?'

'No, son, I . . .'

He put the phone down. Sometimes I think he didn't inherit any of my genes at all. And then I remember that he really couldn't have inherited any of my genes at all, and that the periods during which I forget that fact are getting longer all the time.

I needed a drink. I went down to the bar. Alice found me there an hour later and said, 'You're looking . . . the same.'

'I didn't have time to get changed . . . work . . . Do you want a drink?'

'No,' she said, 'we have to go.'

She turned on her heel. I took a respectable minute to finish my drink, then followed. She'd evidently had some trouble parking; she was a couple of hundred yards away across the car park. She was wearing a short white skirt and a denim jacket. I watched her walk. If I hadn't been married, if she hadn't disliked me right from the start, I would have been quite prepared to give *her* a minute of my time. But I was, and she did, so I waited for her to bring the car to me.

We were destined for Sean O'Toole's Killiney retreat, and we drove there in virtual silence. I managed to find 'London Calling' on the radio. She switched it off. She rolled down her window, I followed suit. She tutted and rolled hers up, then tutted again as she tried to fix her hair, as if the wind from my side was going to ruin it any more than her own.

She had a buzzer to activate the security gates at the entrance to Sean's abode, big solid gates attached to concrete pillars. Two sets in fact, presumably so that you could see nothing of the house beyond, when the first set opened. There was a tall wall around the gardens, but the house itself was built on a slope which allowed it perfect views of the spectacular bay below. It was early evening and the sun was out and the sea was calm. There were boats and yachts and families sitting in the sand. The DART line ran far below and there was a hotel with a large car park, and I'm sure there were people looking up at the house wondering who exactly lived there and wouldn't it be lovely. And it was. It wasn't a particularly big place by movie star standards, I supposed. Madonna would probably have found it quite compact. But it was nevertheless an imposing building by out-of-work-and-owed-a-lot-of-money journalist standards and

I gave a low whistle as Alice drove slowly up the driveway.

'Bet he doesn't cut the grass himself,' I said. She managed a brief smile.

'I'm surprised he's invited you,' Alice said. 'He's got one hell of a lot of work to get through.'

'What, like learning lines?'

'That's the least of his worries. We've one more week of filming to go, then usually you'd have a nice leisurely four or five months in post production. Sean's given himself a month. He's editing on the hoof.'

She pulled the car into a gravelled parking bay. A security guard, one of the two that had accompanied me earlier to the burned-out caravan, appeared from behind a small hedge and gave us the once-over, then disappeared. Perhaps *he* cut the grass.

I said: 'What's the rush?'

'Cannes is the rush.'

'The film festival?'

'The film festival.'

'I don't understand, what's so special about . . .'

She had been in the act of getting out of the car, but she pulled the door closed again and said in a lower voice, '*The Brigadier* is going to be a wonderful film, Sean is a great director and he's written a great script. But it's low budget, it's black and white, there are no special effects and the accents are as thick as shite. No studio is going to touch it with a bargepole, even with

58

Sean's name attached . . . *especially* with Sean's name attached. They worry that it could affect future box office . . .'

'As in, I saw that pile of poo that was *The Brigadier,* he'll probably be just as crap in *Lethal Alien Cop Six*?'

'Exactly. But Cannes is *the* place to take a film like *The Brigadier*. You get extra marks for being black and white, they presume you're an intellectual if you've jazz on the soundtrack and if you resolutely refuse to compromise your art by providing subtitles and they haven't a clue what the hell your characters are talking about, then you're virtually certain to walk off with the top prize.'

'You sound quite . . . I don't know . . . *cynical*?'

'Cynical, realistic. I've been there the last six years in a row. That's how it works. In cinematic terms the continental Europeans like contemplating their own arseholes, but at the same time they're totally in awe of Hollywood. They won't admit it, of course, but when a movie star comes to town they go bananas. Just picture what they'll do when Sean arrives with *The Brigadier*. The best of both worlds. And then the American studios will have to take notice. They'll pay a fortune for it and shower it with Oscars and Sean'll have what he craves most.'

'Respect.'

There was a tap on my window. I turned. It was Sean. He said: 'If you've quite finished, your chips are getting cold.'

It was a line that came back to me much later on when I was drowning in Alice's car. One line that for some reason came to me through the green murk and made me realise that I was dying because I'd chosen to work with Sean O'Toole and I didn't mind at all because he was more than a star, he was Everyman, all things to all people, and just a good bloke.

Your chips are getting cold.

CHAPTER 9

The chips weren't *that* cold. There were Birds Eye Beefburgers from under the grill and a family-size tin of Heinz Baked Beans. It was hardly *nouvelle cuisine*, unless you ate *nouvelle cuisine* all the time, and then it definitely was *nouvelle cuisine*. Whatever the truth was, I'd discovered italics in a big way.

The house was well furnished without being showy. There were works of art on the walls, but they were not originals. There were framed posters for some of Sean's films, other posters lay rolled up, or squashed under cans of film and cardboard boxes that had once contained computer equipment. It wasn't really a home at all. Sean spent most of his life on film sets scattered all over the world, although mainly in America. This was a holiday home, and he evidently didn't take many holidays. A tax shelter, and he evidently didn't pay much tax. There was a vaguely musty smell. When I asked for a Diet Coke with my meal rather than the Californian white he offered he sent me to the fridge. I found a can to my liking, a good year, but I also found plenty of stuff that was past its devour-by date. Yoghurts, salads, coleslaw, milk, nearly all of them still sealed and festering from within. The only item that seemed to have been regularly visited was a jar of Hartley's Seedless Raspberry Jam. I opened it up. Research. It was two thirds empty, and there were butter marks on what was left. I *hated* people who did that, although not enough to kill them.

'My compliments to the chef,' I said when I'd cleared my plate.

'Just a little something I picked up along the way.' Alice had hardly touched a thing. Sean smiled benevolently at her and said, 'What's up with you, Beefy?'

'Worry,' she said.

'About me?'

She nodded. I finished my sip of God's nectar and said: 'You sound like his mother.'

She turned cool eyes on me. 'No, I sound like his *wife*.'

I looked from one to the other. Sean smiled. Alice looked bored. 'Oh, look,' Sean said, 'scoop number two.'

'You're . . . not serious?'

'Am,' said Sean, then added, 'Six weeks.'

'I had no idea.' I began to formulate some apologies for the sordid thoughts that had been lurking beneath my conscience since meeting Alice the previous evening. 'But your . . . surnames are different,' I said weakly, like they had just perpetuated the most amazingly complicated subterfuge

62

since Churchill misled the Nazis into thinking he was just a fat bastard with a cigar.

'We've been trying to keep a lid on it. And we trust you will, for a while.' Sean lit up a cigar. He sat back with a glass in his hand and smiled lovingly at his new wife. 'You'll have to interview her for your book. She's paranoid about my previous lovers.'

'No,' Alice said, 'I'm paranoid about your future lovers. I've seen your record.'

He smiled again and took her hand in his. 'She's not really, not about the girls anyway. The caravan thing spooked you, didn't it, love? Seeing as how you were in it at the time.'

'Seriously?'

She gave a little shrug. 'We'd been married six days. No honeymoon, just a couple of nights in Jury's and then straight to the set. I was relaxing in the jacuzzi when a breezeblock came through the window with a petrol bomb attached.'

'I've warned her about staying too long in the jacuzzi before,' Sean said. 'Whoever it was got clean away. Doesn't exactly fill you with confidence, does it?'

'You've barbed wire and bouncers in that place, *how'd* they get away?'

'Don't know. Inside job, maybe. There's a lot of people on a film crew. But what can I do, except press ahead? I'm not chickening out.' He let out a little sigh and ran his hand through his slightly receding hair. 'I sometimes wonder what the hell

63

I'm doing trying to make this picture. I mean, I'm just an actor; I get paid obscene amounts of money for prancing about a film set, I should be happy with that instead of messin' with bastards like Michael O'Ryan.'

'If you want to direct,' I said, 'I'm sure there are easier subjects.'

He looked at his empty glass for several long moments, then reached out a perfectly muscled arm and poured himself another. He lifted it to his lips, paused for a moment, then said quietly, 'He killed a friend of mine.' He took a sip, then set the glass down again. 'It was a long time ago.'

He fell silent. His eyes seemed to lose focus. Alice took his hand. He half-heartedly tried to remove it, but she held on, then gave it a little squeeze and he relaxed. Their eyes met, and held. His philandering was legendary, but there was a depth and intensity in that lovers' gaze which suggested that there might really be a special connection between them. I had not been able to muster that look since my honeymoon, and then only with the aid of the Guinness brewery. It was the first time that evening that I'd felt like I was intruding, like I should be in another room.

I poured a glass of white wine. I don't usually drink wine at all, but it seemed like the right thing to do. Patricia doesn't like me drinking wine because I tend to consume it in beer-like quantities, and then fall over. She can always tell when I'm drinking it because my neck starts to go red, and

64

the colour gradually rises up my face like the needle on a petrol gauge: empty, quarter, half full, completely pissed. But needs must. I felt awkward, and somehow small. Even with the bags beneath his eyes he was one of the beautiful people, and for Alice it went without saying. I did not move in their world. I sat on beer stools bemoaning my lot, and Little Stevie's ginger hair.

I said, as sympathetically as I could, 'What happened?'

It seemed to break the spell. Alice let go of his hand and poured herself a glass of wine. She even smiled at me as she did. She still wasn't sure of me, but seemed more willing to trust her husband's take on me, at least until sobriety beckoned.

'You know where I grew up, Dan. It wasn't exactly Butlins. Me and wee Danny Murphy were the best of pals. Same gang. Go-karts made of pram wheels and planks of wood. Guiders, we called them.'

'So did we. What has this to do with Michael O'Ryan?'

'He had a bigger guider. He used to steal *our* guiders. Bigger gang. He always had a bigger gang. Not older, not tougher, just bigger. And bigger always wins. David and Goliath was a lot of wank.'

'Although Northern Ireland did beat Spain in the 1982 World Cup.'

'Granted.'

'Tell me this isn't about guiders.'

'No, of course not. Wee Danny joined the civil

service. He was never *involved*, you know what I mean?' I nodded. 'But he had access to information. Information about where prison officers lived, that sort of thing. I think he handled their national insurance payments, something like that. Michael O'Ryan wanted the info, Danny refused. O'Ryan paid him a visit, told him to get the names or else. Danny chose *or else*. Nothing happened for six months, then one morning my friend Danny Murphy, wouldn't harm a fly, turns up with his throat cut. It was a couple of days after a prison officer got topped. Somebody spread the word that Danny leaked the address. But like I said, Danny wouldn't hurt a fly, or give out its address to Mr Spider, y'know?'

I nodded again.

'The thing is, a lot of people regard Michael O'Ryan as some sort of folk hero. Leading the fight against the Brits. Scarlet Pimpernel stuff, life on the run, master of disguise, tunnelling out of prison, daring bank robberies and yet all done with a certain *joie de vivre,* a lightness of touch, a charm, a . . . y'know, Kevin Costner *is* Robin Hood. They tend to overlook the fact that he was and remains a fucking psychopath as well. They seem to think loonies are the fucking preserve of the Protestants. Y'know, our side had plenty of them as well, they just didn't get as much press.' He took his first sip of wine in a while. 'So this is all for Danny.'

We were quiet for a bit. It had grown dark. Alice stood up and drew the curtains and switched on a lamp. A star of his stature, there should have been floodlights outside to scare away intruders. If Big and Bigger hadn't been able to notice a punk with a breezeblock and petrol bomb I wasn't certain that they could master the power of darkness. Perhaps they were monitoring the grounds through night-vision glasses, their fingers itching on the trigger of their Uzis, but I doubted it. They looked like the type who put a lot of faith in *Beware of the Dog* signs.

Sean opened another bottle of wine and we got to talking about growing up in Belfast again. He'd been out of the country for years and wasn't aware that I had once caused Northern Ireland to lose its independence by kissing a girl I shouldn't have. Some time around midnight I realised they were both looking at me and I stopped mid-sentence and said: 'What?'

And they both laughed and for a moment I thought that maybe they'd invited me to join them in a threesome or something but I hadn't heard.

Alice said: 'You do realise you've been talking non-stop for the past twenty minutes.'

'We should write a book about you,' Sean said. 'We have enough material.'

'Sorry,' I said. 'Wine gets me that way.'

'Aye,' Sean said, 'so we heard.'

'What?'

'Sam warned us. He says all literary geniuses have their faults.'

And that stumped me for a moment. To fill the

void, Alice stood up and began to pull on her denim jacket. 'Early start in the morning,' she said. 'Time to turn in.'

'If you need a jacket to walk to the bedroom,' I said, 'you should think about double glazing.'

She smiled at me like I was a fool or a child. 'I need a jacket because I'm giving you a lift to your hotel, and then going on to my apartment.'

'You don't live . . .' I looked at Sean.

'No, we don't,' Sean said. 'We haven't had the chance to move any of Alice's stuff in here yet. Besides, I stay up all night editing, and that doesn't make me very pleasant to live with.'

'So if you're ready,' Alice said, 'let's get moving.'

I stood up. I drained my glass. I thanked Sean for a pleasant evening, put on my jacket and waited for her to lead the way. And then remembered that at least one of them was a young lover, so I said I'd wait in the car and they got down to smooching.

Thirty minutes later she came out, muttering something about she'd had to check tomorrow's schedule with him, but she didn't meet my eyes and her cheeks were flushed. She might have been blowing up party balloons for all I knew. It was none of my business if they'd had sex, and there was no reason why she should be embarrassed by it. But she plainly was, and I found it quite endearing.

That and the way she tried to reverse the car after consuming so much wine.

'Drive slowly,' I said.

She nodded and hiccuped and we both giggled.

CHAPTER 10

Alice said, 'Fuck.'

I followed her gaze. Up ahead, revolving slowly, a red light. Cops. A checkpoint. A country road and the driver drunk. She looked at me, panic-stricken. 'I can't afford to lose my licence, not here. I live here. I drive *everywhere*. I drive Sean *everywhere*. He'll kill me.'

She'd slowed the car to a fast snail's pace. There was one vehicle ahead of us, already stopped at the checkpoint.

I took a deep breath. I was rarely south of the border, losing my licence wouldn't make any difference to me, although Patricia would give me a thick ear if she found out. I said: 'Swap over. Now.'

'But . . .'

'Now.'

She kept the engine running, but stopped the car. Up ahead the cop was shining his torch onto a driving licence. Alice manoeuvred herself over the handbrake and onto my knee. I manoeuvred myself from under her rear and over the handbrake into her seat.

70

'Shit, shit, shit, shit,' she was saying. She began to rifle through the glove compartment. 'There's mints in here . . . there's mints in here . . .'

I told her not to worry. I'd been down the mint road before and knew the inherent dangers. The car in front of us was waved on. I eased us forward. I rolled down the window and nodded. I tried not to breathe. The cop asked for my driving licence and I obliged. He looked at the picture, then at me.

'You've aged badly,' he said.

'Thanks,' I said.

'And the lady?'

'She's hardly aged at all.'

'I mean, do you have any ID, darlin'?'

Even for a cop, it was a bit forward. 'What does she need . . . ?'

'Do you think we're fucking stupid? We saw you swapping seats.'

Alice sucked on a lip and volunteered her driving licence. He examined it closely, then turned and nodded to a colleague.

'I'm not drunk,' Alice slurred, helpfully.

The cop leaned into the vehicle. 'That's okay, I'm not a cop.'

He produced a gun and placed it against my head.

We were in the back, one of the fake cops holding a gun over us from the front passenger seat, the other, obviously, driving. Behind came another car, the getaway car. We drove back towards the city, which was handy for us.

'What's this all about,' I said. 'We haven't any money.'

'Don't be fucking stupid,' the guy with the gun said. He had dropped the southern brogue and replaced it with Belfast hard-man. Beneath his Garda cap there was a flat boxer's nose supervised by small, mean eyes. Alice was holding my hand and shivering. Or it might have been the other way round. I've been exposed to plenty of danger in my time, and I've learned a thing or two about avoiding it. Mostly it revolves around not going out, but staying in and watching television. If you have to invite somebody to dinner make sure you've slept with them at least once and preferably exchanged marriage vows. Quite high on my list of things to avoid is being caught drunk in a car with a beautiful woman by gangsters who have vowed to murder her husband.

I said, 'Are you planning to give us a good telling off, or to kill us?'

'The latter,' the guy with the gun said.

'As a warning,' the driver said, 'not to fuck with the Colonel.'

'We could tell Sean,' I suggested, 'that you're really angry.'

'Shut the fuck up,' the gunman ordered.

We were passing through an area of Dublin I did not know and liked less. It was all dark hulking warehouses and creaking, rusting metal. I could smell the sea. Which would make it the docks. Good things do not happen to kidnap victims down at the docks.

I didn't know what to do. Alice was looking at me as if I should. The rear door did not appear to be locked, but there didn't seem any point in going for it. If it did open, the most we could hope for was that one of us – me, in fact – would hit the ground at speed. If it didn't break my skull I could limp away and spend the next thirty minutes trying to find a phone to call the police or the Samaritans, by which time Alice would be dead. In fact, they would either stop the car, reverse and shoot me where I lay groaning or decide that I wasn't worth the trouble, drive on and kill Alice. Whatever way you looked at it, Alice would be dead.

There was only one thing left to do. Charm them.

'You do know who I am, of course?' I said.

'Yes, you're the cunt writing the book about the film.'

Clearly, we were going to die.

'It's not the sort of book your boss probably thinks it is. It's highly critical of Sean O'Toole. It attacks him for taking liberties with the facts. And for turning the Colonel into some sort of monster. Which we know he's not.'

The driver caught my eye in the mirror. 'Stop fucking squirming, son. You're dead meat.'

Alice said, with admirable calm: 'This will only make Sean more determined. Keep me alive and you have a hold over him; kill me and he'll finish the picture, make Michael O'Ryan into even more of a bastard.'

The driver glanced back. 'Sorry, love, I'm sure you're right. We're only following orders. The Colonel doesn't do things by half measures.'

We came to a halt. We were halfway along a short pier. There was the bulky outline of a ship to our left, and just blackness to our right. The driver and his comrade climbed out. The engine was still running. The second car had pulled up behind and a third man I had not seen before, thin and with a trendy pair of spectacles, stepped out and exchanged some words with our driver. He handed him a coiled rope, then returned to his vehicle. A moment later the driver and his friend returned and pushed the driver's and passenger seats forward, giving them room to step hunched into the back beside us. They tied us up, hand and foot. The knots probably wouldn't have foxed Houdini, but Houdini was dead. When they had finished and we could hardly move a muscle, they stepped back outside. Then the driver leaned back in and said: 'Listen, drowning isn't the nicest way to go, particularly in there, the water's piggin' – do youse want me to shoot youse first, or are you happy enough to go with the pollution?'

I looked at Alice. There were tears in her eyes and her fingers had wriggled free enough to grip my hand extremely hard. I took a deep breath, although not as deep as I would have to make it to survive underwater for a couple of days. I said, 'I've been shot before and didn't much like it. I'll go for the drowning. Alice?'

She nodded.

'Drowning it is then,' said the hood. He held the door open while his mate went to the car behind and opened the boot. A moment later he returned with a breezeblock.

The fake cop grinned in at us. 'I would say, *tonight, you sleep with the fishes,* but they were all poisoned years ago. So sweet dreams.' He nodded at his friend. In one fluid movement the breezeblock was dropped hard onto the accelerator and the door was slammed shut. We shot out over the edge of the pier and we both screamed as we plunged into the darkness.

The thing about drowning in a car, of course, is it doesn't just happen like that. It's not like getting shot through the head or stabbed in the heart. You sit in the blackness and at first nothing happens. You float lazily down. The water seeps in. But unless you've got the windows open you're left pretty much on your own for three or four minutes to contemplate your impending doom.

The water wasn't that deep. Maybe twenty feet. In a few seconds we'd settled on the sea bed. The ocean floor. Outside, it was as black and thick as a Stygian night, whatever that is. They'd left the keys in the ignition and although the engine had died, the electrics on the dashboard were still working.

The clock said 12.35 and we'd half a tank of petrol. Things we didn't need to know. There was no point in struggling, but we did, for one minute, then two, then three as the water started to lap about our feet. But then we gave up. We were tied together, our faces close enough to feel hot breath, but helpless as far as escape was concerned.

I said, 'This is it then.'

She was sobbing. 'Shit, shit, shit,' she cried between gulps.

'If you've any last words, you may say them now.' The water was freezing. It smelled green.

'It can't just end like this!' Alice screamed.

'Fuck!' I yelled, straining again against the ropes.

'Oh Jesus!' she said.

'Fuck it!' I yelled.

Our heads fell back. I started to laugh. She said: 'What?'

I said: 'This is just so fucking ridiculous. I'm trying to think of some profound thought with which to leave this level of existence and all I can think of is Sean saying, *Your chips are getting cold.*'

She looked at me for a moment, then started to laugh. It wasn't funny, yet it was the funniest thing in the world. In seconds we were laughing hysterically. And then we stopped as the water reached our knees.

I said, 'Do you love him?'

'I do.'

'This much?'

'Almost. What about your wife?'

The temptation was to shrug. But it would have been a lying shrug. I nodded. 'Too much,' I said. I sighed. My throat was dry and a headache was beginning to throb across my brow. 'Nothing like a bit of drowning to sober you up.'

'I know,' Alice said. 'I could do with a drink of water.'

We both started laughing again.

The water was seeping into my groin. I looked at her and said, 'I'm of the firm belief that we should not depart this mortal coil feeling angry.'

Her teeth were now chattering, a toxic mix of cold and fear. 'What would you suggest?'

'Well, I can say this because it really doesn't matter if I embarrass myself now, nobody's ever going to know. But even though I'm happily married and you are very obviously recently happily married, I think you're one of the most beautiful people I've ever met. You may have a severe personality disorder as well, but right now I can think of nothing nicer than kissing you right before I die. It would be a nice way to go.' She had the beginnings of a look of complete disbelief on her face when the electrics gave up and we were plunged into total darkness. For several moments there was just the chill lap of the water. 'This is no time to play hard to get,' I said.

Silence.

The water had evidently found a more efficient method of entry. From its leisurely climb up our bodywork at the start of our nightmare, it was now fairly racing up us. Cold and foul.

I thought of Patricia.

And Little Stevie.

And the Clash.

And chips that were cold.

And then there was something moist on my lips and a warmth that was as old as time and as fresh as a daisy. Her tongue met mine and we lost ourselves in a kiss that was as beautiful as our predicament was ugly.

It was the only way to go.

CHAPTER 11

My funeral service was held at Roselawn Crematorium on the outskirts of Belfast. It is a long, low building, almost like a bungalow, but with a chimney that is a little too big for cosy nights in in front of the telly.

Though I'm sure there would have been several ministers fighting over my corpse – there are quotas to be achieved even in God's kingdom – I had not left any specific instructions for my departure, other than taxidermy as my least favoured option. I called myself a Protestant still, but that had bugger all to do with religion. It had to do with culture, football, attitude and land rights. No, it would be a civil service, come full circle from our wedding not that many years before.

I hovered above, expectantly.

There were about two hundred seats within the chapel. There was piped organ music. There was my coffin sitting at the front, waiting to be lowered into the inferno. Mourners were beginning to file in. There came Patricia's mum and dad, he hobbling on the stick, not long to join me. My brother. Journalists from the various papers I'd worked for.

Lee Cooper, the stripping nun. Fat Boy McMaster, studiously ignoring his former manager Geordie McClean. Sam Cameron, whispering to Mouse about the possibilities of writing a book about my life and seeing Mouse's brow crinkle up, torn between telling him to piss off and asking how much. Then Patricia. She was wearing a short black dress and high heels and held Little Stevie by the hand. He wore a black crombie coat and shiny black shoes. They walked to the front of the chapel and stood for several moments before my coffin. Little Stevie lifted his little hand to his brow, and saluted. There were emotional gasps from the congregation.

They took their seats. Patricia glanced round several times, as if she was waiting for someone, then eventually gave a little smile at a man who came down the aisle towards her. I thought at first that he was going to take the service, that he was coming to check some last-minute facts with her – *yeah, great journalist, everyone loved him, fantastic in bed* – when he kissed her full on the lips and sat down beside her. She took his hand. With his other he ruffled Little Stevie's hair, ginger like his own.

Jesus Christ!

Not that I'm religious.

Tony!

Patricia's lover!

Ex-lover, or so I thought!

Couldn't even wait until I was cold – or hot, as it happened.

80

Fuck.

The bitch.

And then heads turned and there were two big, beefy guys at the door, with sunglasses and little earplugs looking about them like the President was about to enter. But it was Sean O'Toole, in a black Armani suit. There were excited whispers from the congregation. Sean paused, looked behind him, put his hand out, then Alice appeared in the doorway in her short skirt and white jacket.

Alice. Looking beautiful.

They began to walk down the central aisle.

As Alice walked she suddenly looked up to the ceiling. She could see me, even in my bat shape, hanging from the rafters. She smiled. She mouthed the words: 'Nice kiss,' then walked on.

I didn't know what the hell was . . .

. . . there was a fat, sweaty man's mouth on mine. Then I spewed green slime onto the dock. There was coughing beside me. There were lights. My chest was on fire. My stomach had come loose. I was rolled onto one side and I continued to throw.

I forced my eyes open. They stung. There was . . . *goo* in them. I dragged an elastic arm up and wiped the mess away and tried to make out shapes. There were angry voices. The crackle of a walkie-talkie. Alice was vomiting beside me.

I was not dead.

I sat up.

81

'Holy fuck,' I croaked.

One of the men turned. The thought had flashed across my mind that these men, these men who had so recently kissed me and brought me back to life, might be the Colonel's men having their fun, ready to toss us back in again unless we swore to bring filming to a halt, but I saw now that they were not, that they were Sean's security guys and that in the harsh light of their car headlamps they were jittery and scared and panicked. They were also both coated in green slime.

I delved around in the polluted byways of my mind for something smart to say, but all I could manage was, 'Thanks.'

The guy closest said, 'No problem.'

I looked at Alice, still heaving, and asked the stupid question, 'Is she okay?'

'As okay as anyone can be, drinking that stuff. You must have a strong constitution.'

It was years of drinking Harp. It had tasted pretty much the same and been considerably cheaper. I raised myself gingerly to my knees. I was dizzy. I was soaked. I was poisoned. But I was alive. 'What . . . ?'

'Sean sent us after you. Well, after Alice. He doesn't let her go anywhere without us.'

'Does she know . . . ?'

He glanced at her. She was too busy throwing up to be listening. 'I doubt it.' He paused, then gave a little laugh. 'Yes, I know what you're thinking, how can fat bastards like us not be noticed

– but believe it or not we're professionals. Ex-SAS.'

It seemed the wrong time to ask why they were *ex*. The other guy helped Alice to sit up.

My hero reached out a hand and pulled me up. There were anchors on my feet and needles in my eyes. 'Okay?' he said. I nodded and nearly toppled over. He steadied me. 'I'm just sorry it took so long,' my saviour said. 'We had to make a choice. Steam in and maybe they would panic and kill you anyway, or wait and see what they'd do. Seeing as they'd made a point of coming down to the water, we figured it was better to wait.'

'I'm glad you did.' I let out a long, bubbly sigh. 'What now?'

He looked up the road behind us, stretching dark and lonely between warehouses. 'We've ordered a taxi for you. We have to get back to Sean. He's by himself out there. Go to your hotel. Wait there. Don't let anybody in. Sean'll decide our next move.'

I looked across at Alice. She was rubbing goo from her eyes. It was stupid question time again. 'Are you okay?'

She gave the faintest of nods. 'I've . . . felt better . . .' she said weakly. She looked at the security guy beside her and then at the water. 'You . . . ?'

He shrugged. 'Yeah. It's not that deep, but it's dark and nasty. Took us a while to find you. Had to cut you loose to get you out through the window. Then went back for him.'

'I'm glad you got your priorities right,' Alice said.

He smiled. 'Well, we stopped for a fag first.'

The taxi came. The driver took one look at us and tried to drive on. The security guys gave him several large-denomination notes. He stuffed them into his shirt pocket then climbed warily out of his car. He removed what appeared to be a paint-spattered curtain from the boot then draped it over the back seat.

We got in. The security guys hurried into their car and raced off ahead of us. The driver looked at us and our dank evening wear in the mirror. 'Where to?' he said.

'Jury's,' I said.

He nodded for several moments, then said: 'No offence, but I don't think you'll get in dressed like that.'

I put my arm round her and we shivered against each other. She said: 'You sure know how to show a girl a good time.'

We were out of the docks and back into the centre of Dublin. There were lots of people on the streets and everything was neon lit, but it wasn't welcoming any more. When we stopped at lights people peered in, as they will at any stationary vehicle. But it felt like they *knew* what was going on, that they were in the Colonel's pay, they were his eyes and ears and trigger fingers. It was paranoia, but who could blame me. I had nearly died, and for no reason. I was incidental to it all, and that was scarier than being to blame. It could have been me or Kissinger in the car with Alice, it wouldn't have mattered to them. It was *all* about Sean O'Toole and his stupid bloody film.

I had come within a millilitre of death, and had no idea why I should be reincarnated as a bat.

'One thing,' Alice said.

'Mmmm?'

'Don't mention the kiss.'

'Okay.'

'Sean's very . . . jealous. He wouldn't understand.'

'That's okay.'

'We were dying. It just seemed such a good idea.'

'I know.'

Her eyes flitted towards me, then quickly away again. She was looking out of the window. We were stopped at a traffic light. There was a multi-screen cinema beside her. Two of Sean's films were showing. There was a poster of him. She took a deep breath.

'It was a lovely kiss though,' she said.

'I thought so,' I said. There was no doubt about it. I was falling for a girl with green slime in her hair.

CHAPTER 12

The sniffy doorman said, 'Are you residents?'
'Protestants, mate,' I said and pushed on past him. We walked up to the desk. I asked for my key. The girl was a professional. She hardly batted an eye. It was an electronic key card, the kind you're meant to carry with you, but I'd never trusted myself with them enough to take them outside. They were too easy to lose track of, particularly when you were submerged under twenty feet of murky water.

We went up to the eighth floor and I let Alice into my room.

'Tidy,' she said.

'I haven't unpacked yet,' I said.

'What do you do, wait until you get home?'

'Usually.'

We looked at each other. We were awkward. It wasn't that we had nearly died together, but that we had kissed. It changed things. Particularly the fact that it was a good kiss. If she'd had bad breath, holes where there should have been teeth and a viper's tongue, it wouldn't have been so bad.

But.

We were soaked. The kiss made it difficult to get out of our clothes. I said, 'Why don't you go in and take a shower? Or a bath. There's a bathrobe. I'll order us a couple of drinks.' She looked at me. I added, 'I'm sure Sean'll be along in no time.'

She nodded. She went into the bathroom. I lifted the phone and ordered three bottles of Harp and a half-bottle of Smirnoff Vodka and a bucket of ice. I held the phone against my chest and shouted, 'What do you want to drink?' through the bathroom door. There came a muffled reply. I added a bottle of white to the tally. Sam Cameron was paying for it. And he would, probably with his life.

I paced. I was soaked through, but I couldn't get out of my clothes yet. I couldn't be standing in my underpants when she came out. It would be too big a temptation for her. To run away. So I paced and switched on the TV and switched it off and looked out of the window at the traffic below and the lights of the city.

I would have to find out how she had met him and why she had married him. Where she came from and where she went to school and how many hearts she had broken, and in learning it all it would demystify her. Since I had married I had only kissed one other girl with passion, and it had killed her, almost literally. I had sworn it would never happen again. Perhaps, in the Big Book of Things, kissing Alice in the back of the car moments from my death wasn't that much of a sin; but the fact of it was that we'd both enjoyed it and neither of us had died. And now it was out there.

I pressed my forehead against the glass. I had to get a grip of myself. I was still half intoxicated. My veins were afire with the adrenaline of a near-death experience. I was letting my imagination run away with me. There must have been a dead dog floating in the stenchy river and I had picked up a bad case of puppy love.

Stop it.

Stop it now.

I tried to concentrate on Michael O'Ryan and why he was getting so upset with Sean's film. He had received plenty of bad press in his time, what difference could a movie make?

Because nobody believes bad press, but everybody believes the movies.

They *become* history. Our take on Nazis, Red Indians and Italians are formed by the movies. Our take on the Guildford Four, the fate of the *Titanic* and the assassination – or was it suicide? – of JFK is irrevocably influenced by the movies. What if Michael O'Ryan had convinced himself that he was a hero? Convinced himself that it was scummy here-today-gone-tomorrow journalists who portrayed him as a murdering psychopath? What if it was only when he read Sean O'Toole's screenplay to *The Brigadier* that he realised that not only this generation, but the next and the next, would come to regard him as a madman?

It seemed far-fetched. It seemed weak. But what

other reason could there be for such an hysterical reaction?

But then, since when did a nut have to justify himself?

The door opened and Alice came out. Her hair was dripping. It had darkened under the shower. The make-up was gone. She had the bathrobe on. 'Thanks,' she said. 'Ahm, there's another bathrobe.'

We passed each other in the gap between the dressing table and the bed. We laughed a little, smiled like teenagers. I paused in the bathroom doorway.

'There's a hairdryer over there,' I said.

'Thanks.'

'Ahm. There's drinks on the way.'

'I could do with one.'

'Do you want to phone Sean?'

'No. He'll be on his way.'

I went into the bathroom and closed the door. I took my trousers off. I removed my wallet from my back pocket. When I opened it up, a small fish fell out.

No, it didn't. But it might have, my life was such a fucking comedy. There was nothing in my wallet but damp money and red telephone bills. I took off my shirt and jacket. They were green, though not with envy. I rolled them in a ball. They didn't need washing, they needed chemo. I doubted if clothes were available on room service, but something would have to be done. In another life I would have had a manservant to go out and replace my wardrobe. Or probably not. In my other life, it seemed, I had been a bat.

I was naked. I looked at my face in the mirror. Thirty-something, now. Stubbled. Hair not noticeably receding. Dark under the eyes. I traced the outline of those bags, then saw in the reflection that my fingernails were caked black and green. Dublin Bay nail varnish. I removed my wedding ring and sat it on the edge of the sink and then unwrapped one of the free minisoaps. I put in the plug, then turned on the hot water. I ran up a lather in my hands and started to scrub and pick at my nails. It wasn't the sort of dirt that would come out under the shower.

There was a sudden knock on the hotel room door.

'Dan?' Alice hissed fearfully.

I turned and grabbed a towel. I hurriedly tied it about my waist then pulled the bathroom door open. Alice was standing hugging herself, looking at the door. 'It's okay,' I said softly, 'it's just the drinks.' She didn't look convinced. 'Who is it?' I called.

'Room service,' a woman's voice replied.

I smiled at Alice. She smiled back and walked to the door. I returned to the bathroom and closed the door. Then I said, 'Fuck,' because the water in the sink had already started to overflow. I reached in and yanked out the plug. I dropped my towel onto the ground and started to soak up the overflow. There wasn't much.

'Dan,' Alice said through the door.

'What?'

'Can you come out here for a moment?'

'I haven't had my shower yet.'

'Could you please come out?'

And then I realised I would have to sign for the drinks, so I pulled the towel up again and tied it. I looked up just in time to see my wedding ring disappear down the plughole.

'Fuck!' I yelled. I made a dive for the sink. I jammed my fingers down the hole. It had one of those three-pronged bases which ordinarily should have been enough to have stopped anything like jewellery getting past, but evidently my wedding ring was thin enough and cheap enough to have failed quality control. It was gone. 'Fuck!' I yelled again.

'Dan!'

'I'll be there in a fucking minute!' I yelled. 'Fuck. Shit. Fuck.' I felt the pipes below, trying to work out if it could possibly have got stuck further down, but there was no easy way of checking. It would need a plumber or, failing that, a deep-sea diver.

I was still cursing when I opened the bathroom door. Alice was standing there, looking a little pale, a little perplexed.

Beside her, looking very pale, very perplexed, and very angry, stood Patricia.

CHAPTER 13

I have noted before that Patricia is not one of those women who look more attractive when consumed by anger. Her eyes widen and turn bloodshot. Her eyebrows knit, usually a funeral veil. Her nose pales, accentuating whatever blackheads she has sought to hide with rouge so that they seem to quiver like poisoned porcupine spines, ready to shoot off angrily in my direction, not as a defence mechanism, but as an attack mechanism.

'Hi,' I said weakly, 'this is a surprise.'

'I'll bet it fucking is.'

I opened my mouth, but nothing further would come out. This rarely happens, and it only made her madder. The fact that I was totally and completely in the right did not seem to matter; I do not react well to being in the right. I go red and I lose the power of speech. I have a built-in guilt complex. I look *guilty*. If there is a police line-up, I will be picked. If there is a roadblock, I will be stopped. If there is an international war crimes tribunal, I will go to the electric chair.

'This isn't what it looks,' Alice said.

Patricia looked at her with disdain. 'What are you, girlfriend or hooker?'

'I'm Sean O'Toole's wife.'

'And I am Dan Starkey's wife. So why are you slumming it with wank features?'

'That's not . . .' I started, but she cut in with: 'Shut the fuck up.'

'Somebody tried to kill us,' Alice said.

'I swear to God,' I added. 'Look – look at our clothes.'

'You're not *wearing* any clothes, that's the fucking problem.'

'*Patricia*, I can explain.'

It was time to take the moral high ground. The problem with high ground, of course, is that it leaves you open to sniper fire. And Patricia was a professional. We raged at each other for twenty minutes, Alice contributing the odd barbed rejoinder, until finally we achieved some sort of understanding.

Alice and I had been in the back of a car, and nearly drowned. There was nothing going on. Patricia had come down to surprise me because I sounded forlorn, but had been surprised herself. She had been waiting for me in the bar, presuming that I would stop there on the way to my room. Little Stevie was with her parents. She had work in the morning. She had driven down on a wild crazy whim and found me half naked with a beautiful woman, although it wouldn't have made the slightest difference if Alice had been a pig in a wig.

93

Patricia sat on the bed, legs crossed, chin on palm, elbow on knee, smoking. I gave her a shot of my vodka and three of my ice cubes. She looked from me to Alice to me and said: 'It's happened before.'

'We've both been bad. But this time I've been good.'

'Swear to God?'

'Swear to Strummer. Trish, you know me. I wouldn't.'

'Not so much as a kiss?'

'Not so much as a kiss. Alice, tell her.'

Without blinking, Alice said softly: 'I'm just married, Patricia. I know it looks . . .' Then her voice hardened. 'Somebody's trying to kill me, for godsake.'

I had told Patricia back home about somebody being after Sean O'Toole, which was a good start. We presented our balled-up clothes as evidence. Patricia examined them with the rigour of a forensic pathologist. Even to her suspicious mind, destroying our clothes seemed a little far to go to hide a clandestine affair. I put my arm round her and said: 'I'm really pleased to see you.'

She softened a little. She took my hand. She looked into my eyes. And then her expression hardened again and she said: 'Where's your wedding ring?'

I rolled my eyes. 'Trish, *please* . . .'

'Please nothing, where the fuck is your wedding ring?'

94

I pulled my hand away. I closed my eyes. 'You're not going to believe me.'

'Try me.'

When I opened my eyes she was looking daggers at Alice. Alice was drinking one of the beers and staring out of the window, pretending that she wasn't listening.

'What's the point?'

'The point is I nearly believed you. You would never take that ring off, not unless you were screwing around. I know you, Dan. You get weighed down by guilt. You take the ring off, you're as free as a rabbit. You've been screwing that bitch.'

'He never fucking touched me!' Alice spat from the window.

'Shut your bake, you fucking bitch!' Patricia screamed.

'You fucking make me!'

Alice turned from the window and squared up with the bottle. 'If I wanted to fucking screw him I could, just like that!' She clicked her fingers. 'But as it happens, it's your lucky day, because I wouldn't fucking touch him if he was the last man on earth! Okay? I'm married to Sean O'Toole, I don't need to fuck around with the hired help, okay?!'

Thanks, I said, mentally.

Patricia spun on me. 'Yeah, sure. Well, where's your fucking wedding ring, then? Those guys that tried to kill you, insist on you taking it off, did they?'

'No,' I said. I sighed. 'If you must know . . .'

'Yes, I must know. Sadly. Because I *care*. Unlike you, you two-faced . . .'

'Listen! I took it off in the bathroom, my nails were thick with that fucking scum from the river. I ran the tap. You came to the door. The water overflowed. I pulled the plug. By the time I got back to it the ring had washed down the plughole. I swear to God.' She was looking at me. Alice was looking at me. 'I swear to God!'

Perhaps they would laugh at it in retrospect.

'That really is the weakest yet,' Patricia said.

'I swear on the Bible.'

'You don't believe in the Bible.'

'I swear on my mother's life.'

'She's dead.'

'I'm telling the fucking truth. I think it's stuck in the pipe. I swear, Trish.'

She gave the slightest shake of her head. 'Okay,' she said. 'Call maintenance. Get a plumber up here. Let's check it out.'

'It's nearly two o'clock, Trish.'

'Don't I know it. Call. Or I'm walking out of here and you won't see me again.'

'Jesus.' I walked across to the phone. I rolled my eyes at Alice. She didn't respond, couldn't really, with Patricia glaring at her. I lifted the phone. I asked for a maintenance man. I explained my predicament. It sounded like the same unflappable girl. She giggled.

'I'm sorry, Mr Starkey . . .'

'*Please* . . .'

96

She hesitated, then said, 'I'll have a word with the night manager. I'll see what I can do.'

'Thanks, you're a life saver.'

I put the phone down. 'They're sending someone up,' I said. There was no way of knowing if the ring really was in the pipe. Even if it was, it didn't prove anything. Alice slumped down into a chair beside the TV. Patricia sat on the bed, her back against the headboard. I took another bottle of Harp and paced.

Alice, with the gentle touch of a bomb disposal expert, looked at Patricia and said: 'I'm sorry. It must look . . .' She trailed off.

Patricia looked at me and said: 'I thought you'd be happy to see me.'

'I *am* happy.'

'Then why bring her back here?'

'Because it was closest,' Alice said. 'And safest.'

'I thought I was being romantic,' Patricia said.

'You *were* being romantic,' I said.

'A two-and-a-half-hour drive, and then you weren't even in.'

'It *was* a nice thought. I'm sorry. I didn't plan on somebody trying to kill me.'

She looked at Alice. She was showing more leg than was decent. She quickly flicked the towelling robe back across. Patricia sighed and looked at me. 'I should have stayed in bed. What you don't know doesn't hurt you.'

'There's nothing to know! For Christ . . .'

There was a slight tap on the bedroom door.

I turned, but Patricia snapped: 'Stay where you are!'

I froze.

'I don't want you tipping him off. I don't want you slipping him a tenner. I want the *truth*. Sit down. Shut up.' Alice started to get up out of her seat. 'You too . . . !'

'Don't you talk to . . .' Alice began.

'Please,' I said, making calming gestures with my hands, 'just sit down.'

She hesitated, then sat back. 'This is one stupid fucking night,' Alice said. I nodded. Patricia walked up the short corridor to the door and opened it.

I turned to the drinks tray and poured a vodka. I asked Alice if she wanted one. She shook her head. She sat back and closed her eyes.

I took a long sip, then looked up towards the bathroom. Patricia had led the guy straight in and was talking to him in clipped schoolmistressy tones. She was saying, 'Where are your tools?'

'I don't have any tools.'

'What sort of a plumber are you?'

'I'm not a plumber.'

'Well, how are you going to get the ring out?'

'What ring?'

'His wedding ring. It's stuck down the drain, *allegedly*.'

'Oh. Right. I see. Do you have a magnet?'

'What?'

'If you had a magnet you could . . .'

98

'Who the hell carries a magnet about with them?'

'I was only trying to help.'

'What sort of a fucking plumber are you?'

'I told you, I'm not a plumber.'

I walked up the hall. Alice joined me, grinning. We stopped in the bathroom doorway. Patricia's face was red and she looked like she was about to slap him.

'Patricia . . .' I said.

'Keep out of it,' she snapped.

'This is Sean O'Toole.'

'Oh,' she said. Her legs seemed to go a little shaky. One hand gripped the sink. Her voice rose an octave. 'I've seen all your films,' she said.

CHAPTER 14

We were driving home. I had a sorehead hangover and the munchies. We couldn't wait for breakfast in the hotel. She had to get to work. A two-hour drive to Belfast. Sean had closed the set down for a couple of days. He was rethinking security. He was going to have to reach into his own pocket to cover the shutdown. It would cost tens of thousands. He said what did money matter as long as his wife was safe.

We weren't speaking, Patricia and I.

Because we had made love. It had been some of the most frenetic and enjoyable lovemaking of our entire married life, and that worried me. It wasn't that old standby, the best part of breaking up is when you're making up. It wasn't the fact that she had me back after my near-death experience. It came to me when we were lying there, no longer breathless but caked in sweat and starting to feel a little cold but still too sticky to pull up the sheets, when we should have been cuddling for warmth. I said, 'You were thinking about him, weren't you?'

'What?'

100

'When we were making love you were thinking about Sean O'Toole.'

'Don't be ridiculous.'

'You shouted his name out.'

'I did not!'

'No, you didn't. But you might as well have.'

'Dan, don't be silly. I was making love to you.'

'Your body was. Your mind was elsewhere.'

'Uhuh. And you're inside my mind.'

'Yes, I am. It was different, it was new. You were thinking about Sean O'Toole.'

'Dan, you are the most insecure, paranoid man I have ever met. We make fantastic love. I should give you a medal. Bronze, at least. And all you can do after it is lie back and fret. I love *you*. I made love to *you*.' She turned to me and kissed my chest. She moved her head up and kissed me on the lips. She was a beautiful woman, especially in the dark.

'You went all wobbly when you met him.'

'He's a film star. I love his films. He has charisma.'

'You tried to get him to unblock the drain. He can't have that much fucking charisma.'

'I didn't look at him, I was that angry.'

'You recovered quickly enough. It's a pity he wasn't a plumber, he could have done something about all that drooling you were doing.'

'I wasn't *drooling* . . .'

'Yes, you were. It was embarrassing. Alice didn't know where to look.'

'Alice. Yes. Now there's another strand. If I was

101

thinking about Sean, then you must have been thinking about her.'

'You mean you were?'

'No, I mean she is a stunningly beautiful woman. I am a dog who has been beaten with a mallet compared to her. She didn't stray across your thoughts while you were making love to me?'

'Don't be ridiculous.'

'Why's it ridiculous for you and not for me?'

'Because I wasn't drooling.'

'Yes, you were; every time you looked at her your eyes went all soft and charmy.'

'Your head's cut. I was *pissed*.'

'All the more reason.'

'At least my nipples weren't erect.'

'*What!?*'

'When he gave you that hug on the way out, you turned away and your nipples were erect.'

'You were watching my nipples?'

'I couldn't miss them. They were up like thimbles.'

'I was *cold*.'

'Aye.'

We lay in the dark. We could hear traffic distantly, the hum of the elevator and somewhere, not next door, but maybe a few rooms along, the sound of a couple larking about in a bath. Patricia stroked my chest.

'Anyway,' she said, 'is it wrong?'

'What are we talking about, fantasies or thimbles?'

'Fantasies. Where exactly is the problem if Sean O'Toole enters my thoughts when we're making love. Are you trying to say you don't fantasise?'

'Yes. No. I mean, the problem is, Sean O'Toole isn't a fantasy. He was in this room an hour ago. *That* isn't a fantasy, that's being unfaithful.'

'*What?*'

'Everyone is entitled to their fantasies. Sure, occasionally I might have one. I'm sure half the world fantasises about getting a movie star into bed. But that's precisely what it is, a *fantasy*. But Sean O'Toole isn't a fantasy. He was in our room. He hugged you. Thimbles. You weren't fantasising about something unobtainable, you were fantasising about something that has suddenly become possible. If unlikely.'

'Did I ever tell you that you were crackers?'

'Often.'

'Dan?'

'What?'

'I'm going to sleep now.'

'That's right. Run away from our problems.'

'What problems!'

'If you don't know I'm not going to tell you.'

'Oh, for Jesus sake!' She reached down and roughly pulled up the sheets. She turned her back to me. She huffed and puffed.

I lay with my hands clasped behind my head. I waited until her breath calmed down, began to steady out into that mellow marshmallow land that precedes sleep, then said: 'I bet he's crap in bed anyway.'

'For fuck sake!'

'To busy looking at himself in the mirror to . . .'

'Dan, will you shut up!'

'It's probably a wig. They all wear wigs. Charlton Heston.'

'Dan, I'm trying to get to fucking sleep!'

'Sean Connery.'

'Dan!' She sat up in bed. She gripped her head and shook it. 'Sometimes you drive me so fucking crazy!'

'Sorry,' I said.

'Just go . . . to . . . sleep . . .'

She slumped back down on the bed. I leant across and kissed her. After a moment's hesitation she responded. I lay back and said, 'Good night.'

'Good night.'

'Sleep tight.'

'Right.'

'Don't let the bedbugs bite.'

'Dan!'

'Sorry.'

I turned away from her. I closed my eyes. I thought about Alice.

We arrived in Belfast just after rush hour. I dropped Patricia off at the tax office. She was on one of those ridiculous civil servicey things called flexitime and could pretty much start when she wanted. We hadn't talked for the best part of a hundred miles.

She was getting out of the car, then leant back in and said: 'Sorry.'

'What for?'

'I have no idea.'

I nodded. We kissed. She left. I drove round to her mum's house to pick Little Stevie up. Her mother looked pleased to be rid of him. He could be a handful. He was advanced for his years and already adept at sarcasm. I asked him what he wanted for breakfast and he said: 'Sweets.'

I asked him if he liked his granny, he said no. 'She puts me in my cot.'

'Were you naughty?'

'No,' Like butter wouldn't melt in his mouth.

We drove in silence. I was going to take him to McDonald's for breakfast. Halfway there he said: 'Dad?'

'Mmmm?'

'Where's Tony?'

'What?'

'Mummy's friend.'

My heart began to speed up. I looked at him in the mirror. I said, 'I don't know.'

He nodded. 'I like him.'

'Good. When did you last see him, son?'

'Don't know.'

'Think.'

'Last night. *He* brings me presents. Did you bring me a present?'

'No, son, I didn't.'

'You're not my friend any more.'

I tried to concentrate on the traffic. Tony. The bastard with the ginger hair.

'Daddy, are we going to McDonald's?'

'No,' I said.

CHAPTER 15

Little Stevie was in a playgroup called Toddlers Are Us, the only one we could get him into. He had an affinity for Lego. They took him three afternoons a week and thought the sun shone out of his bottom, and they saw his bottom more than most. If you're such a friggin' great wee fella and really advanced, I'd say to him when roused, how come you're still in nappies? At which point he'd cry and enquire about fostering. Kids get you that way. You can have a perfectly grown-up conversation with them for five minutes, then they poke you in the eye.

Him being in playgroup left me free. Free to worry. I do that. I know. I have to get to grips with it.

Of course Tony had visited last night. He had every right to. He was Daddy. He had visited before, when I was there, and you could cut the atmosphere with a blunt knife. Of course it made sense to visit when I wasn't there. A little visit. Bring a present for your son. Buying Little Stevie's love. What had he bought him? Whatever it was, my first instinct was to go home and smash it. Or just leave it switched on so that the batteries would run down – it was bound to have batteries. Batteries represented a two-pronged attack on my marriage. One: presents with batteries tend to cost more, they're brighter and flashier than the lump of coal he gets from me, and so he worms his way into Little Stevie's affections. Two: batteries die. Thus, to keep my son happy, I have to go out and buy more batteries, thereby creating a financial drain on my resources at a time when money is not plentiful, leading to rows with my wife, the breakdown of a beautiful relationship and bitter arguments in the divorce court.

I'm convinced he was thinking of all this as he bought Marty the Flashing Robot.

I drove. It was a way of not drinking. There were roadworks on Botanic Avenue, so I turned into the Holy Land and all these memories of Trish and me in our courting days came back. I paused outside our old house. It had seen a party or two in its time and was still standing. Bitten by the nostalgia bug, I drove across town to my old school, and then on a whim sought out the twenty-foot, barbed-wire-topped wall they called the peace line, where we'd gathered as kids to throw petrol bombs at the Fenians on the other side. But it was gone. It had not long been removed. The foundations were still in place in case it had to be hurriedly restored. I parked the car and walked across it. Into no Protestant man's land. I kept walking. After about ten minutes I came to St Bernard's Secondary School. There were hundreds of kids in the playground. I found the secretary's office and knocked on the door. The door remained closed but a smoked glass panel in the wall beside it slid back and a middle-aged woman with short grey hair smiled out.

'Can I help you?' she said.

I told her who I was and what I was doing and her smile remained in place, but her eyes seemed to harden a little. She said I'd need to talk to the headmaster. She pulled the glass panel back across. A couple of minutes later I was shown into a small, cluttered office. The headmaster was called Malachy Corrigan. He had jet-black hair and an eager smile. He didn't look more than about forty-three, but as we exchanged pleasantries I picked out a framed certificate on the wall which showed he'd passed teacher training back in the early sixties, which would put him in his sixties.

'Sean O'Toole, you say?' His voice was soft and lilty and his eyes sharp and I could see how girls might once have fallen at his feet, which would have been a bit dangerous in his line. 'Yes, of course he was a student here. Now hasn't the big fella done well for himself?'

I asked about old photographs of him, school reports, what the young Sean was like. Corrigan said Sean had been a good student, no trouble, hadn't really stood out until he discovered acting, and then he'd just blossomed. He promised to have a root round, see what paperwork he could find. Then he fell silent for several moments. He clasped his hands before him, almost in prayer, then gave a little nod and asked, 'What sort of a book is it that you're writing?'

'A biography.'

'With his approval?'

'He's cooperating with it, yes.'

'So it won't be . . . how should I put this . . . ahm, warts and all?'

'It will be an honest account. If there are warts, I'd like to see them. Hear them, that is.'

'I hesitate to . . .' The prayer-struck hands collapsed a little, from the church steeple to the bunched double fist. 'May we . . . ahm . . . speak off the record?'

'Reluctantly.'

He smiled. 'What's that old John Ford saying, when you have the truth and you have the legend, what do you do?'

'You print the legend. I can't say I subscribe to that particular school of journalism.'

'No, I suppose it belongs to another era. Nevertheless, I would like to keep this off the record. Is that okay?'

I nodded. It was a lying nod. I didn't have to attribute whatever was coming to him, and, besides, if it was juicy enough I was certain I could get somebody else to talk about it.

'You know,' Corrigan said, 'Sean O'Toole isn't the most popular around here.'

'Yeah, I know, some of his films leave a little to be desired.'

110

'No, I don't mean that.'

'You mean, because of his current project?'

'No. What would that be now? More sex and gratuitous violence, I'll warrant. Or is it the other way round?'

'Nah, it's just a gangster movie. So what's the problem?'

'I don't wish to speak ill of any man . . . particularly one who has made such a success of himself, and we're very proud to have educated him here at . . . Well, anyway . . . we had a, ahm, misunderstanding with him, ahm, last year.'

He paused, unsure whether to continue.

'What sort of a . . . ?' I prompted.

He sighed. 'The thing is, Mr Starkey, we've been trying to raise some money for a new computer suite. We've been down all the usual routes, you know, had the bring-and-buy sales, sponsored coffee mornings, a few bank robberies . . . that's a joke . . .' I smiled politely. 'We contacted as many old boys as we could, looking for support, and of course Sean is the most high profile of them all, although we do have several writers and an MP amongst them . . . Ahm, what we had in mind was a gala concert. So we wrote to Sean and he agreed to come along and present prizes at the end of it. He couldn't have been more helpful. We sold hundreds of tickets on the strength of his appearance.'

'But he didn't turn up.'

'Oh God, no – excuse me, I wasn't taking Him in vain, it was just a little prayer – Sean turned up okay. He came in a white stretch limousine. It was quite a sight. He signed hundreds of autographs, had time for everybody. He gave a lovely speech, had the place in stitches. Then he gave us a grand big cheque. We could have given the tickets away for nothing! He paid for the whole blessed computer suite. After the show he was cheered from bar to bar, and I was with him every step of the way.' He chuckled softly. 'A fantastic, fantastic evening it was.'

'So?'

'Well, y'see, the problem was, the cheque bounced.'

'Bounced?'

'Like a rubber ball. We thought perhaps that there had been a mistake, you know, these stars probably have dozens of accounts, probably don't know where their money is half the time. So we tried to contact Sean, but we couldn't get hold of him, we tried and we tried and we got blocked everywhere we turned. His agent, his manager, his accountant, his production company, even his friggin' – excuse me – hairdresser. Every one of them made some lame excuse, promised to sort it out or passed the buck. And then it emerged that he hadn't paid for his hotel either, or for the stretch limo. Bought a load of drinks for everyone, mind you, can't say the man didn't buy his round, but all the same . . . movie star and all that, and his home town, his old school. You shouldn't mess with people like that.'

'Nothing happened to, y'know, make him change his mind? To cancel the cheque.'

'God, no – oops there's another wee prayer, I'll be a popular man up above – he had the time of his life. It wasn't cancelled, it was bounced.'

'So what do you think the problem was?'

'Is. I think the problem is he hasn't got any money.'

'He gets ten million dollars a film.'

'Well, I don't know what the hell he's doing with it, but he shouldn't go making promises he can't keep. Oh hell – sorry – we'll get over it, we'll get the computers. We haven't even gone running to the press. We're just . . . well, we're just disappointed. He shouldn't . . . well, y'know. It's a sore point.'

I nodded sympathetically, then as unsucky as possible said: 'You're still willing to help me with all the old stuff for the book, though?'

Corrigan nodded slowly. 'I don't see why not. That was then, this is now.'

'S.E. Hinton.'

'Excuse me?'

'Nothing, sorry. I appreciate your help.'

He smiled. 'It's just such a pity, he seemed such a wonderful, warm human being. Maybe there's a reason, I don't know. I suppose in the grand scheme of things it doesn't amount to much. It just would have been nice.'

I thanked him for his time and he promised to look out what the school held in its records and talk to the teachers to see if any of them would have a word. We shook hands. On the way out I paused. He remained behind his desk. He was just removing a packet of cigarettes from his desk and checking under files for a lighter. He found it and lit up. 'Do you still have the cheque?' I asked.

The headmaster nodded. He leant back in his chair and pointed up with his cigarette. There was the cheque, framed, screwed to the wall behind him.

'That'll be worth something, one day,' I said.

'I know,' said Corrigan.

CHAPTER 16

I said, 'Is there anything you want to tell me?'
Patricia paused between feeding spoonfuls of Yoplait Toffee Yoghurt to ginger boy and said: 'Like what?'

'Oh, I don't know, undying love . . .'

'I hate it when you get sarcastic.'

'You must hate me all the time then.'

'*Dan* . . . what's the problem?'

'There's an informer in the ranks.'

'What?'

I nodded down at Little Stevie, yoghurt down his front, mouth open, waiting. Patricia recommenced feeding. 'In the old days we would have taken him out and tarred and feathered him. Kneecapped him probably. Maybe he's a bit young for it. Maybe we could leave his nappy on for days or reinfect him with headlice . . .'

'Dan!'

I stopped, I cleared my throat. 'I hear you had a visitor.'

Her brow crinkled a little, and there was the slightest flush. She concentrated on feeding Little Stevie. 'What do you mean?' she said casually.

115

'I mean, gingersnap spilled the beans. Tony was here while I was away.' It sat in the air for a moment. 'I thought we had an agreement.'

'No,' Patricia said, coolly, 'you laid down the law, and I chose to ignore it.'

'Right.'

She sighed. 'Dan, for godsake. He called round, unannounced, what do you want me to do, shut the door in his face?'

'Yes.'

'Dan, he was in a bad way.'

'Nothing too triv—'

'Dan . . .'

'Did you sleep with him?'

'No, I didn't sleep . . .'

'Because it would be pretty sick to sleep with him and then drive all the way down to Dublin to sleep with me . . .'

'I didn't friggin' sleep with him, I . . .' She paused. She'd finished the yoghurt. She wiped Little Stevie's face on some kitchen roll and then lifted him out of his chair. 'You go in and watch some cartoons, darlin',' she said and patted his head. He toddled off. She said, 'Tout,' quietly after him.

She took my hand and sat me down at the kitchen table. She held onto it as she slipped in opposite me. She looked into my eyes. 'On average,' she said – kindly, I think – 'how often would you say that when it comes to reasons for us fighting, you get hold of the wrong end of the stick?'

I shrugged.

'Would you say, like, seventy-five per cent of the time might be about right?'

I shrugged.

'Okay. Listen to me then.' She squeezed my hand. 'You know that Tony comes round from time to time to see Little Stevie. He is Little Stevie's father, like it or not.'

'Not.'

'And that ninety-nine per cent of the time he pre-arranges it and you're here and you just glare at each other the whole time.'

'Right.'

'But you also know that he has not told his wife that he has a son by another woman.'

'Chickenshit bastard.'

'Well, not any longer. He told her. A few weeks ago. Naturally she was devastated. They went through a very difficult time.'

'I'm finding it very difficult to feel any sympathy.'

'But they've come through it. They're going to stay together.'

'And what, pray tell, has this got to do with you or me or the price of fish?'

'They want to play a bigger part in Stevie's upbringing.'

'*What?*'

'They don't have any kids of their own.'

'I don't give a flying fuck.'

'Dan, he has certain rights.'

'He has fuck all squared in a box! He hardly wanted to know before!'

'Dan, you *know* he has certain rights. If it goes to court, he will be granted certain things. You *know* he will.' She had let go of my hand. She was sitting with her chin in her palm and her elbow on the table. 'I don't want it to go to court, Dan,' she said.

'So what are you saying?'

'They want to take Stevie away on holiday with them, so that they can get to know him.'

'No fucking way . . .'

'Just for a couple of weeks.'

'No fucking way.'

'Disneyland. Florida.'

'No fucking way.'

'Dan. He's Stevie's father.'

'No, he's not. I am.'

'Dan . . .'

'I'm his father and that two-timing bastard isn't going to take him anywhere, especially Florida. Have you thought about this *at all*?'

'Yes, of course I have. Dan, I don't want this to go to court. Dan, it's an absolute certainty that they'd get access. But what if they got *custody*?'

'How on earth would they get custody?'

'I'm not saying they would. I'm saying that if we insist on going to court there's a remote possibility that they might. They might take a very close look at our lives, turn up every stone, and let's face it, Dan, between you and me we haven't exactly been

God's little angels. *They* have a nice settled family life, he made one mistake and now he wants to make amends. He has a good job. They have lots of money. They will be able to afford a shit-hot barrister to handle their case, and thanks to Sam Cameron we will only be able to afford some fluffy-faced kid who doesn't even remember *Crown Court*. *Think* about it, Dan.'

'I am. I'm thinking about all the newspaper stories I've read about fathers borrowing their kids for holidays like that and never coming back. They go to America, we might never see Little Stevie again.'

'Don't be ridiculous.'

'I'm not being ridiculous. It happens all the time. Can you guarantee that it won't?'

'Yes.'

'How? Are you going to make them *promise*?'

'Dan, you're being unreasonable.'

'I'm being sensible. What I don't understand is how you could even contemplate letting him go. For Jesus sake, Trish, you're his *mother*.'

'I know what I am, Dan.'

'Do you? I'm telling you this now, darlin', he's going nowhere. Or if he is, it's over my dead body. And probably yours.'

'Are you threatening me?'

'Yes.'

I got up. As I walked out of the kitchen Patricia was wiping a tear from her eye. I went into the lounge. Little Stevie was watching *The Magic Roundabout* on the Cartoon Network.

119

I sat down heavily beside him and he clambered up onto my knee. I ruffled his hair. He pushed my hand away.

'I used to watch this when I was a kid,' I said, nodding at Florence and Dougal.

'Why?' said Little Stevie.

'Because it was good.'

'Why?'

'Because it made me laugh. It still does.'

'Why?'

'Because although it is a nice happy puppet show, there are a lot of barely concealed druggy references in the script for adults to appreciate.'

'Why?'

'Because it was kind of a rebellious thing to do in the sixties, and the grown-ups never caught on. Everyone does it these days. We have a thing about elevating ancient kitsch kids' programmes into iconic intergenerational talismans.'

'Why, Daddy?'

'I have no idea, but I think I might be heading towards a nervous breakdown.'

'Why?'

I lifted Little Stevie off my knee. Florence was just telling Dougal it was time for bed. 'Don't ask,' I said. 'Go and see Mummy, she's in the kitchen.'

Little Stevie motored off. I sat back on the settee and closed my eyes. The fairground music at the end of *The Magic Roundabout* seemed more annoying than usual, sinister almost. Who the hell did Tony think he was, wanting to take my child to Florida? Patricia didn't understand. It was something that would have to be sorted out between me and him and a crowbar.

I groaned. Who was I kidding? I could barely lift a crowbar.

I sighed. Northern Ireland had come a long way since I'd started my journalistic career. Ancient enemies sat at the same table and discussed arms decommissioning. There were no longer soldiers on the streets and there hadn't been a bomb in months. Tony was a reasonable man, and so was I. Patricia was partially right. He should have access, and we would work out a compromise. Just as long as he understood there was no way that my son was leaving the country for two weeks, or indeed our house for anything more than a few carefully chaperoned hours.

There was a tiny hand on my knee. I opened my eyes and smiled at Little Stevie, back already from the kitchen.

'Dad,' he said, 'what's a wanker?'

CHAPTER 17

We spent the weekend shouting at each other. By the time I left for the drive back to Dublin on Monday morning nothing had been sorted, although I remained in the right. Little Stevie gave me a kiss and a hug goodbye and out of Patricia's earshot I warned him about getting into cars or airplanes with strange men.

I listened to three tapes on the way down. The Clash, for old times' sake. The Geoff Love Orchestra's Big Western Movie Themes because it was classical music with horseshoes and the closest I could get to old culture without falling asleep. And a free CD from *Q* magazine of the best songs of '98, a last desperate attempt to familiarise myself with music outside of the punk era so that I could sit in bars again and tap my foot along to something I recognised and which was only three years out of date.

I checked back into Jury's. I even got the same room. I enquired if a wedding ring had shown up but there was nothing to report. I would have to start looking for a new one, though first I would have to decide if I wanted to remain married to someone who was willing to give my child away to a complete stranger, though of course he wasn't a complete stranger, he wasn't my child and she wasn't going to give him away.

Sometimes there's too much goes on in my head.

Concentrate.

Concentrate on unpacking. We'd been rowing, but she'd still folded everything perfectly. I took out the shirts and the T-shirts and put them away. I changed from my Oxfords into a pair of black baseball boots, black jeans and a zip-up black suede bomber jacket. I looked pretty cool, which was accidental but fortuitous seeing as how I might have to attract a new wife.

I drove back out to the set. It was the final week of shooting *The Brigadier* and I had barely scratched the surface of the research for my biography of Sean O'Toole. He had thus far been affable, open and chatty, but I had hardly made a note. By the time we had gotten past the chit-chat it was always time for him to go back to work. I already had in my mind a vague plan to climax the book with Sean's triumph (or humiliation) at the Cannes Film Festival; it would provide a suitably glamorous backdrop, and it would also nail Sam Cameron for several thousand more in expenses. I made a mental note to phone his secretary as soon as I got back from the set. She could organise a hotel room for me out there; in fact Sam could bloody well pay for Patricia and Little Stevie too.

That's what we needed, a break, a holiday, just the three of us. There was no need to call Patricia with the good news just yet. It would be a pleasant surprise for her when she caved in. A reward. But it would be mean to dangle it before her like a carrot, or a free holiday.

Before even contemplating Cannes, however, I had to find Sean the man, not Sean the star, and already I had the first indication that the two might be very different.

The star stuff was easy. The facts of his movie career could be picked up over the Internet; there were a thousand and one newspaper and magazine profiles, there would be the industry newspapers that would give me the lowdown on his films' box-office performances, and of course there would be the reviews. If I could read enough of them I might even be able to avoid sitting through all of his movies. It was tempting.

It was getting behind the PR sheen, however, that would make or break the book. Not that I was trying to do a Kitty Kelly or Goldman hatchet job. I wasn't prepared to print every salacious rumour I came across. I would need documented verification, or at least scout's honour, before I'd do that. His headmaster had already intimated that Sean wasn't as Britney as he appeared. A bounced cheque wasn't that important, but from someone who liked to be thought of as a nice guy, it was surprising, unusual and definitely worthy of further investigation.

But how? Confront him and risk him withdrawing further cooperation? Bang on his caravan and shout: 'You cheated the kids out of thousands, you fucker!' Or leave it to the very end of my association with him when it no longer mattered? Would *not* raising the subject colour my opinion of him anyway when there was possibly a perfectly reasonable explanation?

As I arrived at the gates to the warehouse where *The Brigadier* was filming it became immediately apparent that Sean had doubled security, at least physically. There were now four big bouncers on the gate. They demanded I climb out of my car and be searched. They were Dubliners. They rooted through my trousers with the suspicious scowls and unconcealed enthusiasm of halfwits who think everyone with a northern accent is a terrorist, whereas it's actually only about thirty per cent.

This time they were filming indoors. They'd constructed a mock-up of a cell within an RUC station, and Sean O'Toole's version of Michael O'Ryan was combating some savage police brutality with a steely smile and a ready wit. There was a palpable air of tension. But it wasn't anything Sean was managing to create in front of the camera. It came from the crew. It was the eighth take of this particular scene. Sean wasn't happy with his own performance and he was taking it out on the technical staff. There was too much noise. Not enough light. When somebody dropped a cup

125

during filming he got fired on the spot and only reinstated when everyone else threatened to walk out. This had happened before I arrived. Karen, the make-up girl, told me all about it. She had walked past and smiled and told me she used to read my column up north. She had short brown hair and attractive freckles and I thought she was examining me with a little too much appreciation until she started to suggest creams I could use to sort out my skin problem and I said, 'What fucking skin problem?'

'Take it easy,' she said, 'it's more common than you'd think.'

She produced a mirror from her bag of tricks and held it up for me to see. It was one of those super-powered efforts that they use to magnify hair follicles and DNA, so of course it looked like I'd a skin problem. She suggested a moisturiser, I suggested I might as well write *homosexual* on my head. She said times had changed, I said not that much. She said I was taking the piss and I said I might be. She said Sean was a sweetheart to work with and I asked if she'd managed to cash her pay cheque yet. She looked at me oddly and I looked at her oddly back, though her back wasn't oddly at all.

Then Sean, way behind us, said: 'Cut!' and followed it with, 'That's the one, check the gate!'

But there followed an uneasy silence during which Sean's relieved smile faded. The camera-man whispered something in Sean's ear, and Sean checked out the monitor, touched a finger to his nose, then nodded. Evidently all was not well. Then the focus puller announced there was a hair on the lens as well. Sean issued an angry 'Fuck!' The assistant director bellowed: 'Right, let's get set up again. Karen! Sean needs sorting!'

Sean retreated towards his caravan. Karen hurried across after him. I tagged along. As I passed amongst the crew I detected angry murmurs. I couldn't quite pick up what they were saying, but it sounded like *murmur-murmur-murmur-murmur*. Karen skipped up the steps into the caravan and I followed most of the way. I put my head around the door and said: 'Okay if I come in?'

Sean looked angrily across. Then he sighed and nodded me in. Karen had lifted his chin up and was holding a tissue to his nose. There was blood seeping into it. 'I know what they're fucking thinking,' Sean growled. 'I know what the fuck they're slabbering about.'

'What?' I said, innocently. Karen looked across and rolled her eyes.

I had an inkling. I'd never practised myself, but I'd seen *Scarface*.

'Can't get a fucking nosebleed without them thinking I'm a fucking coke addict!' Sean shouted. 'Jesus Christ, I could have a fucking brain tumour and they'd still be thinking I was doing coke! Fucking hell. They *know* how hard I'm working! They know somebody's trying to kill me! And all they can do is bitch about every fucking thing . . .'

127

Karen pulled the tissue away. 'I think that's it, Sean.' She began to re-apply his make-up. 'I didn't hear them say anything, Sean,' she said softly.

'You think I'm paranoid?' Sean snapped. He pushed her hand away. 'That's just another way of saying I'm a coke addict. Jesus Christ.'

She pulled his chin forcefully back towards her. He seemed a little surprised. 'Just sit where you are, Sean. You're worse than a little boy sometimes.'

'I'm working my fucking guts out and all they can do . . .'

'Shhhhh,' Karen said.

He looked at me and he sighed, a common enough occurrence. 'Fuck,' he said, 'I'm screaming around here like Elton John, and Johnny Boswell is here to record it.'

I shrugged. 'You're under a lot of pressure,' I said.

'Dead right I am.'

Karen pulled his chin to one side. He resisted a little this time. It was, evidently, the side of his face he was not happiest with, and perhaps he had a point. With the light coming through the small caravan window, it did not cut quite as perfect a profile as the world was familiar with. Any other man would have been deliriously happy with such 'defects', but Sean was A Movie Star, which required nothing less than perfection, unless you were Kathy Bates.

Karen, evidently aware of his feelings, finished re-applying the make-up quickly. As she let go of

128

his chin it snapped back into his more usual profile like it was on a tight spring.

When he spoke again, Sean's tone had lightened a little. 'What was it Forrest Gump used to say: life is like a box of chocolates, you never know which one you're going to get?'

'Something like that,' I said.

'Well, I always know, it's always the fucking coffee cream. Nobody ever likes the coffee creams.' He smiled, at last. 'You know, I know people who stick it up their arse.'

Karen gave him an odd look. 'Stick what up their arse? Coffee creams?'

'*No,*' Sean laughed, '*cocaine.* Their noses can't take it any more, they have to find some other way. Just thought you'd like to know.'

'You've never indulged yourself?' I asked. 'I mean cocaine, not up the arse.'

'Of *course* I've indulged.' Karen offered him the same nuclear-powered mirror and he began to examine his face intently. 'I've had my wild days, but I've settled down now. Love of a good woman, all that.'

'It's about six weeks since you met her, Sean,' Karen said.

'Love of several good women, then.' He slipped his hand around her waist. She removed it. 'Chance would be a fine thing,' he said. He smiled round at me. 'Write this: Sean said that once he realised he wouldn't be able to wear his trademark sunglasses without his nose caving in, he decided to quit taking cocaine. Now he's an occasional social user, but much prefers a nice cup of tea and a Paris bun. Write that.'

I said, 'Do you have any money problems, Sean?'

He hesitated for a moment. His brow furrowed ever so slightly, just enough to send off a little flurry of powder. Karen tutted. 'You mean on this film?' Sean asked.

'No, I mean generally.'

We looked at each other for several moments. Karen detected a chill and said, 'Do you want me to leave?'

Sean shook his head. He looked into the mirror. His voice went deep. 'Mirror, mirror, not on the wall, who's the fairest of them all?' He closed his lips, then let out a passably good ventriloquist's 'You are!' before turning his gaze upon me. 'Now who have you been talking to?' he asked.

'Headmaster. Your old school.'

Sean nodded slowly. 'I see.' He took a deep breath. Then he clapped his hands together and let out a loud whoop. 'Class!' he shouted. 'Didn't I show those bastards!'

CHAPTER 18

He made me wait, of course. Five minutes. He cruised out of his caravan and performed the scene to absolute perfection and with a warmth and style he had not previously mustered. He even earned a round of applause from a relieved crew, and without a hint of sarcasm about it. It's amazing what hearing some good news can do for a guy, and getting one over on his old school seemed to do the trick.

Sean checked the tape, then had a brief discussion with his team about the next scene, which, although it was set just a few yards away in another part of the mocked-up police station, would still require the best part of an hour to get the cameras and the lights shifted and set up.

I took a Diet Coke from the small fridge. I have a thing for exploring fridges. Knoweth the fridge, knoweth the man, as Oscar once said. There wasn't much else in there. A bottle of vodka. Half a dozen oranges. And three syringes.

I closed the fridge quickly. Footsteps. When I turned, Alice was in the doorway. I generally do look suspicious, so her quizzical expression was to be expected. 'Should you be in here by yourself?' she asked.

'Yes,' I said, 'he's on his way.'

She looked at the fridge.

'I was just getting a drink,' I said, holding the can up for evidence. I opened the fridge door again. 'Can I get you one?'

'No.'

'What about an orange?'

'No.'

'What about a syringe, so we can shoot some heroin together?'

She took a deep breath. 'I don't know why the hell he ever agreed to this book,' she said.

I closed the fridge door. I crossed to the little lunch table and slipped in behind it. I opened my can and took a long drink. 'Just how well do you really know him, Alice?' I asked.

'Better than you ever will.'

'Did you know about the . . . well, y'know?'

Alice nodded. She glanced behind her. Sean was approaching. As he came up the steps he looked at her and said: 'What's wrong?'

Her voice faltered endearingly, to me anyway. 'Sweetie, it's Dan. He's . . . well, he found your syringes.'

'Christ.'

'I know,' Alice said.

'I was just . . .' I began. 'I didn't . . .'

'Fuck,' said Sean, 'I need a shot right now. Will I get you one too, love?'

Alice nodded. She pulled the caravan door closed and started to roll up her sleeve. Sean crossed to the fridge.

'Will you join us, Dan?' Alice asked.

'No,' I said. 'I don't . . .'

'Och, Danny,' Sean said, 'you should learn to live a little. Y'know, one blink of the eye, your life's over, you should enjoy it while you can.'

'I . . . no. No thanks.'

Sean was holding the bottle of vodka. He removed the top, then lifted a syringe from the fridge and dipped it in. Disinfecting it. Good. At least he was a health-conscious junkie. He began to draw the vodka up into the syringe. When he had filled it he set the bottle down on the worktop above the fridge then leant back into it and removed an orange. Then he plunged the needle into the fruit and squeezed the plunger. When the last drop had been injected into the fruit he removed the needle, then tossed the orange across to Alice. She caught it in one hand, then started to peel it. Sean reached for the vodka bottle again.

'Oh,' I said.

'The problem with journalists,' Alice said, 'is that they invariably jump to the wrong conclusions.'

'I didn't . . .'

'You did.'

Sean finished squeezing again, then tossed the second orange across to me. I fumbled it and it rolled across the table and off. I reached under to retrieve it but misjudged the available space and

133

cracked my head. The impact knocked the can over and a bubbling lake of Diet Coke sopped over the edge and into my lap.

I had an orange vodka in my hand, and damp trousers. I looked at the two of them, quietly giggling into their fruit, and said: 'Sorry.'

Alice got some kitchen roll and mopped up the mess.

'We both enjoy a wee tot of vodka once in a while,' Sean said, 'but it's not good to drink in front of the crew, or reporters, for that matter. It's a little innocent subterfuge.'

He crossed to Alice. They clinked oranges. I cleared my throat and tried to forget about my trousers. 'You were going to tell me about your old school,' I said.

Alice kissed Sean on the cheek. 'I just came to tell you that George Bijoudeux is coming on Friday. He wants to see what you have.'

'Fuck,' said Sean. He gave Alice a little hug.

'It'll be fine,' she said. She glanced across, gave me the tiniest smile, then exited.

'Fuck,' said Sean again.

'Who's . . . ?'

'He *is* the Cannes Film Festival. He'll want to see as much of *The Brigadier* as I can cut together. I'm a star, but I'm not a star director. He has to satisfy himself I haven't made a complete crock of shite before he accepts it for the competition. Though of course he's French and would probably say it in a much nicer way.'

'Is there a problem with that? *Is* it a crock of shite?'

'Not for me to say really. It just means working even harder than I have been. From little sleep to no sleep. Shit. Still, it's better than being beaten with a big stick, which is what happened at my old school.'

He moved into the seat opposite me.

'Really?' I said.

'Really.' He took another suck on his orange. 'Y'see, Dan, it might seem petty to you, but sometimes it's just not enough to drive past the old place in a big car and say, look how well I did despite what you did to me. You have to get out there and beat *them* with a big stick. So I did.'

'Were they really that bad to you?'

'Not just me. Others. Catholic education, old style. Beat it in to them, or knock it out of them. Turn the other cheek, boy, 'cause we've already thrashed the other one.'

'It *was* years ago, though.'

'The pain stays with you. The sensation of having a grown man's hand down your shorts, that stays with you too.'

'You mean Corrigan . . . .'

'He was one of them. Of course he wasn't headmaster at the time, and he wasn't the worst, but they were all at it. Even the priests. Dan, always be suspicious of a man who volunteers for celibacy.'

'I was conscripted,' I said.

He shook his head slowly. 'I'm not a brave man

135

meself, Dan. I went there full of great intentions to expose them – the way they'd exposed me . . .' He laughed softly. 'But when it came to it I couldn't do it. I was going to stand on that stage and accept all the plaudits, then I was going to tell everyone what grasping little perverts they were. I chickened out. There were little boys in that audience and I knew just to look at them that they were still going through it. It wouldn't help them. The sad thing was their parents were there with them, parents who were with me when I was at school so they must have known what was going on, yet thirty years on they've sent their own kids back to the same fucking place with the same fucking teachers. And that makes me sick. But that isn't why I stayed quiet either.' He drummed his fingers on the table. When he looked at me there was the merest hint of a tear in one eye. His voice sounded like a damp winter's morning. 'I stayed quiet because when I looked at Corrigan and the rest of them – do you know what I felt? Scared. *Scared.* Still scared of fucking Corrigan and the fact that he might tell my parents.'

'I thought your parents were . . .'

'My parents *are* dead. And that shows you how scared I felt on that stage.'

'So . . .'

'So bouncing the cheque was just my stupid little way of letting them know that I haven't forgotten.'

'To an outsider though, who doesn't know the facts, it just makes you look mean.'

'That's why you're here, Dan. To set the record straight. Isn't that what it's all about, getting at the truth, writing about the man behind all this . . . shite?'

I nodded. I took the first bite of my orange.

'I always find it's better to peel it first,' Sean said.

He had a point.

CHAPTER 19

I spent most of the last week of filming talking to everybody involved in *The Brigadier* but Sean O'Toole. Shooting was running behind schedule because of the enforced break after the attack on Alice, and the last person he wanted to talk to was me, the fool who didn't know how to eat an orange.

There was no shortage of interviewees. Making a film requires only slightly less planning and coordination than the invasion of Normandy, and the consequences of getting it wrong are only marginally less serious. Low-budget film-makers face arguably a greater foe than Adolf Hitler – not the weather, not lack of resources, not even Michael O'Ryan, but lack of time. You have so long, and then your window of opportunity passes. At Normandy, they *could* have waited for another week or two, though history likes to claim otherwise. In a big studio film, sure, you can keep people hanging around for weeks or months on the payroll; if it goes over budget you get more money, if it goes over time you pay them to stay on. But on a low-budget number like *The Brigadier* there was no such freedom; the crew was being paid minimum wage and they all had other jobs to go on to. It was a case of getting it done, getting it done *now*, or not getting it done at all.

I talked to set designers, dialogue coaches, the continuity girl, the costume designer, the grip, the gaffer, the best boy, the rigging gaffer, the art director, the storyboard artist, the unit production manager, the production coordinator, the choreographer, the boom operator . . . there were dozens. Even a doctor. An American called Abel Fruitke who was known to one and all as Fruitcake.

I said to him, 'I take it you gave him the syringes?' and he looked at me blankly for a moment until I added, 'For the oranges in the fridge.'

Then he smiled and nodded, though I wasn't entirely sure if he knew what I was talking about. Not that it mattered. It was only small talk. He was Sean's personal physician, had been with him for years, following him from movie to movie.

'He's not sick, is he?' I asked.

'Healthiest man I know,' said the Fruitcake.

'Easy job then.'

'My job is to keep him that way. He goes down, the whole picture closes, insurance companies have to pay out millions. It's not exactly Vietnam, but he keeps me busy. Combination of nutritionist, physiotherapist, psychologist, MD, personal trainer, chiropody . . . you name it, I see to it.'

I left it at that. I'd been speaking to people all week and all I was getting were variations on

what a swell guy Sean O'Toole was. Notwith-
standing some Catholic child-abusers in Belfast
and a psychotic gangster, Sean was held in genuine
affection by everybody, everywhere.

Finally, on a sunny Friday evening, just after
seven, Sean shot the final take on the final scene
of *The Brigadier*, waited for the gate to clear, then
called out in his distinctive tones, 'It's a wrap!'
There was a round of applause. He made a short
speech thanking everyone and taking the piss out
of himself. He had managed to claw back the time
he'd lost and completed filming just under budget,
which meant, he said, that there was enough left in
the kitty for a party. Everybody was happy.

The wrap party was to be held that night at
Sean's house out at Killiney. It was strictly cast
and crew only. Invitations were handed out only
to those named on them. There were to be no
guests, no wives, no hangers-on. Not even any
biographers. I was sitting on a bench, staring at
a wall, telling myself I wasn't bothered, when
somebody sat down behind me.

I turned. She was looking wonderful. Her cheeks
were flushed from the early summer sun. Her hair
was tied back in a little ponytail. She wore a leather
jerkin and tight black jeans. I hadn't seen her all
week but I hadn't forgotten how nasty she'd been
to me or how great a kisser she was.

She said, 'Are you coming tonight?'

'That's a leading question.'

She tutted. 'To the party.'

140

'I haven't been invited. Cast and crew only.'

'Oh, right enough. Oh, well.'

She hopped down from the bench and walked off around the corner. When, after three minutes she hadn't popped her head back round and laughed, 'Only joking, here's your ticket,' I got off the bench myself and looked for her, but she was gone. Nearly everyone was gone.

I had been part of the scenery for the best part of two weeks, but who invited scenery to a party?

I tramped back to my car. On the way out one of Sean's security guards waved at me. It was the one who'd sucked green slime out of my mouth. I didn't want him to think I was that easy all the time, so I looked away.

Back at the hotel, there was a message to call Trish. We had spoken a couple of times during the week. Cordial exchanges for the most part, marred only by my insistence that she put Little Stevie on the phone to prove that he was still with her. This time, she seemed pleased to hear from me, but for all the wrong reasons.

'Dan,' she said, 'I'm worried.'

'Don't. I'm fine.'

'About Stevie.'

'Is he sick?'

'No ... I ... this sounds silly. But I think somebody tried to snatch him.'

'*Snatch* him ... ?'

'At his playgroup. A man said he was supposed to pick him up. Of course they didn't let him ...'

I took a deep breath. I'd guessed it was coming.
'I told you Tony would try and . . .'

'It wasn't Tony.'

'How do you know?'

'The girls there know Tony, they wouldn't
stop . . .'

'How the fuck do *they* know Tony?'

'Dan – not now, please! For godsake, somebody
tried to take Stevie, and all you can think . . . shit!
Dan, please. I'm frightened. I . . . thought I saw
somebody outside the house. I might have been
mistaken. But what if . . . I don't know. With
all that's happened before . . . I'm just a bit . . .
y'know.'

I shushed her. I told her everything was okay.
These things happened all the time. The papers
were full of them. 'Is there anybody outside now?'

'No. I checked. It might just have been . . .'

'Where's Stevie?'

'He's here, he's okay. But why Stevie, why would
anybody want to . . . ?'

I couldn't hold it. I snapped, 'It's not me you
should be asking. Why don't you call lover boy?'

'Dan, he's not . . .'

I put the phone down.

I got two bottles of beer out of the mini-bar and
drank them down. I phoned back and apologised.
To the answer machine.

I didn't know what to do. Filming was finished.
I should go home and make sure everything was

142

okay. It wasn't like Patricia to get upset over nothing. It was more like me. But there was a party going on. And Patricia had been lying to me about Tony, or at the very least she'd been hiding things from me. I had no idea how much of Tony she was seeing, or whether he was wearing his trousers at the time.

She could go whistle for her wedding ring.

I filled my pockets with mini vodkas from the mini-bar and took a taxi out to Killiney. I got it to stop at the hotel below Sean's house and drank several pints at the bar on the off-chance that some of the party-goers would stop in for a quick one on the way there and I could sneak in with them, but nobody showed.

I walked up the hill towards his house. There were no street lights. It was pitch black. I would have to use my charm to get in. For the first time I regretted blanking the guy who'd saved my life. If it came to it I might even kiss him again if it meant getting into the party, but strictly no tongues. A taxi came along the road behind me, then stopped at the security gate. I hung back in the shelter of an overhanging tree while three girls in high heels and low dresses climbed out. I recognised two of them as set decorators, but hadn't seen the third before. They were all dressed to the nines. Maybe even the tens. They were laughing and giggling excitedly as the outer gate swung open and one of the security guards came out, though not my friend. There was some kind of disagreement. At first I couldn't make anything out, but it gradually became clear from the way their voices rose that the girls only had two invitations between them. They tried flirting. They tried bribery. Then they resorted to curses and threats, at first aimed at the security guy and then amongst themselves. Finally one of the girls climbed back into the taxi and drove off. Sisters, except where Sean O'Toole's involved.

I wasn't going to get in that way.

I retraced my steps, then followed the perimeter of the wall for a hundred yards in the opposite direction as it snaked up towards the top of Killiney hill. It was nowhere less than eight feet tall and there was razor wire strung along the top. Distantly I could hear music, chatter and cutlery. I had long ago downed the vodkas. I was parched and there appeared to be no way over the wall that wouldn't involve a blood transfusion. What was I thinking of, leaving a perfectly good hotel bar to hang about in the dark outside a film star's party? Fuck 'im.

But first, a piss.

I peed against the wall. Sean's house was too high up the hill and too far out of Dublin for there to be graffiti on the wall, so I ended up watching the stream of pee roll back down towards the bay. Except it didn't. It flooded happily under a bush cropping out from the wall, but then failed to materialise on the other side. Perplexed – because at that time of night and in that state of sobriety these things sometimes seem important – I delved into the bush to see what the obstruction was and discovered a narrow drainage channel running out from beneath the wall. Behind it, set into the stonework, there was an archway which was blocked by an insubstantial wooden gate.

It seemed, indeed, a fortuitous piss.

Bent nearly double, I pushed through the bush and placed my hands on the gate. It was old and flaky. With one good shake it came loose in my hands.

I stepped through. There was another bush planted on the other side to obscure the gate from that side as well. I was through it in a moment and into Sean O'Toole's garden.

Almost immediately I stumbled over a couple making love in the grass. It was dark and I couldn't make out who it was. Their clothes were sitting in an untidy pile. I mumbled an apology and walked on. They giggled. I had his jacket under my arm. I quickly located his invitation and pocketed it. I hid the jacket under another bush and sauntered on. I needed a drink.

The house was still a hundred yards distant. I could see dozens of people standing both within and without. I was moving as casually as I could down towards them when I heard a commotion to my right, a little joyful scream and then a splash. I hesitated, then walked towards the sound. I came upon a thin circle of pines, and beyond them spied a hot tub and a small summerhouse.

Sitting in the hot tub was a young girl I recognised from the costume department, which was ironic, because she wasn't wearing one. Her breasts were being massaged or measured for a brassiere by one of the supporting actors from the film. I watched for several long moments, then edged around the trees towards the summerhouse. There was light within; the curtains had been drawn across the main window, but they were so old that they did little to mask the fact that there were people within. I decided to get closer, in case they needed me.

I moved further round until I was at the back of the summerhouse, and facing a much smaller, dirt-streaked window. It was located so close to the pines and at such an angle that it would never catch the sunlight and thus had not been cleaned. I crept up to the window and, after a moment's hesitation during which I debated the ethics of looking through it and came out on the side of the nosey bastards, I peered from the darkness into the light.

It took me several moments to work it out, to decide exactly what I was seeing; it was a combination of the grime on the window, the orange glow of the light within and the complete shock of observing such a heaving mass of flesh. A conglomeration of shuddering, flouncing, vibrating, sucking and fucking body parts, the most recognisable of which belonged to Sean O'Toole.

I counted and divided and came out at four women, two men. Alice was not amongst them. I did not recognise any of the women, though it took me a while to see their faces. I was prepared to wait. I did, however, recognise Sean's male companion. It was Dr Fruitcake. One of the women was performing oral sex on him, but he seemed to be giving more attention to the syringe he was plunging into his arm.

CHAPTER 20

I found Alice in the kitchen, lifting a tray of sausage rolls out of the oven. As she set them on the worktop she smiled at me and said, 'Good, you got the ticket then.'

'What?'

'I sent one of the security guys after you with your ticket. But you'd left. You looked so hurt when you didn't get one. It was just a mix-up. I had it sent down to the hotel.'

'Oh. Right. It was you. I wasn't sure.'

She offered me a sausage roll. I declined. She said: 'Have you seen Sean?'

I had seen more of him than I ever wanted to, but I shook my head and lifted a can of Harp from a plastic-wrapped crate sitting on the kitchen table. *Alice, your husband is having group sex in the garden shed. Mower or less.*

I stayed long enough to see him shoot heroin into his veins.

They were sharing needles, too.

'No, I haven't.'

'You sure you won't have a sausage roll?'

The house was crowded. There were people

148

slow dancing and smooching to Frank Sinatra in the lounge. Alice was the perfect hostess. She glided about spreading laughter and happiness everywhere. I would have been quite happy to gaze at her all night if I hadn't known that she was being fucked around by her film star husband.

Or maybe she did know about it and turned two blind eyes.

Maybe it was par for the course.

She was a self-confident woman. She wasn't naive or unworldly. Although she had not known Sean for a great length of time, she only had to read the papers to know what the lifestyle could be, to know what was available to somebody in Sean's exalted position.

I returned to the kitchen. I made small talk. The girl from the hot tub came in all giggly, her hair wet. There was no sign of the actor. She cosied up to me for several minutes, but she could tell I wasn't interested and soon moved off. I went out to find a toilet, but there was a queue of five women, so it would be at least an hour. There were stairs, but a chair had been set across the base of them and a handwritten PRIVATE taped to it. I stepped over it and hurried upstairs.

For some reason few stories of high adventure focus on the lack of bladder control which comes with advancing years. It's a gap in the market I am perfectly happy to exploit.

My wife always says to look in a bathroom to find out what somebody is really like. Whereas I maintain it only tells you whether they've bad skin or their hair is receding. Sean's bathroom – Sean's and Alice's, that is – was large and smelled like it had been freshly decorated.

It was done in peach. There was a circular bath, big enough for five or six people, which was handy for Sean. There were gold-plated taps, there was a bidet and a power shower in a separate cubicle. There were no hairs in the bath. There were some Bic disposable razors, toothpaste, toothbrush, Mum deodorant, a damp towel and very little else. Alice, of course, had not moved in yet. It wasn't glitzy, I would tell Patricia, and he used the same toilet roll we did. I had my pee. I exited the bathroom and walked quietly along the hall, opening doors.

There was another bathroom, but it appeared not to be in use. There were five bedrooms, but only two of them with beds. Sean's room was the biggest. There was a giant television. There were several dozen video tapes piled to one side of it. The temptation, of course, was to play some of them. See whether they were porn or he'd been recording *Coronation Street*. The bed was queen size, but didn't look like it had recently been slept in.

I came to the locked room at the end of the landing.

There is always a locked room at parties. Where the stuff you don't want anyone to see gets put. I have never been to a party where there has not been a locked room. It may contain something as inoffensive as ironing you haven't done or paperbacks you don't want your intellectual friends to see, or it may contain your stuffed mother-in-law, but there is always a locked room at parties.

I knew immediately that getting into the room by any means other than force would be impossible. I traced the outline of the lock with my fingers. If I'd had a hairpin I could have pinned back my hair. Frank Sinatra was coming to the climax of 'New York, New York'. There was nothing else for it. I put my shoulder to the door and pressed firmly against it, then a little more; then I was getting angry so I gave it a good kicking. Since I was as weak as a kitten, that didn't make the slightest difference. Then I remembered Patricia, and the cunning way she hid keys around our house. I reached up and ran my fingers along the top of the door frame. Bingo. I was inside in seconds. I closed the door, flipped on the light. I was in Sean's study. I could tell that by the desk and the computer and the shelves full of books, but there was more. There were bottles of pills everywhere. Boxes of them. Vials of liquids. Syringes. Powders. The only studying he could have done in here was for his pharmacy exams. But there was none of the tidiness one associates with a pharmacy. The desk, the chair, the computer, they all boasted a rainbow covering of medicinal dust. It was fingerprint heaven. There were several white-encrusted razor blades.

Silver foil. Matches had been stubbed out on the desk.

I opened the top drawer. It was stuffed full of prescriptions. They were far dated. They were made out in Sean's name, and they had all been signed by Dr Fruitcake. I took a notebook from my back pocket and started to jot down the names of the medicines to check out later, just in case I was getting hold of the wrong end of the stick and he was really into vitamins. Any self-respecting journalist on the espionage trail would have had a miniature camera, but I had never been a self-respecting journalist.

I would learn later what they all were, that Sean had been prescribed daily injections of Toradol for pain, Librium to control mood swings, Ativan for agitation, Valium for anxiety, Depakote to counter acute mania, Thorazine for anxiety, Cogentin for agitation, Vistaril every six hours for anxiety, lorazepam every six hours also for anxiety. He was also taking additional doses of Valium, plus Vicodin, diphenoxylate, diphenhydramine and Colanadine, nystatin, Narcan, haloperidol, Promethazine, Benztropine, Unisom, Atarax, Compazine, Xanax, Desyrel, Tigan and phenobarbitol. It was surprising that he had any time left to indulge in heroin.

Behind me, the door opened.

The way doors behind me always open, and the way I am always surprised in dark corners and revealed in embarrassing situations.

It is my life and I should be used to it.

But you never get used to that first sick sensation when you realise that you have let yourself down again, and everyone else for that matter.

There was Sean, looking hazy-eyed, and by his side, Dr Fruitcake.

I tried an old one, but I knew it would not work. 'I was just lookin' for the bogs,' I said, and gave a little stumble. I let go of the collection of prescriptions in my hand and watched them float to the ground. 'And for a rich man,' I slurred, 'your toilet paper's fuckin' crap.'

They didn't speak. Sean just looked behind him, then nodded and stepped back, and instead of a movie star there were his man mountain body-guards coming into the study. Downstairs Frank Sinatra was doing it his way, and upstairs they were about to do it theirs.

They didn't beat me up, they just carried me through the party to the front door. The guy who'd kissed me at the docks had one hand on my kisscurl and another on my left ear. It wasn't very pleasant. The other security guard took a foot with either hand. As I was carried through the lounge, everybody had a good look, especially Alice.

Sean came down the stairs behind us. I saw Alice hurry across to him. The music didn't stop, but the talking did. 'He was going through our stuff,' Sean said, and even in the midst of being carried out like the garbage I thought how calculating it was to describe it as 'our stuff'. It would have been so much more truthful to say he had discovered me going through his illicit drugs mountain.

They had to wait half a minute, swinging me between them, while the first gate hummed open, and then the second. Then they threw me. I landed on my head. Gravel grated down my face.

From the gate Sean shouted: 'You can consider the contract cancelled.'

'Look at me,' I shouted back, pulling myself up onto grazed knees, 'I'm crying.'

'You write a fucking word of this, you're a dead man.'

'You don't scare me,' I yelled, and then added, 'although *they* do,' for the benefit of the two big bastards advancing towards me with their fists clenched.

I ran.

I put several hundred yards between me and his heavies before I chanced turning and giving them the fingers. But they had already gone back inside. The gates were closed and the road was pitch black.

It was a warm, pleasant evening and my knees were bleeding. I was shaken and thirsty and had been made to look like a low-life sleazeball in front of over a hundred people.

They had taken my notebook and my dignity, but they had failed to locate the half-pound of heroin in my shoe.

CHAPTER 21

It was because I was drunk, of course. And because the opportunity presented itself. And for badness. There were so many drugs in his study he might never notice it was gone. All I knew was that it was difficult to walk with a shoe full of heroin. Every time it hit the ground a little powder puff shot up through the lace holes, like it was a steam train setting off.

I limped on. I was almost entirely sober. I needed to sit down with a beer and think this through, because my first inclination, once I accepted my stupidity in stealing the drugs, was to throw them away.

It would be right, but it would also be wrong.

Right in the context of heroin is bad and nasty, wrong in the context of me retaining a semblance of good health.

Because he would notice the heroin was gone.

And he would know who had taken it.

And because he clearly had connections in the nefarious world of drug-dealing, he would send somebody to get it back.

Mr Gunman, honestly, I thought it was talc.

155

I could not go back to the house and ring the bell and say, 'Sean, half a pound of your finest heroin fell into my shoe.'

I could not even ring the bell and run away, just leaving the shoe, because they would not understand. They would think it was a prank, or worse, an unexploded brogue bomb, and have the army there in seconds.

Why had I done it?

Over three pints in the hotel down below I could not answer that question. The only person I could implicate in drug dealing was myself, by virtue of what still sat uncomfortably in my shoe, so going to the police was pointless. I could get the stuff verified by an independent witness for the purposes of my book, and then dispose of it, which still left me open to getting shot. Or I could sell it to somebody, make enough money to cover the cancellation of the book contract *and* the vast amount of money that Sam Cameron owed me anyway, which would make me financially buoyant enough to hire a gunman to kill whichever gunman Sean hired to dispose of me.

Or was I overreacting? If Sean O'Toole was so drug-addled, he wouldn't even notice that the heroin was gone. Or if he did, he was so rich he could just write it off and order some more from Dr Fruitcake.

I took a taxi back to Jury's. The chances were that Sam would not discover that Sean was planning to withdraw his cooperation on the book for some considerable time, so I didn't yet have to worry about settling the account. Filming was over and Patricia was expecting me back home, but it would scarcely do our custody campaign much good to be discovered crossing the border with half a pound of heroin.

I bought some Johnson's Baby Powder in the hotel shop. The girl behind the counter looked at me curiously. I smiled at her and said, 'Don't you find that new underpants chafe your thighs desperately.'

She nodded.

I went up to my room and called Patricia about the situation. She was my rock. My Simon and Garfunkel. My Gibraltar, minus the SAS and dead IRA bombers. The answer machine responded and I thought it best not to leave an explanatory message. I told her I loved her and missed her and trusted she had not given Stevie away to the gypsies. I went into the bathroom and emptied the bottle of Johnson's Baby Powder down the toilet, and refilled it with the heroin.

I lay on the bed and tried to sleep but it would not come. I watched television into the early hours of the morning and only switched it off when *The French Connection* came on. I drifted off with dawn breaking and woke at nine with a sore head. I swallowed half a dozen paracetamol and opened a can of Diet Coke from the mini-bar. I watched the traffic below for a while. I was no nearer a decision. All I could do was press ahead with what I was doing and figure it all out later. Just write the book, write the best book I could. I had never intended it to be an affectionate portrait of the man, simply an honest one. Nothing had changed. I just knew more, and needed to know more still. The extent of Sean O'Toole's addictions was obvious, but how had they come about? Exactly where did Dr Fruitcake fit into the prescription? Equation. How had Sean managed to write, star in and direct an entire movie while under the influence of such a variety of drugs? All questions I would no longer be able to put directly to him.

I went downstairs and ordered an Ulster fry.

Of course, they didn't call it that. They called it a *full Irish breakfast*. I preferred to think of it as *the twenty-six-counties-of-Ireland-we-haven't-got-yet fry*, but I suspected it would always be too early in the morning for them to appreciate my wit or unionism.

I was luxuriating in the pleasure of mopping up the leakage from the fried egg with a slice of toast – Patricia won't let me do it at home because she thinks it's bad manners, whereas I think she talks a lot of shite – when I saw Alice appear in the entrance to the dining room. She was looking about for somebody, and I could only presume that it was me. I was in a corner, and partially hidden by a family of Italians, so I stood up and waved. She saw me immediately and hurried over.

She was wearing a white denim jacket, white jeans and red-rimmed eyes. She pulled a chair out and sat down. Before she spoke she lit a cigarette and inhaled deeply. I finished the last of my fried egg and sat back. She took another puff of her cigarette and then stubbed it out on my plate. 'I've been thinking,' she said, 'about that kiss.'

'Oh,' I said.

'I haven't been able to get it out of my mind.'

I nodded. 'My kisses are good,' I said, 'but they're not that fucking good.'

She smiled. 'Maybe it was the time, the place, the fact that we were dying.'

'You've been up all night,' I said.

'I know. We've been fighting. You found his cache.'

'And he sent you to get it back.'

'Jesus, no. He doesn't know I'm here. You can pour it in the fucking Liffey for all I care.'

'So why are you here?'

'I don't know.'

'How long have you known about the drugs?'

She shrugged. 'I suspected. I've only known him a few months. I love him. He's a lovely man. He doesn't use them when he's working. He *couldn't* use them when he's working. It was the wrap party for godsake, he was just letting his hair down.'

'Alice, he could keep the National Health Service going for weeks on that lot. Don't delude yourself.'

She rubbed at an eye, she gave a little shake of her head. 'I know,' she said.

'Do *you*?'

'Do I what?'

'Indulge.'

'God, no. I don't even take Rennies when I've a sore head.'

'Rennies are for indigestion.'

'See how crap I am?' She smiled weakly.

'So why are you here?'

'I don't know. A shoulder to cry on.'

'My shoulders are thin and bony. You want to ask me not to write about it in my book.'

'I don't care what you write. I don't think he'll be alive to read it anyway. Not taking that lot *and* Michael O'Ryan on his tail.'

'You think they're connected?'

She started to say no, then paused. 'I don't know. I don't know *anything*, Dan. All I know is that I got lonely one night in my apartment and I went up to the house to surprise him and I found him unconscious. I thought he'd had a friggin' heart attack, but then I found the heroin, and then I found his little room and realised what had been going on. Knew why he kept disappearing into his study. Why he'd blow hot and cold. Why one moment he'd want to sleep all day and the next go out paragliding.'

'And you confronted him?'

'I confronted him, and he promised to sort himself out. And he will. He swore, once the film was over, once he had one last blow-out. He loves me and he's going to clean himself up. We went into his room this morning and gathered everything up,

160

the pills, the coke, the uppers and downers and painkillers, the speed, the dope. We flushed it all down the bog.'

'The fish'll be singing tonight then. Salmon chanted evening.'

'I'm serious.'

'I know. But you don't give them up that easy. I've never taken heroin in my life, Alice, but I've seen the movies. Cold turkey and all that palaver.'

'He's locked in his bedroom now. He's doing it, Dan.'

'Tell me that in three days. Although it only took Gene Hackman about five minutes.'

'Gene . . . ?'

'In *French Connection II*.'

She sighed. 'Life isn't a movie, Dan.'

'Mine is.' The waiter appeared at my elbow and lifted the plate. His upper lip quivered when he saw the cigarette embedded on it. He asked if we wanted coffee. I declined. Alice shook her head. She kept her eyes on the table. She was trying to stop herself from crying.

'What about Dr Fruitcake?' I asked.

She didn't look up. Her fingers played with the unused cutlery before her. 'I threw him out of the house. I never liked him. He's on a plane back to America.' She gave a sad little chuckle. 'He's the only doctor I know whose writing I can read. Still, I suppose it has to be decipherable. He wouldn't want Sean to get something that was bad for him.'

'So why are you here?'

'I don't know.'

'Do you want to go upstairs and lie down?'

'Yes.'

Sometimes it's as easy, and as terrible, as that.

CHAPTER 22

Sean O'Toole was shivering and shaking and vomiting his way through cold turkey, and I was making love to his wife.

It's a crap world, and it's not often I come out on top. Even when I do, it rarely lasts more than a few minutes, as Alice discovered. But it wasn't the performance or the length of it that was important, it was the fact of it, that it had happened, that we were happy about it, relaxed and cuddly and snuggly and all the things neither of us could be with our chosen partners. Because Patricia and I were constantly at war and our interludes of love-making were few and far between. Because Sean O'Toole was a drug fiend whose heart could give out at any moment, and whose penis had given out long before his marriage.

'You mean you never . . .'

'We never consummated the marriage. No.'

'He should try Viagra.'

'Do you really think Sean needs another drug?'

'At least you know he's not being unfaithful.'

'No, I'm the one being unfaithful.'

It didn't seem the right time to tell her what I

163

had witnessed in the summerhouse. Maybe Sean could only perform if there were several women present, or perhaps only under the influence of hard drugs.

I cupped her face in my hand and said, 'We're not being unfaithful.'

'Yes, we are.' I started to say something else, but she took my hand and brought it away from her face and rested it on her breast. 'Please,' she said, 'don't try to justify it. It was wrong, but sometimes you have to.'

'Sometimes you have to more than once, just to get it right.'

She smiled, and we made love again. I did better on the timing front, though not by much. When we had finished, and we were back into nestling, I said, 'I'm worried about the pain in my stomach.'

'You've a pain in your stomach?'

'No. And that's what worries me. When I do something wrong, I get guilt pains. Usually I'm in a constant state of pain. But not now. What does that tell me?'

'That you haven't done anything wrong. Or that you've finally got used to the pain.' She kissed me. 'Relax. Nobody but us will ever know.'

'You mean you're not going to leave Sean and set up home with me?'

'No.'

'We'd be the talk of the town.'

'No.'

'You're not going to trail all over the world after me like a sick puppy?'

'No.'

'Well, can I trail after you, then?'

'No.'

'Well, what then?'

'We stared death in the face, and we'll always have that, and now we'll always have this.'

'You mean like we'll always have Paris.'

'You can be Bogie.'

'That's a relief. Most times I end up being the darkie playing the piano.'

'The *darkie*?'

'It's just a turn of phrase.'

'It's just racism.'

'No, it's not. It's just a jokey expression because I can't remember his name, apart from Sam.'

'It was Dooley. Dooley Grey.'

'Really?'

'Really. It's my favourite film.'

'Whatever. I'd rather be a darkie than a Dooley. Do you remember the Dooleys? That really crap Irish band?' Alice shook her head. 'They were like a poor man's Nolan Sisters, who were crap as well. Either way, I'm sorry, I didn't mean to call him a darkie. I'm harmless, and occasionally gormless. Sometimes I open my mouth and all this shite just comes out, especially when I'm nervous, and I'm quite nervous now even though we've just made love; in a way that was the easy bit because now I have to look you in the eye and

165

figure out the whys and wherefores of what we've just done.'

She kissed me.

An hour later she went in for a shower. I lay back and thought about nothing, which doesn't happen often. I listened to the water, and the sound of her singing 'As Time Goes By'. Bogie, eh?

And then the bathroom door opened and she said, 'Is it okay if I use some of your talc?'

I coughed and said: 'Sure.'

She left at lunchtime. We kissed in the door-way, but we really didn't say anything. We might never see each other again, unless it was in the libel courts.

I took a shower. She had doused herself liberally with my talc. I had no idea what the street value of heroin was, or how many streets you could buy with it, but it seemed reasonable to assume that she had gone through several thousand pounds' worth of it. Still, no matter. One thing I wasn't about to do was stand on a corner trying to sell it. I had seen *Midnight Express* and knew the consequences.

We had put the *Do Not Disturb We're Screwing* sign out. A minute after I changed it back there was a knock on the door and I shouted hold on a minute while I struggled into my trousers and pulled on a white T-shirt. I opened the door and was already in mid-apology for keeping the cleaners back when I realised that the short fat man with the gun was not the least bit interested in cleaning my room.

He said, 'Dan Starkey?' Belfast accent, not hard, not soft, somewhere in the middle.

I said, 'No, he's just popped out to the shop, I can take a message if that's any use.'

He wasn't falling for it. He walked me back into the room and closed the door. He was smartly dressed. He wore a cream suit. The muscles in his neck bulged against the collar of his black shirt and tie; there were cuff links, a Rolex, sharp Italian-looking shoes, a close, spiky haircut. His skin was tanned, his eyes were black and confident, his nose had once been broken, there was a diamond stud in one ear. You take in a lot of information when someone points a gun at you. He pushed me down onto the bed and then pulled out a chair and sat down.

'So,' he said, 'you're having carnal relations with his wife.'

'Whose wife?' I asked.

He raised an eyebrow. I held his gaze, and then he shrugged and said, 'No matter. You'll be wondering who I am and what I want.'

'Yes,' I said.

'Michael O'Ryan,' he said, and for a moment it didn't register because he was nothing like I had imagined. He was more slightly upset football manager than psycho gangster.

I said, 'Ahm, I don't wish to be rude, but can you prove it? I mean, do you have any ID? A driving licence or something?'

'I was told,' he hissed, 'that you fancied yourself

as a funny fucker. Well, perhaps these will wipe the smile off your face.'

He reached into his jacket and produced a series of six Polaroids. He spread them out before him on the table, face down, like he was dealing cards, and in a way I suppose he was. It crossed my mind for a moment that he had contrived to snap Alice and me in action and was intent on some kind of blackmail, but it seemed a little petty for a man of his pedigree.

He nodded down at the photographs and said, 'Go on, take your pick.'

I hesitated. 'I'm not writing the book any more, if that's your problem.'

'It's not my problem. Pick a picture.'

'I'm going home today. Sean chucked me off the project. It doesn't concern me.'

'It doesn't concern me either. Take a peek.'

There was nothing else for it. I turned over the first Polaroid.

It was Patricia.

She was sitting in a chair; there was a white wall behind her with some sort of graffiti on it. One eye was partially closed, like she'd been thumped, and her hair was all over the place. She was wearing the white vest and green army fatigues she used to doss about the house in when she was sure nobody would visit.

My heart was pumping hard. There was a vacuum cleaner working in the corridor. Outside there was a plane dipping down towards Dublin Airport.

Inside there was a smile of relish slowly making its way across Michael O'Ryan's face.

I took a deep breath and turned over pictures two and three.

They were variations of the same.

In the fourth her nose was bleeding, and in the fifth she seemed to be unconscious and somebody was holding her head up by the hair for the camera's benefit. I swallowed and turned over the sixth.

It was Little Stevie. He was being held down on a table; his mouth was open wide and I didn't need to hear it to know he was screaming at the man looming above him and brandishing a hammer over his outstretched little hand.

CHAPTER 23

I had him on the ground with the gun in his mouth. I was screaming, 'You tell me where they are, you cunt, or I'll blow your fucking head off!'

He couldn't, of course, with the gun in his mouth.

My wife, my son.

This man in the cream suit, not fazed at all.

'An understandable reaction,' Michael O'Ryan said as he got back to his feet and patted his suit down. I slumped back on the bed. He took his seat again and ran his fingers over the Polaroids. 'I don't like doing things like this, believe me, but you know, a means to an end and all that.'

The gun lay on the bed beside me. He knew, and I knew, that there was no point in threatening him. His people had my wife and child and would kill them if I did not do what he wanted. I could threaten Michael O'Ryan until the cows came home. I could shoot him in the head. I could dangle him from the hotel window until he revealed where they were. None of these things would stop his people from killing my family, because that is what they did best, that was what they enjoyed most.

I said, 'Why me?'

'Because,' he said.

I lifted the photographs off the table and examined them again.

'She's a remarkable woman,' O'Ryan said. 'Stands up well under torture.'

'Why the fuck would you need to torture her?'

'Because,' he said again.

'Why the baby?'

'Wouldn't you? If you were me? Look at the reaction it gets. By the way, I read your last book, thought it was wonderful. I thought that libel action was a terrible shame.'

'I don't give a fuck what you think, just tell me what you want.'

'What do you think I want?'

'I'm not in the mood to play fucking games.'

'It doesn't really matter what mood you're in, Dan, now does it?'

He had a point. I sighed. 'I *don't know* what you want. If it's about the book, consider it done.'

'Dan, now, if I didn't want you to write the book I would have broken your fingers. And your toes as well. I've seen *My Left Foot*. Didn't he do well now for a fucking crip? And that Daniel Day-Lewis, now isn't he a fine young fella? *Last of the Mohicans* – wasn't that a great wee movie as well? Now there's a man could have played me, don't you think?'

I nodded. He was as much like Daniel Day-Lewis as Van Morrison, and that's still an insult to Van. His hat had come off in our little set-to and he had not replaced it. He had hair, but it was Bobby Charlton hair, a few dying strands desperately combed across the top of his chrome dome in an invaliant effort to make it look like he still had some. Sean was playing him with a full head of hair. Perhaps baldness wasn't big at the box office. Perhaps it had only recently fallen out. I was thinking too much about hair. My wife and child were being held hostage.

'What do you want me to do?'

'I want you to take that gun and shoot Sean O'Toole. Kill him.'

'I can't do that.'

'Yes, you can.'

'I can't just kill him.'

'Yes, you can. You point the gun and you squeeze the trigger. It's easy.'

I took a deep breath. I looked at the gun. I picked it up again. I set it down. There is something magnetic about holding a gun in your hands. It's why policemen always look so fulfilled.

'Y'know,' I said, 'if you kill him . . . if *I* kill him, somebody else will only come along and make the film. Daniel Day-Lewis, maybe. There'll be dozens of books, there'll be journalists, you'll be hounded to death.'

'No, *you'll* be hounded to death. It'll have nothing to do with me.'

'They're not going to believe I killed him.'

'After getting thrown out of his house? Sleeping

172

with his wife? Stealing a large quantity of drugs from him?'

'You've been paying close attention.'

'Well, of course I have, Dan. Now think about it. There's three motives. And you will have murdered your wife and child first, so deranged were you. Dan, I'm quite good at planning these things. It's all in the detail. It's why they call me the Colonel. I'm not exactly Action Man, y'know?'

I shook my head. I lifted the photo of Stevie. My hands were shaking. The terror in his face was . . . I put it down. Face down. I couldn't look. I sighed. 'This is all about a fucking movie?'

O'Ryan gave a little laugh. 'Is that what you think?'

'Well, I presumed . . .'

'Or is that what he told you? Well, yes, of course it was.'

'I . . . well, I heard you read the script, didn't like it.'

'On the contrary, I think it's a wonderful script.'

'So what's the problem?'

'Sean's the problem.' He took out a packet of cigarettes. He offered me one. I declined. He lit up. He inhaled. I reached an ashtray across from the bedside table. He smiled a thank you. He exhaled. 'Do you know he came to me a year ago and told me about the movie he was going to make? He didn't have to do that. I admired him for doing it; it isn't everyone would walk into Michael O'Ryan's den and tell him he was going to

173

make a movie about his life and didn't really give a fuck what he thought about it. He had balls. He said he was going to make it as factually correct as he could, but he wasn't going to pull any punches. He said there'd be a certain artistic licence, but that you had to expect that with Hollywood movies.'

'Will you get to the point?'

'Hold on to your horses, Danny boy, you're working on my time now. It's not Greenwich mean, it's just plain old-fashioned mean. So where was I? Oh, aye. I was happy enough to let Seanie go ahead with the movie. To tell you the truth, Dan, I like movies, and I understand the requirements. I mean, look at me, I've a face like a bucket of shite, then look at Sean. We're not exactly peas in a pod, are we?'

'No, you're not.'

'But we hit it off, hit it off well, y'know? Before he even wrote the script, he came and stayed with me. Six weeks in all. He interviewed me. He hung about with the gang. Do you know, he even came on a bank job with us.'

'He robbed a bank?'

'Not quite. We had a back-up car, in case our getaway one broke down – planning, y'see – and he sat in that. We didn't need it as it happens, but he was there. I suppose he could be charged if anyone ever found out. An accessory. Y'see he's desperate to win this Oscar – he's told you that?'

'Not in so many words. Others have.'

'Well, he is, so he's giving *everything* to this

174

film. He told me that when he makes films he just turns up on set, rehearses the day before, just goes through the motions. But for this he was going the whole hog. Method acting, like Brando, like Hoffman. He wanted to *become* me.'

'And did he?'

'Well, it seems that he did. Y'see, Dan, like I say, I'm a bit of a movie buff. And to tell you the truth I was a little bit in awe of this big movie star when he arrived. But he was so open and down to earth, we became good chums. In amidst all our chats about me, we got chatting about him. About how the roles have been drying up for him, how he's not earning what he used to, how this movie is really going to put him back on top.'

'So?'

'So as the weeks went by, people started to see him change. My people – even though he looks nothing like me – they started to see the mannerisms, the talk, but, more importantly, the *mind*.'

'You mean he became a psychotic.'

The Colonel smiled weakly. 'Please. Remember that I have your son.'

I nodded. 'Sorry.'

'So he went off then to write the script. Back to LA, Los Angeles. Sent me a postcard. A few months later he comes back, shows me the script. I was not entirely happy with it, I suggested certain changes, he promised to consider them. In fact, he made those changes, he *showed* me those changes, though I now understand they were for my benefit alone and he's been shooting from the original. However, the script isn't the fucking problem. Two weeks before shooting was due to begin he came to me, and he was distraught. He was in tears. The financiers had pulled the plug. For reasons not associated with the film. Currency, I think; the dollar dropped in value, something like that. He was putting some of his own money in, but it wasn't enough, the whole project was going to collapse. So he . . .'

'He asked you to invest?'

O'Ryan nodded. 'I have certain financial reserves. And there's only so much you can spend it on. Why not invest in a little immortality?'

'So you bankrolled a film about yourself?'

O'Ryan nodded. 'The ultimate vanity, is it not?'

'But if it got out . . .'

'He'd be ruined, yes, of course. But it wasn't a case of handing over bags of cash, Dan, you know it doesn't work like that. I operate through various companies, most of them outside of Ireland. The money could never be traced back to me. Not one penny. Three million, in all.'

'That's a lot of pennies.'

'It is. Particularly when you discover that none of it has ended up in the film. Y'see, as it turns out, the financiers never did pull out. It was all baloney. I taught Sean O'Toole everything about my profession, and he learnt well, 'cause he turns round and screws me out of three million.'

176

'Jesus.'

'He knows I'm not going to go running to the cops complaining.'

'Jesus.'

'And to make it worse, he uses *that* three million to finance a fucking drugs deal. He meets *my* connections, the wise guys *I* introduced him to, and strikes a fucking deal with them using *my* money. Can you believe the man?'

'Jesus,' I said again. I shook my head. 'Now *that's* what I call method acting.'

'Call it what you want, all I know is he's got three million worth of heroin stashed somewhere. Is it any wonder you were able to walk out of his place with enough horse to run in the fucking Derby and he hardly even fucking noticed? Is it any wonder I want him dead?'

I nodded. I swallowed. 'Would you not settle for just getting the money back?'

'It's beyond the money, Dan. I don't subscribe to that honour amongst thieves shite. I don't believe in *respect* and all that Mafia bullshit. He fucked me, good and simple, and now I'm going to fuck him. Or rather you are.'

He stood up. He lifted his hat and placed it firmly back on his head. He smoothed a crease in his trousers. 'You know what you have to do.'

'What if I bring him to you, you can kill him.'

'No, Dan, that's not how it works.'

'But why *me*?'

'Because.'

He gave a little nod, then walked out of the room.

I lay back on the bed.

I screamed, but it was a silent scream.

CHAPTER 24

I had a gun, six bullets and a decision to make. Kill Sean O'Toole or search for my wife and child.

Sean O'Toole was locked in a bedroom at his country retreat. There were security guards. They claimed to be ex-SAS. One of them had kissed me. There was a hidden access gate I'd already successfully used. Once through that I could probably get into the house. Sean would not be expecting me. He would be in another, vomit-filled world. I'd be doing him a favour. It would be like shooting fish in a barrel, whatever that was like. Sure, I'd get arrested for it, probably do some time, but people would understand.

Or I could go hunting for Patricia and Stevie.

I could go from house to house, calling their names.

They were somewhere in Ireland, north or south. Rumour had it that the Colonel had retired to rural Wicklow, but he still pulled strings up north. Sure, I could track him down, given time; I could track down the members of his gang, given time; I could probably even make an heroic *Taxi Driver* style entrance, given time and some courage, but nobody was giving time, and courage would always be in short supply.

It was a choice that was no choice.

Sorry, Sean, but it's for the best.

I packed my bag. I had a decision to make about the talc. Dump it, hide it, take it with me. I'd be doing the world a favour by dumping it; hiding it didn't seem very practical – third tree from the left, then dig – and taking it with me had its own dangers, but at least it might come in handy as a bargaining tool. I had no idea of its street value, but it seemed reasonable to assume that it was worth more than all my worldly possessions cubed. Take it. You never know. I tried packing it in several different positions, trying to make it look as if it had been haphazardly thrown into my washbag like it was just talc and not a Class A narcotic. Eventually I just closed my eyes and chucked it into the bag, then zipped it up without looking.

I pulled on my bomber jacket and slipped the gun into the side pocket. I picked up the Polaroids from the table. I looked through them again. I winced at the pain in Patricia's eyes, and the horror in Little Stevie's. I went to the mini-bar and opened the door. I knelt beside it, thought for a moment, then took out a Diet Coke. Then I closed the door and lifted the phone. I dialled Belfast, and Mouse.

Mouse, my oldest friend, who I rarely saw. He was married, but he had no children, and there is an invisible line that comes down between men who do and men who do not have children. Not so much an iron curtain as a crocheted one. There are lots of holes in it, through which to see other people having a social life. A man who has a child can stand and talk for hours about how wonderful he or she is, and providing the other man has a child too, he can quite happily listen, and respond accordingly. Talk to a man who doesn't have a child about what it's like, you might as well be talking to a post. Except a post can't walk off, or yawn. Mouse and I would always be the best of friends, but talking about kids pissed him off. 'He's not even yours,' he would say.

Mouse answered on the third ring. He was at work. Sub-editing at the paper. Direct line. I said, 'Hi,' and he was surprised that it wasn't something stupid.

He asked me what was wrong, and I said nothing was wrong.

He asked me what was wrong again, and I said nothing was wrong again.

He said, 'HOW'S TRISH?' He had a problem with volume.

'Kidnapped.'

'AND LITTLE STEVIE?'

'Likewise.'

There was a pause. And then, because he'd been through things with me before, he said: 'ARE YOU SERIOUS?'

I told him what had happened. When I'd finished

he said *FUCK* seven times in a row, then added:
'WHAT CAN I DO?'

'Turn down the volume, for a start.'

'OKAY.'

'Lower.'

'Okay.'

'*Okay.* Mouse, I'm going downstairs now to check out. Then I'm going up to Sean O'Toole's place.'

'Are you going to kill him?'

'I don't know.'

'If he's got you into all of this because of fucking method acting, he deserves it.'

'I'm not convinced he has. He told me a while back about a guy called Danny Murphy, some childhood friend the Colonel topped for no particular reason. He made the film because of him. It crossed my mind he might have ripped O'Ryan off for revenge. I don't know. Maybe it's a mixture of the two. Anyway, that's not your problem, your problem is finding Trish and Stevie.'

'Dan, I'm not Sherlock fucking Holmes.'

'I know, you'd be dead, and English, although it's a pleasant combination. I'm going to fax you up these Polaroids. Take a look at the background. There's some graffiti on the wall. All I can make out is the word *ANGER*. It's a long shot, but it might mean something to someone.'

'I'll do what I can.'

It was worse than a long shot, but it was better than no shot at all. I wished Mouse good luck, and he wished me good luck. There wasn't anywhere else for the conversation to go. Downstairs the nice receptionist faxed through the Polaroids for me. They were face down the whole time, and she didn't take a peek. She printed me out a nice long list of items that had been charged to my room, I signed and told her to put a couple of drinks on there for herself. It was the condemned man being generous with other people's money.

The security gates were lying open. Both sets. I was just going to drive past for a quick look, then park half a mile away and walk back to the not-so-secret entrance, but the fact that the gates were open made me stop. I sat in the car for five minutes, just watching, but there were no signs of life. I knew how security-conscious Sean had become since O'Ryan's people had tried to drown Alice down at the docks, so it was more than suspicious.

I drove in. The security guards would see me, and stop me, but they wouldn't be expecting a gun. At worst they'd have their eyes peeled for a notebook and I would tell them the pen was mightier than the sword even as they set about throwing me out. Then I would pull the gun and say I'd lost faith in the written word and get those hands up. Except I drove up to the front of the house unchallenged. I parked and climbed out. I stood on the gravel for several moments, listening, but there was nothing to hear. I rang the front door bell, but there was no response. I skirted round the house, peering through the windows, but there was nothing to see. The back door was locked, but there was a window to the left which was open just a couple of inches, wide enough to give me a grip. I gave it a good pull and it came open. I climbed in. I didn't set off any alarms. I called, 'Anybody home?' as I stood in the kitchen. 'I've come to read the meter.'

Nothing.

Sean was the boss. Perhaps in the dementia of cold turkey he had sent everybody away. Perhaps he didn't want anyone to see or hear him in the degradation that came with weaning yourself off drugs. Perhaps it was just him and me. I drew the gun and mounted the stairs.

If he was being torn apart by vicious spasms, he was enduring them quietly. There was no sound, not even the ticking of a clock. I walked along the hall. His bedroom was at the end, door closed. I knocked on it. There was no response. I tried the handle. It wasn't locked. I pushed the door open and entered, gun stretched out in front of me. I would shoot him and shoot him again if it meant keeping my wife and baby alive.

But the room was empty. And the bed was made.

I didn't know much about going cold turkey besides what Gene Hackman had taught me, but I suspected graduates of the school of dead fowl didn't make the bed when they were finished.

184

There was no blood on the walls, no sick on the carpet, it didn't smell of disinfectant.

There was no cold turkey.

More likely, somewhere else, a strutting peacock.

I cursed. I felt strange: an odd mixture of disappointment and relief.

I checked the wardrobes. His clothes were hanging there. I left the room and tried his study door. It was open as well. There was no sign of any drugs. Alice had said they'd been flushed down the toilet. I tried the drawer in his desk. All of the prescriptions were gone as well.

I sat in Sean's chair and tried to work out what to do. Clearly there had not been time for him to go through cold turkey. Alice had left him alone, so he'd gone straight out to score some more drugs, taking his security team with him. Possible, but it didn't feel right. The house felt too empty. Even though his clothes were here, there was a finality about it. The gates had been left open. That was more than carelessness. Any fool could have detected that he'd left in a hurry. But of his own accord?

I stared out of the window, trying to work it out. He hadn't taken his clothes, but he was rich enough to have wardrobes full of clothes in properties all over the world. Then again: he had paused long enough to take the stacked cans of film from *The Brigadier*. Or had somebody stolen them? Or had Alice returned full of guilt from our little fling and found Sean in such a desperate state that her resolve had broken and she'd spirited him away to some better place? And how would O'Ryan react to my failure? He had left me his number. All I could do was call and tell him what had happened. Would he say *tough* and kill my family, because that was what psychos did, or *you did your best so I'll let them go?*

There was a strong, cold breeze blowing outside and it was causing the parasols surrounding the swimming pool to rattle like the masts at a yacht club. As I looked down towards them my eye caught the tail end of something floating across the pool. It was visible for just a moment, then hidden by the bank of parasols. I looked away, then back as it drifted momentarily into sight again. And a shudder ran down me.

Legs.

Bare.

I ran out of the study and down the hall. I took the stairs six at a time, half-sliding on the banister, then through the kitchen and out the way I'd come in.

I slowed as I approached the pool. It did not seem the weather for swimming, but there was no accounting for when a junkie might go paddling. So approach with a certain nonchalance then shoot him as he lolled on his lilo.

But I knew he was not swimming. The clatter of the parasols seemed to increase, like they were giving a round of applause for my entrance.

186

All the world's a stage, and my life's a fucking comedy.

The body was at the far end of the pool now, face down and blue.

I hurried along. I picked up a long pole with a net at the end which they evidently used to extract leaves from the water. I reached in with it and pulled the body to the edge.

I didn't drag it out.

I had touched dead people before, I had no wish to repeat the experience.

I pushed down on one side, submerging it briefly but also turning it round so that when it floated back to the top it was face up.

I looked down and sighed.

Dr Fruitcake had written his last prescription.

CHAPTER 25

I stood by a cool pool with a cooler floater and pleaded with Colonel Michael O'Ryan for my family's life. He was having none of it.

I was using Sean's mobile phone. He had left it behind in his hurry to depart. It was easy to check the last number he'd called. Not the emergency services. Not even Alice, but KLM, the Dutch national airline. I called them and gave them some crap about being Sean's agent and there being a mix-up and wanting to confirm what flight he was on, but they denied any knowledge of him. I persisted and they said *don't you think we'd notice if we had a movie star flying with us?* and then I had a very small brainwave – bleedin' friggin' obvious, Sherlock might have said – and told them he might be travelling under an assumed name. Did they by any chance have a Dr Fruitke listed, and bingo. His flight for Amsterdam had taken off an hour before. I asked if he was flying alone. She said no, there were two hundred and sixteen other people on the flight. I thanked her for her time. I had no way of contacting Alice. I could only assume that for now she remained blissfully innocent.

'He's in Europe,' I told the Colonel. 'I have no idea where to start. I've never *been* to Europe. I don't speak European.'

'I don't give a flying fuck, find him.'

I said, 'I've no idea where to start. It could take me the rest of my life.'

'You were a reporter, you find out.'

'I was never that sort of a reporter.'

'What were you then?'

'A satirist.'

'Ah. That's the kind takes the piss out of other people's troubles.'

'That's it,' I said, not wishing to pick a fight, though he wasn't a million miles away.

'Then fly to fucking Amsterdam and start looking, and see how fucking funny that is.'

'What about my wife and child?'

'The sooner you kill Sean, the sooner you see them again.'

'But it could take months.'

'Well, you don't have months.'

'How long do I have?'

'How long does it take to starve to death?'

'I don't know.'

'How long did it take Bobby Sands?'

'I don't know. I think they sneaked him ham sandwiches once in a while.'

'I wouldn't take the piss, satirist. I'll tell you this. I have them in an underground bunker. You will never find it. Tonight I will give them their last meal. Then out go the lights. I will supply them with water. You ever see a hamster drink water from a bottle? That's how they'll get it. They don't get any more food until I have proof Sean is dead. And bear in mind, satirist, little kiddies die quicker than grown-ups, you hear?'

He cut the line.

I slumped down beside the pool.

Dr Fruitcake stared up.

Physician, heal thyself.

Satirist, dying is easy, comedy is hard.

No, comedy is easy, dying is hard.

I took out the gun. I weighed it in my hand. I wondered how many people it had killed before. Or if you could really say it had killed anyone. Guns don't kill, only men kill. I'd heard that in a film some time, and it sounded like the truth. I threw the gun into the pool. I wouldn't be able to take it where I was going.

It took an hour to negotiate the city centre traffic and get to the airport. On the way I phoned Sam Cameron and told him I was pursuing Sean O'Toole to Amsterdam.

He was surprised. 'I was sitting here thinking you'd probably turn in a crappy cut'n'paste job just to get back at me. But I'd overlooked the fact that though you get on like a wanker, you do actually care about what you put your name to. Then again, Amsterdam? I admire your enthusiasm, but is it strictly necessary?'

I didn't tell him why it was so urgent that

I fly to Amsterdam, I just assured him that it would add a million copies to his sales of the Sean O'Toole book.

He said, 'You wouldn't just be trying to fleece me out of more money, Dan? I got them to fax me the hotel bill. You hit room service pretty hard.'

'I want the ticket waiting for me at the desk, I want hotel accommodation laid on in Amsterdam.'

'Did you hear what I said? I'm not made of money, Dan.'

'Yes, you are, Sam. Now please do this for me. It's important.'

And maybe he heard something in my voice. 'Is something wrong, Dan?'

'Yes.'

'What can I do?'

'What I ask.'

'Do you need me to contact Trish?'

'No,' I said.

I cut the line. Sam was okay. He had a heart of fool's gold.

I reached the airport and turned into the short-stay car park, which was optimistic of me, and probably misplaced. I hurried to the desk and asked about my ticket. It was waiting for me, business class, and so was a voucher for the Hotel Ambassade, which according to the small map on the back was right in the centre of Amsterdam. I asked the girl on the KLM desk if she'd managed to get Sean O'Toole's autograph earlier and she kind of smiled before saying, 'Sorry, was he here?'

She asked if I'd anything to check in, but there was just my small travelling bag and I could take that on as hand luggage. I had two hours to kill until my flight. There was the bar, and then there were all the other places: the shops, the restaurant, the amusement arcade, but they all reminded me of the family I didn't have; only the bar seemed to suggest the abject loneliness I was feeling. So I headed there. I would have one to steady my nerves, and another couple just for the hell of it. That would be it. I needed to remain clear-headed. I had to find Sean O'Toole somewhere in mainland Europe, then kill him. I was an assassin. The least well-prepared assassin in the history of assassins. But I would stick with it. I would not be disheartened. I would keep after him like a dog after a bone. And if ever I did write a book about it, it would be called *The Day of the Jack Russell*.

I sat over a pint trying to figure out why Sean was flying to Amsterdam. Was it purely in panic over the death of Fruitcake, the first flight out of town? Had he been involved in Fruitke's death? Or had he merely gone all wobbly over the potential bad press of having a junkie dead in your pool? If Fruitke had been thrown out by Alice, how had he ended up in the pool? And how much of it had to do with the fact that Amsterdam was the centre of the European drugs trade? Had Fruitcake been involved in Sean's three-million-pound drugs deal? Had they argued over that? Had Sean drowned him? There'd been no blood in the pool, so it wasn't immediately apparent how the bad doctor had died. His apparent addiction to heroin could not have helped him swim – it wasn't one of the stimulants or steroids Olympic athletes were routinely tested for – but it probably wouldn't have robbed him of his ability to swim. Perhaps it had been bad gear. Perhaps . . . There were too many questions and not enough answers.

Something came to my ears, vaguely, far away. My name, and then last call for flight . . .

And I looked at my watch and it was time for take-off and I'd barely touched my drink. I snatched up my bag and ran.

My bag was going through the X-ray machine when I remembered the talc. I broke out in a cold sweat. The guy said, 'Can I just take a quick look inside your bag, sir?'

I nodded. I thought about *Midnight Express* and prison rape. I wondered if he could detect a racing pulse. I swallowed with difficulty. I told myself that people did not smuggle drugs out of Ireland and into Amsterdam, it was the other way round. He wasn't looking for drugs, he was just doing his job. He lifted out my nicely folded shirts and pressed underwear and set them on the table and checked through them one by one. He opened my wash bag and squeezed the toothpaste. He shook the bottle of talc. He looked up and said, 'Did you pack this bag yourself, sir?'

It was time to run. But he would catch me, and my wife and child would die. I smiled. I kept my head tilted slightly back so that the sweat would run down my back and not my face. 'Are you joking?' I said. 'It's far too neat. My wife did. But I watched her.'

He sighed. He shook his head. 'I'm afraid I won't be able to pack it all back in quite so neatly. They give us a course in it, but it's never really been my strong point. Here goes.'

He lifted the shirts and began to stuff them back in.

In truth he wasn't doing a great job, but at that moment I didn't give a damn whether he got a couple of creases in them or tore them into shreds and stuck them in his ears.

He zipped the bag shut, smiled apologetically and said, 'Have a nice trip.' The pun wasn't intentional, or appropriate, but I mumbled my thanks and picked up the bag. A moment later I was racing down towards the gate and Amsterdam.

CHAPTER 26

'**M**r Starkey?'
Uhhhhhhhhhhh . . .
'Could you put your tray table up and your seat forward and fasten your seat belt? We're experiencing a little turbulence.'

'Uuuuuh thanks . . . enjoyed the movie . . . uuuh . . .'

'We haven't shown a movie.'

'Uuuuuh . . . sorry . . . *somebody* did.'

Daymare.

A horror movie with a happy ending.

Trish was in it and Stevie and it was horrible and traumatic but we'd been reunited on a beach at the end; I felt warm and loved and optimistic; my personal in-skull movie house.

See, I know about movies. They don't make movies with unhappy endings any more. They don't do well at the previews. People want to feel good coming out of the cinema. Uplifted. Ready to kick the world in the shins and romance that girl into bed. They don't want to be depressed. They don't want the hero's wife and child to die. They want sunsets and beaches and reunions.

195

We all do.

Life isn't a movie, Dan.

Oh, but it is.

You just pay more for the popcorn.

Philosophical, I.

I, philosophical.

I, on the verge of breaking down because once again I had been thrust into a situation over which I had no control, a situation not of my creation. This year's Nobel prize for *Being in the Wrong Place at the Wrong Fucking Time* goes to . . . Get a job, Dan, earn an honest living. Nine to five. Go wild and try nine to half five. Do some overtime! But get a job. Oh, what I would give!

I was being served a little meal in a little plastic tray on a little fucking table and my wife and child were . . .

I sighed, loudly, and began to peel the foil top off the hot meal, but it wouldn't give. I tried it this way and that. I opened the plastic bag containing the plastic utensils and tried to cut my way through the foil with the flimsy knife, but it still wouldn't give. I sighed again. The nun beside me looked over.

I shrugged. I have a thing about nuns. It's a long story. I'd checked the outline of her habit for gun shapes as I sat down. She was gone sixty, but you're never too old to start. I was brought up never to trust nuns and only learned later that the same applies to hippies.

'Are you all right, son?' she asked. 'First time?'

The obvious answer was, *Fuck off and die, anti-Christ bitch*, but I nodded helplessly.

She reached across and peeled the foil off.

She said, 'You poor dear, your hands are shaking.'

I examined my hands.

I gave a little laugh. 'I'm not even hungry,' I said. She nodded sympathetically. I tried to be nice. 'So what's a nun doing flying business class?'

'I'm going to a convention.'

'A convention of nuns? Is that the correct term?'

'I mean . . .'

'Like a coven of witches, although, of course, you're not. What is it, like a record convention? You know, you trade rare habits and those difficult-to-find rosary beads?' I giggled nervously. I tried to apologise. 'Sorry. I'm not anti-Catholic, it's just such an entirely alien culture to me. Like Aborigines. They go walkabout, you go to conventions. I'm sorry, I'm babbling. I've a lot on my mind. It's not the flying. You're not a priest, but you're probably governed by the rules of the confessional, aren't you? You know, you can't tell the police if I tell you something?'

'Well . . .'

'What I mean is, can you say a prayer for me? Not for me, in fact, but for someone else. Prayer by proxy. Can you do that? And then keep it a secret – not that you said a prayer, but what I'm going to tell you, because it's a life-or-death situation.'

'I . . .'

'My wife and baby are being held hostage and I'm going to Amsterdam to try and save them.'

She looked at me for several moments. Her hand jerked suddenly, but stayed in place, gripping the armrest. She was fighting with herself about pressing the assistance button. I shut my eyes. I forced myself to be quiet. If I was carried off the plane in a straitjacket I would not be able to kill Sean O'Toole and my family would die.

When I opened my eyes again the plane was coming in to land at Schiphol Airport, jerking about over the final few hundred feet before bumping down to a round of applause from a loud Italian family near the back. As I lifted my bag down from the overhead locker the nun nodded at me. I wanted to apologise, but my upbringing prevented me. She said, 'I don't know if you were serious, but I said that prayer, and one for you.' I said thanks.

My head was throbbing. I had the ultimate painkiller in my hand luggage but I tried not to think about it as I walked through passport control and then cleared customs without a second glance.

I got a taxi to the Ambassade. It wasn't a long drive. I sat with my eyes closed. I'd never been to Amsterdam before, but I wasn't there for the view. Besides, I'd seen *Van Der Valk*. All you really needed to know you could learn from TV. I found cities boring anyway. All cities. The reality of them was invariably disappointing, boring and hard on the legs.

Amsterdam: canals, tulips, drugs and red lights. There you go. Just saved you five hundred pounds. Throw in some Dutch masters and windmills if you want to be exceptionally bored.

Perhaps I am unduly harsh.

But probably not.

I booked into my hotel. It was charming. Made up of ten historic canal buildings knocked into one. The architectural school of higgledy-piggledy. Old and quaint with stairs leading everywhere. A nightmare to negotiate. I didn't need charm, I needed comfort and efficiency and a guidebook that told me exactly where reclusive film stars were likely to hang out.

I needed to shed blood to save blood.

Relax.

I didn't even need a hotel. I should be out pounding the streets looking for him. I should not rest or eat until my mission was accomplished. There was a room service menu, it was early evening, it was time to eat, I'd had nothing on the plane, I felt ill, I needed sustenance and energy, but I couldn't bring myself to order. My wife and son. No food for them. Sucking water from a hamster bottle. Jesus!

Find Sean.

Find Sean!

I didn't even know if he was in Amsterdam. He'd flown into the city, but he could just as easily have flown straight out again. My decision to stay was one fifth intuition, and four fifths desperation. He had to be here. Any other possibility rendered my mission impossible. I was no Tom Cruise. I could not possibly search all of Europe. He *must* be here. And if he was, I would find him. If he was not, my family was dead. Of that I was convinced.

Amsterdam. He's here. Definitely.

O'Ryan was right. I was a journalist. There were things I could do. Using what I already knew about Sean O'Toole I could track him down.

It was a fair bet that he'd chosen Amsterdam so that he could complete his drugs deal. If that was true, then he was in a world I knew nothing about, and to blunder into it would surely be suicidal. But unless his ambitions had radically altered in the past few days, he would also be determined to complete the post production on his film. Cannes was only two weeks away. If he didn't make Cannes with it, then it was odds on he'd have a financial disaster on his hands. If he was in Amsterdam then he would need access to an editing suite and a recording studio, he would need engineers and sound effects people and he might have to fly in actors to dub in lines and musicians to provide the score. Outside of porn, the Dutch film industry wasn't big; if he was here, the word would be out.

It would be easy.

I would find him.

I would save my family.

I checked the telephone directory in my room. I settled on twenty-six possible companies. I tried the first six, but either they weren't answering or

I got through to a machine. It was getting late. People would still be working, but the reception- ists would be away home. There was no point continuing. I would achieve nothing in the hours of darkness.

Eat.

No.

I will not eat until I find my family.

You'll starve to death and they'll survive.

Eat, stay strong.

I put on my coat and went out. I didn't have a map, didn't need one, I didn't know where I was going. I just started walking, I noted the street signs and followed my nose. I crossed over the Herengracht and Singel canals and padded along Paleis straat until I came to a huge cobbled square in what I took to be the city centre. Dam Square, the sign said. There was a character in a kilt playing the bagpipes. There was an empty hat before him. He was surrounded by pigeons. I turned left. A hundred yards along I found an Irish pub. The world was getting predictable. Everywhere the lan- guage was English, only the accent was different. Wax works, McDonald's, Guinness and begging Scots. The bar was mock old and quite dark. It was packed with Irish tourists, ex-pats and Germans. I didn't talk to anybody. I drank a Harp and left. There were no particular signs for the red light district, I just followed everyone else.

I was depressed, and it was depressing. There were hundreds of beautiful scantily clad women flaunting themselves in red-lit doorways and a lot of men walking past, half averting their eyes, pretending they were off to the shops but had taken a wrong turning. And that was the problem. It reminded me of shopping. *That* erotic. Patricia was a mistress of shopping. I detested it. She could spend hours going from clothes shop to clothes shop, trailing me with her, asking my opinion and then shooting it down in flames, but if I spent more than five minutes in a bookshop she would storm off over my selfishness. I looked at the windows and wanted to ask *how much for a hug*, but I was too embarrassed.

A big black girl in a small white bikini leant out of a window and shouted, 'Mister – come and talk.'

I walked across. She dipped down as I approached and gave me a view of the biggest mountains in Holland. I thanked her for the view but said my climbing days were over. I said I was a stranger in town and asked her if she had any idea where I might sell half a pound of pure heroin. She screamed something in Dutch and slammed her window.

I repeated the question in a coffee bar a few doors up. One of *those* coffee bars with the ganja sign outside, the Jamaican colours and the international aroma. They looked at me like I was a fucking loony or an apprentice cop, and I was made equally welcome.

I wasn't serious. I was just looking for a reaction.

Outside I leant on a railing and stared into the neon-lit canal and thought about how desperate it was to be alone and friendless in a foreign country and how for thirty quid I could purchase the pretence of both. I had the money, but not the inclination.

There was no company and no friends like those starving in a bunker.

I spat.

CHAPTER 27

From day one I had a Moroccan taxi driver called Maurice. He was small and weedy but he had close-set dangerous eyes which grew steadily narrower as the day wore on. By the time we hit lunch time the meter had all but run out of digits. He pulled over and asked me to *show him the money*; he wasn't going to drive me about all day if I was going to do a runner at the end of it, although of course he said it in a mixture of broken English and Dutch. For all I knew it was broken Dutch as well. He had sharp predatory teeth which looked like they'd bitten off an ear or two in their time. I was pissed off irritable. I gave him a mouthful of abuse then put my hands over my ears for protection as he fired a similar stream of venom back at me. But it seemed to do us both good to let off steam; he finally rolled his eyes, then turned the meter back to zero and started again. He spent the rest of the day muttering under his breath. Finally he took me back to the hotel and shouted some ridiculous figure at me, and I halved it and he swore at me and upped it and we bartered along like that for five minutes

204

until eventually we came to an agreement that made us both deliriously happy, although neither of us let on. I scowled, he scowled. I didn't give him a tip. He roared off. Next morning he was waiting for me, and the next. The pattern was exactly the same: distant but efficient until lunch time, muttering and suspicious until pay time, and no tip.

On the morning of the fourth day I hung about hotel reception waiting for him for half an hour. I wasn't eating breakfast, I was missing lunch and barely picking my way through a room service dinner. I'd lost ten pounds in three days. I stepped outside and flagged down another taxi. I was just climbing in when Maurice roared up and blasted his horn. I looked at my new driver. He smiled pleasantly, and I looked at Maurice growling over his wheel and sharpening his teeth on a cigarette. I apologised to the other driver. I didn't say anything to Maurice as I climbed into the back. I passed him a sheet of paper with a list of addresses on it and he perused it briefly. Then he looked round at me and said: 'We did these already.'

'I know. Now we do them again.'

He muttered something and pulled out.

The pattern was: I walk into a film company, give them some shit about making a documentary on Amsterdam and wanting to check out their facilities. I'd get a free tour of their offices and the chance to see if Sean was around. They were

205

all keen for my business, but there was no sign of Sean.

By the fourth morning I'd exhausted the possibilities. There was no alternative but to start over again. I'd called Mouse to see if there was any news. He had people looking, but there was nothing. He urged me to go to the police. But the Colonel had warned me that any hint of police involvement and he would shoot my wife and son. I couldn't take the chance. He told me Irish police were playing down the death of Dr Fruitke. Although there were a variety of illegal substances in his body, his death appeared to have been an accident. There had been some lurid headlines in the papers – Mouse had written a couple of them – but the police were satisfied Sean had been staying with his wife at her apartment in Dublin at the time of death and would only seek to talk to him when he was next in the country.

I called Sam and asked him to advance me some more money. He asked how much and didn't have a heart attack when I told him. He said it would be done within the hour. I said, 'You're being unusually helpful,' and he said, 'I talked to Mouse.'

'I didn't think you even knew Mouse.'

'You'd be surprised who I know. Is there anything else I can do?'

'You can find me Sean O'Toole.'

'I have my eyes peeled and all of my connections looking for him.'

'Thanks.'

The eighth stop on the fourth day was at a company called Paralog Films. It was a bright, modernised three-storey building overlooking Prinsengracht. I walked in and told them I was Neil Jordan and I was sick to death of working with the big film studios. I wanted to make an indie film set in the red light district with Leonardo DiCaprio and what could they do for me. It was a vaguely hippie kind of place, like most of Amsterdam, but I could see the dollar signs light up in their eyes as I talked. 'Loved *Interview*, man!' '*Butcher Boy*! Fucking A, man!' I smiled and took another man's plaudits and they gave me the tour. I dropped a bit of gossip. I said Leonardo was a pain to work with and I was thinking about axing him in favour of Sean O'Toole. I'd heard he was in town.

They hadn't.

I stalked back out to the cab and slumped into the back seat. We didn't move off. Maurice was looking at me in the mirror. I said, 'What?'

'Mister,' he said, 'each day you get smaller.'

'What?'

'Whatever you got on dem shoulders, you just get smaller.'

'Yeah, well,' I said.

'I put word on radio, anyone seen dis Sean-o-toole, but nobody.'

This was a surprise. We hadn't exchanged more than half a dozen words that weren't *fuck you*. 'Maurice,' I said, 'do you want a cup of coffee?'

He looked at me for a moment, then gave a slight nod. There was a café just opposite the film company and there were seats outside it, looking over the canal. Maurice drove over the bridge and parked next to the tables. I said, 'Leave the meter running, somebody else is paying for it.'

He shook his head and switched it off. We sat at a table. I bought him a cup of coffee and got myself a Coke Lite. Tourist barges were cruising past. Some kids waved and I waved back. I said, 'Maurice, do you have any children?'

He smiled and held up his hands. He spread the fingers. 'You have ten?'

He shook his head. 'Eight.' Then added helpfully, 'Two thumbs.'

'Must be expensive to feed.'

'I work hard. You have one son?'

I nodded.

'He is kidnapped?'

'Yes, kidnapped.'

'And you must find this Sean O'Toole, he knows where your son is?'

'Something like that.'

'To have a son is a very wonderful thing.'

I nodded.

'And to lose a son also, is a very terrible thing.'

I nodded. 'You've lost a son?'

'I have lost three sons. Morocco is not an easy place.'

'I'm sorry,' I said.

He shrugged. We sat silently for several moments.

I looked into the canal. He sipped his coffee and then said, 'Mister . . . would you like a camel?'

I cleared my throat. 'Ahm, no. Thank you very much for the kind offer. But I would have nowhere to keep it.'

His brow furrowed slightly. He leant forward and raised his eyebrows. 'You could keep it behind your ear.'

I cleared my throat again and took a drink of my Coke Lite. I wondered if the waiter had dropped a lump of hash into his coffee. 'No, thank you. My wife, she would not like the . . . smell.'

'You . . . get used to it.' He sat back. 'I hope my offer . . . does not . . . offend you?'

'No . . . of course not.' I nodded appreciatively at him. God love his cotton socks. Trying to make me feel better. In Morocco perhaps a camel was as valuable as a son. Or perhaps he was a camel agent in his spare time the way others sold water purifiers and Tupperware. I set my glass down. As I did so he picked up his packet of cigarettes from the table and removed one. I saw that it said Camel on the box.

I started to explain, and then thought, *fuck it*, let it lie. I laughed to myself, at myself, and he laughed to keep me company. I glanced back across the canal just in time to see Alice hurry out of the front door of Paralog Films and climb into a waiting cab.

CHAPTER 28

I said, 'Follow that cab.'

The thrill of saying it was probably lost on Maurice. Perhaps there was a Moroccan equivalent – follow that cart, follow that hashish, follow that under-achieving World Cup team. For obvious reasons I avoided *follow that camel.*

Thankfully most of the narrow canal streets in central Amsterdam are perpetually choked with cyclists, making it a place of slow progress for vehicular traffic. Alice's driver laboured, while my own was something of a master, and we were able to close in on her relatively quickly. Alice's head was down, she appeared to be studying something in her lap. From the front Maurice said, 'This lady – who she is?'

'Sean O'Toole's wife,' I said.

'Ah. And do you . . . know her?'

Intimately. I nodded. Her cab turned right and skirted along Brouwersgracht, then turned onto Prins Hendrik opposite Centraal Station. A couple more turns and we were into the red light district. Her taxi pulled over. We slipped in behind it. I kept low. Alice climbed out, but no money exchanged hands. The driver reached into the back and removed a newspaper, which he began to read. Good. It meant the meter was still running. I asked Maurice to wait for me while I went after Alice.

She was wearing flat black shoes, sunglasses though it was now starting to rain, a short white jacket and a knee-length black skirt. There was a black leather handbag over her arm, which was large, but blew in the breeze like there wasn't much in it. It was early afternoon. Although the district was comparatively quiet there were enough single men for me to blend in, and few enough single women for Alice to stand out. I stayed close. She was studying house numbers, and ignoring the girls in the red-lit windows which fronted them. She stopped several times to consult a sheet of paper she held in her hands, then peered back up at the houses. After walking several hundred yards she stopped abruptly; evidently she had passed the address she was looking for. She turned on her heel and started coming towards me. Luckily she was concentrating on the houses and not the sex tourists on the footpath; I ducked quickly down a set of stairs. At their foot there was a bouncer in a DJ standing before a garishly illuminated box office.

'Come in, come in,' he said. 'Girl will do what you want with banana.'

I heard the clip of Alice's shoes pass above and behind me. I smiled at the bouncer. 'Can she make me a banoffi?' I asked.

211

His brow furrowed for a moment, but he recovered quickly. He grinned. 'She do *everything*, sir,' he said and opened his palm to shepherd me to the window.

I shook my head. 'Not like my wife,' I said.

I hurried back up and peered out before stepping onto the footpath. Alice was twenty yards away, looking up at a doorway. She was folding the sheet of paper back into her handbag. She ran a hand through her hair, then quickly mounted the steps. She rang the bell, then turned away from it for a moment and looked back down the street. I ducked down, gave it five seconds, then chanced another glance back up towards her.

The door was just closing. I couldn't see who had opened it. Or who had closed it, for that matter. I walked back up onto the path and looked along to the house. There were two red-light cabins on the ground floor with girls touting for business; but to either side of the door at the top of the steps the windows were curtained. There was nowhere on the nearside of the canal to get a proper view of the house, so I crossed over the bridge and began looking up at terraced houses on the other side, working out which one might give me the best perspective. It wasn't exactly rocket science. There was a bank of three red-lit glass doors, each with a bikini-clad girl perched on a stool. All three of them were reading paperback books, which reflected well on the Dutch educational system. Or indeed, the English educational system. The centre girl pushed a smile onto her face when I knocked and said, 'Thirty-five for oral, sixty-five for full sex,' in dulcet Essex tones when I enquired how much.

'I like to watch,' I said.

'Fifty,' she said.

I nodded. I gave her the money. She ushered me inside her cabin. She had mousy brown hair and a small chest. She had red nail varnish on one foot and black on the other. There was a single bed and a small lamp. There were several paperback books on the floor, and a large packet of condoms. She moved to close the curtains, but I told her to leave them; she said no way, I said yes way and offered her another fifty. She said okay as long as I stood in front of the window so that others weren't getting a free show. I said okay.

She lay back on the bed and removed her bikini top. She made a kissy face and asked me where I was from. I said Dublin. Generally the English can't tell the difference, and it's better to get Dubs a bad name than innocent little Ulstermen. She took her knickers off and spread her legs. I asked her if she happened to have a pair of binoculars. Her mouth fell open slightly and she said, 'Your eyesight must be fucking appalling.'

I told her what I was about and she closed her legs. 'You a cop?' she asked.

I shrugged. I told her I was a spy in the house of love and we spent five minutes trying to work out what song that line came from while we looked at the house across the road. She was quite content to join me in my observation, although she pointed out it would cost me fifty guilder for every fifteen minutes. It was going to get expensive, what with the hooker and the meter still running on Maurice's cab, although at least he could give me a receipt.

There was nothing to see. The door and the curtains across the way remained resolutely closed. She pulled a kettle out from beneath the bed and made me a cup of tea. She said on a good day she got through about thirty customers. The temptation was to say, *ooh, you must have a really sore crack*, but I'd already left secondary school. She didn't have a pimp, she was a member of the Amsterdam Prostitutes' Union, and she wasn't working in the red light district to finance her education or set up her own business or even to support her children. She was doing it because it was a job and she enjoyed it. Also, she didn't believe for one minute that I really was watching the house across the road. She thought it was just me playing out my little fantasy. I could tell by the way she agreed with everything I said, and I've never come across that in a woman yet.

I asked her if she knew the girls working in the windows across the road. She shrugged noncommittally. I said, 'Will you go across and ask them what they know about the people upstairs? Please?'

Her eyebrows rose a little. I opened my wallet and took out 100 guilder. She shook her head; I was about to add another fifty when she raised her hand to stop me. 'You just want me to leave you alone, then you'll have a wank in my bed when I've gone. I know the score, mister.'

'I swear to God, I won't.'

'You can swear to whoever the fuck you want, I know your type.'

I folded my wallet closed and threw it on her bed. There was a lot of money in there, and none of it mine. 'Look,' I said, 'I'm serious, I need to know about the people across the way. I swear to God. Take the wallet with you; if I do anything when you're gone, keep it. There's stacks of cash in there. There's a credit card. There's a kidney donor card if you fancy trying a different organ for a change.'

She looked to the window, and across the road. 'Straight up?'

'Straight up.'

She let out a sigh, then packed everything of value she had into a handbag and pulled on a black knee-length leather coat over her bikini. She pushed my wallet into a side pocket in the coat. She went to the glass door and opened it a fraction, then looked back. 'If you're going to have a wank, use one of the condoms. And I'll check the place out when I come back, inch by inch. No wanking in my shoes. Or between the last two pages of my book. Okay?'

'Okay. I'm not a wanker.' Though, of course, it was common knowledge in Belfast that I was.

She nodded once and slipped out. She locked the glass door behind her. I stood and watched as she went down the steps and along the path to the bridge. She paused on it for several moments, just long enough to check out the contents of my wallet. Her fingers flicked over the notes, then she extracted a photograph. It was one of Patricia and Little Stevie. As she replaced it, she glanced back up at me. I nodded. She continued on across the bridge and then along the cobbled pathway to the house opposite. One of the two red-lit windows was curtained now, but the other was still open for business. A black girl in a red wig smiled as she approached, then hopped off her stool. The glass door opened. A moment later, with my girl inside, it closed over and the curtain was pulled.

The temptation, of course, was just to have the wank. For badness. And to do it somewhere she wouldn't think of looking. But I didn't. It would be breaking my word. It would be disgusting. And married men don't. I looked at her books instead. She was reading the latest Michael Crichton. The three on the floor were a biography of George Michael, Salman Rushdie's *Midnight's Children* and *The Little Book of Panic*. Her taste was in her arse, as I'm sure a lot of people had found out.

She was back in ten minutes. I smiled at her as she came through the door. She glowered suspiciously back and took it as a challenge. When she'd searched high and low she breathed a sigh of relief and refilled the kettle. She asked me if I

216

wanted another cup, I said no. When it had boiled again and she was stirring, I said, 'Well?'

She took her first sip, hummed appreciatively, then sat on the bed. 'They're Irish,' she said. 'Three of them. Arrived about a week ago. There's some woman upstairs with them now, don't know where she's from. Says they keep themselves to themselves, but look heavy duty. She thinks it's drugs, but she doesn't really know.'

'Much coming and going?'

She shook her head.

'I mean,' I said, 'if somebody famous, say a movie star, was in there, she'd know, right?'

'Guess so.'

'But she hasn't seen anything unusual.'

'No.'

'Okay, thank you. I appreciate it.'

'No trouble.'

There was movement across the road. The door was open and Alice was standing on the top step. She was talking to somebody, but I couldn't see who.

'Gotta go,' I said.

'Okay.'

I hurried to the door. Alice was halfway down the steps. I paused. 'Oh,' I said, 'my wallet.'

'Shit – sorry,' she said, not very convincingly. She reached into her coat pocket and extracted it. She reached it across.

It felt a lot lighter. I flipped it open. More than half of the notes were gone. I raised an eyebrow.

'I had to pay the girl for her time,' she said, then added, 'There's nothing free round here.'

She took another sip of her tea. 'Fair enough,' I said, and pulled the door open. Alice was already twenty yards up the street, heading in the direction of her waiting taxi. I paused in the doorway. 'Oh,' I said, 'that wank? You should have checked the kettle. See ya.'

I closed the glass door and hurried down the steps in pursuit of Alice O'Toole.

CHAPTER 29

I tagged Alice just as she was reaching for the taxi door handle. She twirled, holding her bag protectively against her. For a moment she didn't realise who it was, then she let out a surprised 'Jesus, Mary and Joseph.'

'And I thought you were a good Protestant girl,' I said.

'Dan . . . what're you . . . ?'

'Tulips,' I said. I took her by the arm. 'Come for a ride, Alice,' I suggested, then added, 'In my taxi.'

Maurice was out of the car and had opened the back door for my benefit. We were becoming quite a team, although he may have just been angling for a tip.

'But my . . .'

'Send him on.'

Alice opened her bag, removed her purse, then settled up with her driver. She got into the back of Maurice's cab and snapped an address. She gave me a long, appraising look, then said, 'This isn't going to turn into one of those *Fatal Attraction* things, is it?'

I shook my head.

'Good.' She reached across and kissed me. Her tongue pressed against my closed teeth. She sat back. I caught Maurice watching in the mirror. She said, 'What's wrong?'

'You tell me. You left without calling.'

She shrugged. 'This *is* going to turn into *Fatal Attraction*.'

'Except instead of a boiled rabbit there's a drowned doctor. What about Fruitcake, Alice?'

She sighed. 'Dan, c'mon. I told you about him. He was a bad guy. I sent him away. He came back high as a kite and drowned. Sean saw it all from his bedroom. He panicked. He called me. I panicked. We ran away. End of story.'

Maurice pulled out into the traffic. He caught my eye in the mirror again. I gave a little shrug. I looked back to Alice. She was watching me.

'Except you can't see the pool from his bedroom,' I said.

She tutted. 'Don't be so fucking pernickety, Dan. That's what happened. We didn't do anything wrong.'

'So why Amsterdam?'

'Sean's a drug addict and he's high profile. He's not stupid enough to try and take stuff through customs. Amsterdam is drug central, it's the natural place to come.' She smoothed out her skirt. She ran a finger along my leg. 'So why are you here? I can't believe you're that enthusiastic about the book.'

'I don't like leaving a job half finished. I need to talk to Sean.'

'Well, he doesn't want to talk to you. You fucked him over, Dan, you betrayed him. You betrayed me.'

'I was drunk.'

'It's no excuse.'

'I'm sorry. Look. I've come all this way.'

'And you can go all this way back. He won't talk. He's up to his eyes in the film, you know the sort of deadline he's up against, and all this shit about Fruitcake has hardly helped. He hasn't the time. He hasn't the time for me, let alone you.'

'So who's looking after you?'

'Don't even think about it.'

I tapped my knuckles against the glass. I said, 'I can't keep this drug stuff out of the book, you know that?'

She nodded. 'It'll just be dismissed as gutter journalism. You don't have any proof. Besides, he's an artist, people take it for granted.'

'Who was that you were visiting?'

Her eyes turned sharply towards me. 'You were following me?'

'I like to hang out in red light districts. You walked past. I shouted, you didn't hear. You knocked on a door, you disappeared. I'm only asking.'

She sighed. 'Okay. I'm sorry. I'm nervous. I'm not used to all this shit. Jesus. I had to go out and buy gear for Sean. Heroin. Fuck. Look what I'm reduced to.'

'Love is throwing your husband's heroin fix in the canal.'

'I can't. Not yet. We've tried cold turkey once, we'll do it again when the time is right. When the film's finished.'

'So until then you'll have to take your life in your hands going to buy smack for him.'

She gave a little shrug.

'What was it like? Were they scary? Did they try to rip you off?'

'They were fine. Maybe they sensed a regular customer.'

'What were they, Moroccans? I hear there's a lot of them involved.' There was the merest twinkle from Maurice upfront.

Alice shook her head. 'I don't know what they were. Black guys. Nigerians, maybe. Does it matter?'

We had driven down onto the canal where Paralog Films was situated. Maurice pulled into a parking space several doors down. Alice put her hand back on my leg. 'Sean's working his guts out. He's been through a rough time. Please don't complicate matters. Let him finish his film. Come to Cannes. I swear to God he'll speak to you there. And I swear to God he'll be clean.'

'I find generally that God is quite busy.'

She smiled. She leant across and kissed me on the lips. The tongue didn't try anything this time. 'You're nice, y'know, Dan,' she said.

'And we'll always have Dublin.'

She nodded. 'You're not hurt, are you?'

'No. Of course not.'

'Good.'

She opened the door and climbed out. She didn't look back. When she'd gone through the door into Paralog Films Maurice looked back at me; I asked him if he wanted another cup of coffee and he nodded. We went back across the canal and took our original seats.

This time, when he offered me a Camel, I took it. 'Maurice,' I said, 'you look like a man who has connections in this town.'

He stirred his coffee with one hand – or, indeed, a spoon – and cupped his cigarette with the other. He kept his black eyes steady on me.

'I need to buy a gun.'

A pained expression. 'Why you need a gun, mister?'

'You know why I need a gun. Can you get me one?'

'A gun, I think yes. But is expensive, yes?'

'I don't have much money. But I have drugs. Heroin. Lots of. I'll swap the lot for a gun and some bullets.'

'I not think . . . you were into heroin, man.'

'I'm not. I have it by . . . accident.'

'How much you have?'

'About half a pound.' He looked confused. I had no idea what it was in grams or even if Moroccans or Dutchmen used grams. I was of the ounces and pounds generation. I raised my cup of coffee.

'About this much,' I said and levelled my hand across the top of it, 'and then some.'

'Plenty heroin,' Maurice said. 'I talk to right people. Get you gun okay.' Then he gave a little cackle. 'Get you six guns and . . . rocket launcher!' He smiled expansively.

'I'll settle for the gun. You can keep the change.'

'Keep . . . ?'

'Whatever is left, after buying the gun. You keep.'

'That is, I think, very generous.'

'Well,' I said.

Across the road the door to Paralog opened again and three men in big suits and dark glasses emerged. They checked north, south, east and west. Then Sean appeared, with Alice on his arm. Behind them came two more heavies. One of them had kissed me before, though it hurt that he hadn't called since. A limo came around the corner and stopped before the little group.

Beside me Maurice continued to stir. 'This, I think, is the man you want to kill.'

I nodded.

'I have seen his movies. They are not good.'

'No, they are not good.'

'But not so bad, that he should die.'

'Maurice, I have no choice.'

He nodded slowly. I got up. He followed. We got back into the taxi and tailed Sean's car along the canal. At Wester straat the limo pulled off the road and approached a set of electronic gates which barred entry to a small car park facing a block of expensive-looking apartments. There was a guy in a cap guarding the gates. Evidently he knew the car. The gates opened without any checks. Maurice pulled his cab to a halt a few hundred yards down the road. We watched as Sean's guards shepherded him and his wife into the apartment block.

'I think,' Maurice said, 'he will be difficult to kill in there.'

'I think,' I said, 'he will be difficult to kill full stop.'

'That woman,' Maurice said, 'I not trust her.'

'No,' I said, 'me neither. You'll get me a gun?'

'I will get you this gun, you will do right thing.'

I wasn't so sure. I was more Robert Morley than Robert de Niro. It floated across my mind for a moment that I was about to give this taxi driver the tip of his life and that the least he could do would be to kill Sean O'Toole for me in return. My Travis Bickle.

But no. It was something I had to do myself. He had his own wife and many children, not to mention the camels.

I had one wife, and one child, and they were dying. I had to get to Sean.

CHAPTER 30

Three thirty AM. We were back on Prinsengracht. There were no cyclists, no coffee shops, no tourist barges. Even the hookers had closed their legs for the night. Maurice was wearing a new jacket and smoking a cigar. He could now afford to put his children through medical school, though he still insisted on keeping the meter running. I had a Glock automatic in my pocket and fear in my soul. Just over the bridge Paralog Films sat in darkness. I sat in a pool of sweat. There was a plan in my head, a simple plan for a simple man.

I grasped the door handle. 'Wish me luck,' I said.

Maurice nodded back. 'Break your leg in a horrible accident,' he said.

I climbed out. I was wearing my black zip-up bomber jacket, black jeans and black Oxfords. I was going for a black look. If I'd owned a balaclava I'd have worn it, but they'd stopped selling them in Belfast since the ceasefire.

I bent back into the car and said, 'Twenty minutes.' Maurice nodded. I closed the door and he drove off. I lurked in a doorway for several moments until I was sure there was nobody about, then hurried across the bridge and along the few yards to Paralog. I had reconnoitred the building before and was fairly certain that there was no alarm system. Certainly on my earlier tour none had been evident. After escorting Sean home, I had returned with Maurice and watched the staff leave for the night and it had taken them a while to secure the locks. It seemed evident they trusted manual rather than electronic security.

I was convinced that my earlier escorted tour had not missed out any rooms in the three-storey building. Which left the possibility of a basement. One hop over a low wall at the rear of the building confirmed it. There was a long, narrow window which ran the width of the building at about foot level. At the far end, where it joined the next building in the terrace, there was a set of steps leading down. They were strewn with rubbish and the door at their base had been barred by planks of now rotting wood. The whole area was damp. Of course it was. There were canals all around.

I pulled at the wood. It came loose easily. Then there was the door and a grimy window. The door was locked. The window was already cracked, probably from the contractions of its damp wooden frame. I pressed against it and it came away in my hands. I was able to place the glass on the ground without making a peep. I reached inside and opened the door. A moment later I was inside Paralog Films.

When I'd started looking in the early evening for a shop to buy a flashlight, I had not been able to locate one. In Amsterdam, however, there is no shortage of hippie emporiums and I was able to lay my hands on an aromatherapy candle and a box of matches made from a tree which had died of natural causes. It was a relief that there was nobody around to see the most embarrassed burglar in western Europe lighting up in the basement of Paralog Films.

There were four rooms. Only one of them was locked. The other three were used for storage. I found that the fourth, after I'd kicked the door in, had been recently tarted up; it smelt of fresh paint and the carpet was crisp and springy. The room was dominated by a large desk on which sat a Lightworks Editing System, a computer-based program editors use these days as an alternative to the mechanical restrictions of working with film in a cutting room. Sean had told me that the main advantage of the Lightworks system was that it allowed a numbskull like him to edit and re-edit to his heart's content. He could change scenes and their running order without having to strike another cutting copy of the negative, which in turn left him free to be more creative. I had asked him to explain the process to me both as a requirement for the book I was writing and out of a film fan's curiosity. I had not thought then that what he told me about the process of film making might help me to lure him to his death. For Sean had also made the mistake of deciding to keep all of his eggs in one basket. Sitting stacked in one corner were a dozen cans of film, each one of them marked with a logo for *The Brigadier*.

I'd struck gold.

Foolish, big man. If I didn't get to him first, the insurance company would string him up. He had not only brought the telecine transfer he was using on the Lightworks with him to Amsterdam, but also the cans of master negative. They were all there together in that little room where anything could happen to them, particularly if some bitter hippie burglar happened to break in.

The room was soundproofed. So I smashed up the Lightworks and didn't mind how much noise I made. I hurled it around the room until I'd reduced it to little bits. There was no need for it, of course. I could simply have wiped the disks. But I enjoyed it. Maybe I was getting my anger and frustration out. Maybe it was the aroma. Maybe in amongst the rows of calming candles in the shop I'd accidentally picked out something made from mayhem berries.

When I'd finished I turned to the cans of film negative. They were not only heavy but awkward to carry. I went into one of the storage rooms and rooted about. I came up with a sack of discarded film scripts. From the titles and the few lines I read I guessed that Paralog had got its start by producing its own porn films. I emptied them all out and returned to Sean's room with the sack. I filled it with the cans of negative and then threw in the telecine transfer for good measure. As I pulled the sack up onto my back it jarred against the desk and knocked over the aromatherapy candle. It rolled off the desk and into a set of files nestling in the corner. As I left the room I saw that the files were beginning to smoulder. I paused, but then thought, fuck it, why bother, it'll burn itself out.

It had taken less than fifteen minutes. Master burglar.

I exited Paralog, sack on my back, and heaved it over the low wall. I started walking. As I stepped onto the bridge I saw that there was a young fella already crossing. He was meandering somewhat. Drink or drugs. He said something as I passed and I said sorry, no speako da lingo.

Moments later, back on solid ground, I was thrown up against a wall. The kid from the bridge, and another guy, bigger, out of nowhere, but brandishing a knife.

Muggers.

They were jabbering something and pointing at the bag. Robbing a robber. I had the Glock in my pocket, but there was a knife against my chest and my hands were pinned back by the bag.

'Look,' I said, 'there's nothing of value in here.'

They started to pull at the bag. I held tight.

'Look,' I said, pulling back, 'my uncle fought at Arnhem.'

The bigger mugger paused. 'What?' he said.

'My uncle saved your fucking life and all you can do is rob me!'

The other one, the smaller one, looked up at his partner and said something. The big guy spat back. He moved the knife up to my face. 'We are Turkish, what do we know about Arn-ham?'

'On the other hand,' I said, 'my grandfather died at Gallipoli, so you've had your fun.' I gave another pull at the bag. The big guy zipped the knife down my face and I felt blood begin to run. 'Jesus fuck!' I spat and pushed the bag out at him. He stumbled back with the weight of it and fell onto the cobbles. The bag came open and cans of film began to roll out left, right and centre. Several sat up on their rims and made for the canal. The muggers stared perplexedly at their booty as it made for freedom. As I pulled at it my gun snagged in the lining of my jacket pocket.

Across the canal the windows of Paralog Films exploded outwards with a deafening crash. Flames licked out.

My two muggers stood frozen for a moment, then looked from the fire to me to the cans of film scattered on the ground. Then they ran for it. My gun finally came free. I raised it. I aimed from one to the other, then thought better of it.

I was scrabbling around the ground trying to get as many of the cans as possible back into the sack when Maurice screeched to a halt beside me. His window was down and there were a thousand questions written on his face, highlighted by the glow of the rapidly escalating inferno across the canal. Thankfully he asked none of them. He jumped out and helped me gather up the last of the cans. Then we lifted the sack together and dropped it into the boot. We slammed it shut and hurried back into the cab. We could hear a police siren somewhere in the distance. Maurice kept his lights off as he began to negotiate the backstreets away from the canal.

We didn't speak.

I sat with my eyes closed and thought about my next move.

CHAPTER 31

Sean came to survey the damage in the first light of dawn. In fact, he wasn't the slightest bit interested in the damage, but in the fate of his film. When he saw the state of the place he threw a fit. Paralog Films was a charred wreck. What was still standing didn't look like it would for long. Men in hard hats surveyed the smouldering ruins and tutted. As Maurice reported it, idling in the coffee shop across the way, smoking one of his new cigars and sporting another new jacket, Sean ranted and raved. He would not be consoled.

Understandable, of course.

Alice tried talking to him, but he marched about, tearing his hair out, which was a bad move for a middle-aged man marching down route Bobby Charlton. His security guards, many hundreds of pounds of solid muscle and sunglasses, stood helplessly, nervously fingering their ears for urgent messages over non-existent earplugs. They had once worked for somebody important. Sean, clearly, no longer was. His chance for an Oscar was gone. He had just proved himself unemployable by breaking the cardinal rule of the film business: don't fuck

233

with the insurance. He could lose as many millions as he wanted at the box office, that was to be expected; they could write that off; sometimes it made more sense for a film to bomb, depending on what part of the tax year it came out. But in the movie business, insurance was God. You couldn't write off something that didn't exist, and *The Brigadier* might as well never have existed. The insurance companies weren't going to pay up for something so patently stupid as keeping all of the negatives and their copies in the one room, a room next to a paint store, in a building that was equipped with neither burglar alarms nor a sprinkler system. Sean had thrown his lot in with independent films, and would never be able to raise a cent again. His name was mud. He couldn't go back to the big Hollywood studios, they didn't want him. He was past his best. He couldn't open a movie any more. He had once been on the A list but had long ago slipped to near the bottom of the B. With this disaster he would be automatically relegated down into the Ms and Ns, the nether world of showbiz; he'd be presenting weekly aerobic workouts on cable television or providing the commentary for videos like *You Won't Believe These Crazy Golf Shots Volume 5*. Within a couple of years he'd be shooting up methadone in a shop doorway on Rodeo Drive and telling everyone he used to be big in pictures and wailing a second-hand *I didn't get small, the movies did.*

Something like that.

Then the boy, not more than twelve, but already passing hash on the streets, slipped through the security guards and ran up to Sean. He was just about to swipe him away when the boy produced a can of film with *The Brigadier* written on the front from inside his jacket. And everything changed.

Sean hungrily opened it, realising already that it was too light to actually contain film, but suddenly hopeful that all was not lost. A light at the end of the tunnel.

A note. *Love the movie, let's talk.*

I had guessed he would think it was Michael O'Ryan behind the fire and wouldn't swallow the bait. No point in getting the film back if he was going to get killed. Posthumous Oscars weren't half as much fun. I had debated several ways to reassure him and settled on the simplest. *Don't worry, I'm not the Colonel.* O'Ryan, master of machiavellian plotting and dastardly deeds, would not have come up with anything quite so straightforward.

The note was in Maurice's handwriting, just to throw the curious off the trail. He volunteered willingly, and plainly didn't realise that doing so implicated him in blackmail, burglary, arson and murder, which just goes to prove that big tippers can be right cunts as well.

After the message, the instructions.

Alice was looking at him, the guards were looking at him, the boy had already slipped away, forgotten. Maurice was waiting in his taxi on the other side of the bridge. Sean said something to his wife Maurice couldn't hear, then walked straight across the bridge and climbed into the back of the taxi.

Maurice roared off before the door was closed. He saw the security guards scrambling for their own vehicle in the mirror, forgetting Alice, who stood stunned and abandoned.

I stood and waited on a bridge over Herengracht. It was only a few hundred yards from my base in the Ambassade Hotel. I had had enough of misty country roads at dawn. It was a fine bright morning and the canalside was already busy with bicycles and the first of the tourist barges were cruising past, their bug-eyed passengers blissfully unaware that I was contemplating murder.

Ordinarily I might have considered compromise. But it wasn't like I was dealing with a good guy, and, besides, the news from home was not good. In his time Mouse had dealt with some of the biggest scumbags in Ireland, and Sam was one of them, but between them they hadn't turned up the merest hint of a clue to my family's whereabouts. If the graffiti I'd pointed out to him in the Polaroid still existed, it wasn't in a location frequented by anyone with a criminal record.

They called in the police.

I exploded.

'Dan, we had no choice.'

'He said he would kill them if . . .'

'There was nothing else we could do. We've tried everything.'

'You're condemning them to death.'

'No. You are. By not telling the police. They've promised nothing will leak out.'

'Things always leak out.'

'They won't. Dan, it's for the best.'

I sighed.

'How're you doing, Dan?'

'I'm on the point of murder, thank you.'

'You're going to go through with it?'

'What choice do I have?'

He shrugged. He was on the phone, but I could tell by the silence that he was shrugging.

'Okay then,' I said.

Mouse told me the police were searching high and low, but mostly low. Anybody who asked was told they'd been tipped off about an undeclared IRA explosives dump in a perilous state. Sinn Fein denied all knowledge, about the IRA, and the dump, but assisted in the search by sending out kids to throw stones.

It was their fifth day without food.

It was pleasant in the early-morning sun. I remained in black and, despite a shower, still smelt of smoke and mayhem berries. Maurice's cab pulled up and Sean got out. If he'd bothered to look, he would have found his precious cans of film in the boot of the cab. If he was surprised to see me standing there with my hands in my pockets, it didn't show. If he could see that one of those hands was shaking through the jacket as it gripped the Glock, he didn't say.

Sean walked straight up. Behind him Maurice parked the car, then stepped up onto the bridge; he nodded at me, then leant against the fence half a dozen yards away, and lit another cigar. He was smoking them like they were coming into fashion.

Sean smiled. 'I didn't think the book was that important to you,' he said.

'It wasn't,' I said.

'So what's the problem? Don't tell me you're hurt. Don't tell me you haven't been thrown out of better places than mine. Don't tell me you object to my little social addiction. Worst of all, for godsake, don't tell me you're a film critic.'

'Right on all four counts, actually, but it's not why I'm here.'

'Perhaps it's because you've been fucking my wife.'

'No, it's not that.'

'I don't mind. Habitual drug addiction routinely leads to impotence. She's young and she's beautiful but she'll never leave me for you, not in a million years.'

'I don't want her to leave you. I'm not fucking her. She's very concerned about you.'

'So taking the film, it's meant to achieve something, it's meant to encourage me into Betty Ford?'

'Michael O'Ryan is holding my wife and son hostage.'

238

He looked at me for a moment; his square jaw dropped a little. 'Oh. Shit.'

'Shit indeed.'

He gripped the guardrail and looked down into the canal. 'Are they okay?'

'I presume not. He says he's starving them to death.'

'Seriously?'

'Is there any other way?'

He shook his head. 'I'm sorry. The bastard. He'd go to those lengths to get the script changed?'

'No, of course he wouldn't.'

'I mean, I can do a lot in the editing, but even so . . .'

'It's not about the film, Sean. It's about the money.'

'Money? What money?'

'The three million you ripped off of him.'

'*What?*'

'Don't fuck me around, Sean. Don't give me any of your acting bullshit. You fucked him over, and O'Ryan's not the kind of guy you fucking fuck over.'

'I don't know what the hell you're talking about.'

'You're not making this easy.'

'I'm not making *what* easy?'

'The fact that I have to kill you.'

He straightened back from the guardrail. 'What the fuck do you have to kill *me* for?'

'So that my wife and son can live.'

He blew air up into his cheeks and out. 'Look,'

he said, his voice softer, 'I don't know what bull-shit Michael's been giving you, but as far as I'm concerned we've had a bit of a tiff about the interpretation of his character. That's as far as it goes, Dan. I don't know where that stuff about three million comes into it, and I don't know anything about your family. You think I can afford to have drug money in a picture about a gangster? Seriously?'

'No, I don't think you can, but what I think hardly matters. What matters is you ripped him off. I know what method acting is, and you probably deserve your Oscar, but not at the expense of my wife and child.'

'Dan, I killed three thousand aliens in *Light Years from Home*, I healed the sick in *Messiah*. I don't think there's life on other planets and I don't walk on water in real life. I have not ripped anyone off.'

'Well, I'm sorry,' I said, 'but I don't believe you.'

I removed the Glock from my pocket.

'Dan, I'm only an actor. You're not a murder-er.'

'You're not, and I am.'

My finger was on the trigger. I thought of Trish and Little Stevie, and bending for the soap in prison. I thought of making love to my wife and a tiny white coffin and wondered how many it would take to carry it.

Kill him.

A car door slammed to my left. I glanced around. Three men getting out of a car. Another car on the other side of the bridge. More men. Sean took a step back.

Fuck it. Squeeze the trigger.

They were hurrying, but not racing.

They were still far enough away.

Sean's eyes were wide with terror. He had hidden it well, right up to the point where he would die.

So die.

But even as I squeezed the trigger, there was a gun at my ear.

Impossible, the men were still coming up onto the bridge . . .

A familiar voice, yet more coherent than before, hissed, 'Police! Put down your weapon!'

I turned ever so slightly.

Maurice, with a gun in his left and a badge in his right.

'Police! Put down your weapon!'

CHAPTER 32

Those time-stands-still moments.
They can be as innocuous as a driving test decision or a bluff at poker.
Or as vital as a baby's first cry, as long as an old man's last breath.

Pull the trigger, save my wife and child.

But die myself.

Or hold off, seek another way, live to fight another day.

Ultimately, we are all selfish.

I dropped the gun. Maurice said, 'Well done.'

'Your English suddenly got good,' I said.

'Better,' he corrected.

Sean O'Toole blew out of his cheeks and stepped back into the arms of the plain-clothes police officers. Before he could speak they bundled him back over the bridge and into one of the cars.

Maurice bent to pick up my gun. He opened it, showed me it wasn't loaded, smiled, then slipped it into a jacket pocket, and holstered his own.

I said, 'What's going on?'

'You don't kill movie stars in our town, Dan, that's what's going on.'

'But why . . . the gun . . . if you weren't going to . . .'

'Because we wanted to see what you would lead us to, and you've done very well.' There was the merest hint of sympathy in his voice, but I was in no mood to appreciate it. 'We understand why you're here,' he said, 'but that's out of our control. You're a lucky man; if we wanted to we could put you in prison for importing heroin into Amsterdam. We've been following you since Dublin, Dan. You were the worst courier the Garda ever saw. We could add another ten years for burning down Paralog Films. But as it is, you've led us on to bigger things, so we're prepared to look the other way.'

'What bigger things?'

'It has nothing to do with you any more.'

'It has everything to . . .'

'No, it hasn't. I'm sorry.'

I sighed. I bent down and rested my head on the guardrail. A barge emerged from beneath the bridge. Tourists waved up. Maurice put a hand on my shoulder, 'Go home, Dan, back to Ireland, find your wife and child. You can't do anything more here.'

'You are killing my family.'

'No, I'm not, I'm doing my job.'

'They're starving to death.'

'I'm sorry. Go home, Dan. Sean's ours, you won't get near him.'

He turned and walked back across the bridge to

his taxi. He opened the door and slipped into the driver's seat, then glanced back at me. He reached up and switched off the meter.

'You're killing my family!' I shouted.

He shook his head, reversed the cab, then drove off. The car with Sean in it followed behind. The other one had already driven off. In a few moments there was only the lap of the water and the rhythmic hum of the bicycles meandering along on either side of the canal. I stared into the water.

I had saved myself. Even if the gun wasn't loaded, I could still have clubbed Sean to death with it. But I'd surrendered, thrown in the towel, put up my hands without so much as an angry word, let alone a fight.

And condemned my family.

Perhaps they were already dead.

Or they were crawling across the floor of some freezing concrete bunker, skin and bones, too weak to even suck at the brackish water in the hamster pipe. Too slow to catch an insect and gobble it up. Too tired to fight off the rats.

Selfish.

I tramped back to the hotel. I asked if there were any messages. There were none. I went up to my room and ordered drinks from room service. Four bottles of Amstel. It was early to be drinking, even for me. I took out the Polaroids and stared at them.

My wife, and the hell I'd put her through over the years.

244

My son, not my son, but nevertheless my son.

Tony. He wouldn't even know what was going on. He would read it for the first time in the newspapers, or hear it on the television news when he was having dinner with his wife. Nobody but his wife knew he was the father. He would come to the funeral alone. We would look at each other and not know what to say. We had shared a beautiful woman and I hated him for it. They had made a beautiful child, and I hated him for it. And now we would bury my wife and his child, and I would give anything for her to be alive and living with Tony, and for Little Stevie to be alive, and living with them.

I looked at his Polaroid. Being held down on a table. Screaming.

In the background *ANGER* scrawled across the wall.

Anger indeed.

I would never get to do his homework for him. Never take him to the cinema. Never go out drinking with him or clear up the mess of his first drinking session. Never kick a ball with him in the back garden. Or take him to his first match – scarves and cold hot dogs and screaming curses at the referee.

I stopped. I flipped through the photographs again. The fourth. Patricia bruised. ANGER behind her. Except beside the last letter, the merest hint of white. The beginning of another letter? Cut off by the edge of the photograph.

I stared at the word.

A clue, Sherlock?

Could it mean something beyond *anger*? I raced through the alphabet, adding letters: *angera, angerb, angerc, angerd* . . .

S. The only one that made a word, and yet still no sense. ANGERS . . .

Why would some vandal write *ANGERS* on a wall?

Because there was another letter missing, at the start of the word, cut off by the edge of the photograph in exactly the same way as the last. And in looking at it, it was immediately obvious what it was.

RANGERS.

Glasgow Rangers. The Scottish football team worshipped by hardline Protestants everywhere.

Republican Michael O'Ryan had chosen to hide my wife and child where nobody would think to look for them, in the heart of enemy territory.

It wasn't an address, but it was a narrowing of the possibilities. It was the merest pinprick of light at the end of the Channel Tunnel. I phoned Mouse. There was nobody in. I left a message on his answering machine. I phoned Sam. He wasn't in either. I left another message. I called Mouse at work, but he couldn't come to the phone; I left the information with his secretary with the strict instruction that she deliver it immediately. Frustrated still, I pulled out my laptop and plugged into the Internet. I posted an appeal on as many newsgroup sites relating to Ireland and Rangers as I could. It wasn't much, but it was something.

I sat on the bed and drank my four bottles.

There was nothing more I could do. Maurice had advised me to go home. Big of him. He was prepared to look the other way. Big of him. Because I'd led him on to bigger things. Sure.

Bigger things?

Like what? What had I done but burn down a building and fail to murder someone?

Something, or why say it? Something to do with Sean, and probably something to do with drugs. Sean had seemed genuinely surprised when I'd mentioned the money he'd ripped off from the Colonel. But then he was an actor, and an addict, professional liars both. Yet they'd rushed him away, and surely not out of fear for his safety. I had been defused. Where had they taken him? To a police cell to flush out names. But could you do that to a movie star? More likely they'd give him a lift to rehab and shepherd him through cold turkey, then charge him with something minor in return for some information. He wouldn't serve any time. He wasn't stupid. Nothing was written down, nothing was in his name. He didn't even venture out to get his own fix, he sent his wife to do that, sent Alice into the heart of the red light district to buy heroin from Nigerians.

Or the Irish, if you believed a shop-front hooker.

I rolled off the bed.

CHAPTER 33

I tapped on the glass and said, 'Any chance of a wank?'

She lowered her book, recognition dawned and she raised it again. She was reading *The Eagle Has Landed*. She said, 'Fuck off,' from behind it.

I tapped again. I now had my credit card out. 'Please,' I said.

She rolled her eyes. She opened the window a fraction and asked me what I wanted. I asked what had been happening across the way. She said why should she care. I said she was bound to be curious after we'd spent so much time watching the place. By way of encouragement I told her I hadn't really come in her kettle. She said she knew I hadn't, and by the way, she didn't have credit card facilities, unless I wanted her to run it down her crack.

I said no thank you. I gave her what few notes I had left and she opened the door. 'You look like you've gone downhill,' she said.

'I have.'

'Drink or drugs?'

'Both.'

'I don't do neither.'

'Neither do I. Apart from drink, and then not much.'

'So what the hell are you talking about?'

'Do you really want to know?'

'It's your money.'

I stood by the window, peering across at the Irish or Nigerian drugs den. The curtains upstairs were open now, but there was no sign of life. She lay on the bed, resting her head on her arm. She wore a black bikini and heels. 'My wife and baby son are being held hostage at home in Belfast,' I said. 'An Irish gangster called Michael O'Ryan is starving them to death. He won't give them up until I kill somebody for him. I'm not a killer, but I have no choice. Actually, I think it doesn't really matter any more, I reckon they're dead already.'

'How old is your son?'

'Three.'

'Oh,' she said.

I glanced back at her.

'Are you shitting me or what?' she asked. I opened my wallet. I showed her the Polaroids. I don't know why. She studied them intently. 'You can buy pictures like them in any of the sex shops. Maybe you'd have to pay extra for the kid ones, but you can. You could still be fucking me around.'

I delved further into the wallet. Folded way in the back behind the autobank receipts and the cinema stubs was a picture of Trish and me on our wedding day. I looked younger and healthier. Patricia looked alive. 'Satisfied?' I asked.

She shrugged. 'Lot of people coming and going,' she said, 'across there.'

'What sort of people?'

'People. That girl you followed, two or three times. Others.'

'Any, like, internationally famous film stars?'

'No. You asked about that before, didn't you? Who're you expecting, Robert Downey Junior?'

'Sean O'Toole. That's who they want me to kill.'

'Really? You should do us all a favour then. *Light Years from Home* was a crock of shit.'

'It did well at the box office.'

'So did *Mission Impossible*, doesn't mean it's any good. Special effects, that's all; the acting was shit.'

'You a movie buff?'

'Kind of. Do some acting as well. Been in some movies.'

'Seriously?'

'Seriously.'

I watched the house silently for a couple of minutes. She watched me. There were guys on the canal bank in yellow overalls testing the purity of the water. Some of the girls were shouting come-ons at them from their windows. Maybe they could have done with testing the purity of the girls. Their souls and what this life did to them. I glanced back at what's-her-name. 'These are the sort of movies where you keep having to put coins in the slot, right?'

'Right, but it's a start.'

'Fair enough.'

'Last year I was at Cannes.'

'The film festival?'

'The porn film festival. Happens at the same time. It was brilliant. I met Candi Stripper and Debbie de la Crutch. You don't meet them every day.'

'No. Indeed.'

'Would you like a cup of tea?'

'Sure.'

'Okay. This time *I'll* fill the kettle.' She smiled. It was a nice smile. Pleasant, though I didn't doubt she was as hard as nails. We talked. Hours passed. It got dark. Every time I got back to it, she steered the conversation away from my dying family. It was nice, and quite skilfully done. I looked at my watch. She looked at a little alarm clock she kept beside the bed.

'I know,' I said, 'I've run out of time.'

'You've been on a freebie for the last half-hour.'

'Is it my scintillating company or my sad story?'

She laughed. She shrugged. 'I should get back to my book.' She picked it up. 'I have to see if Churchill gets killed in the end.'

I cleared my throat. 'He's from Belfast, so he is.'

'Winston Churchill?'

'Jack Higgins.'

'Oh.'

'Like anybody else with talent, he left. Brian Moore, he left too.'

251

She nodded thoughtfully. 'Well, I suppose he had to.'

'Yeah.'

'I mean, there can't be much football in Belfast.'

'No, I suppose not.'

'Sean O'Toole, he left too, didn't he?'

'Yeah.'

'I suppose he's the exception to the rule.'

'What rule?'

'About talent.'

'Oh, right. Fair enough.'

A light flipped on across the road. I'd been distracted discussing literature and Jack Higgins with the happy hooker and missed whoever it was approaching the house. At first I wasn't sure what I was seeing. There were one, two, three figures moving, but I only caught brief glimpses of them as they passed the windows. Two men, one woman, and then the woman paused for a moment, framed, and I knew it was Alice: the hair, the shape, the profile, all lovingly memorised. She was gesticulating at the men, and then she was rifling in her handbag and where in other people's lives it might have been a brush or a compact she produced, in mine it could be nothing less than a gun, which she raised and pointed at men I couldn't see.

'Fuck,' I said. The girl joined me at the window.

'Fuck,' she said.

'You read the thrillers,' I said, nodding across. 'Read that.'

'Usually when I get to this point, beautiful woman in distress, the pages are stuck together. Occupational hazard. She's either protecting herself, or she's pulling a fast one.'

I nodded. 'Either way I have to go to her.'

'Why?'

'Because.'

Because I'd slept with her and she was in danger.

Because she was a direct line to Sean.

And Sean was a direct line to my family.

She pressed my arm. 'Is there anything I can do?'

I shook my head. 'Unless you happen to have a gun handy.'

'I have a fourteen-inch dildo which is pretty deadly, but I guess that's not what you mean.'

'I want to help her, not give her an orgasm.'

'Believe me, you wouldn't.'

There was a lot of talk across the street. Alice was waving the weapon; the men, with their backs to us now, seemed frozen to the spot.

The girl hurried across the room, bent and reached under the bed. She pulled out a small vanity case and flipped it open. She removed something, closed the case and pushed it back under with her foot. She came back and pressed the object into my hand.

'Switchblade,' she said. I pressed the switch. The blade shot out. 'The last line of defence.'

'Thanks,' I said. I bent to kiss her, but she pulled away.

'We don't kiss, ever.'

I smiled. 'You don't know what you're missing.'

'Yes, I do.'

I retracted the blade and slipped it into my jacket. I pulled open the glass door and stepped out.

CHAPTER 34

I hesitated at the bottom of the steps, to all intents the shy sex tourist, riddled with guilt and insecurity. The girls on either side of the door invited me up. One was black, one was a Thai or Filipino. I stood fingering the switchblade; it was woefully inadequate, and so, usually, was I.

What the fuck was Alice playing at?

I was trying to do what might one day be construed as either the noble or foolhardy thing. I would barge in in my usual foolish way and hope to cause enough of a distraction to ensure that no harm came to anybody, that Alice was protected and so, indirectly, was my search for Sean. She had a gun, but what did that say except that poor innocent love-struck Alice had been sucked into the sick world of celebrities and their drugs.

Except she'd never come across as being either poor or innocent.

What if Sean wasn't the only addict in their partnership? What if she'd been lying to me all along? What if she needed the drugs as much as he did, and now she was in the midst of an argument with her suppliers? They were haggling over money or purity and a gun had been pulled. Paranoia and violence, they went with the territory.

There was a smell. It shouldn't have distracted me, but it did. Any excuse, perhaps, not to go in. I turned. There was a man standing behind me. At least, I think it was a man. It was difficult to tell under the mass of matted hair and twiggy beard. He was wearing a trench coat that had once been black but was now so slimed and grease-stained that he must surely have stolen it from the floor of a chip shop where it had been employed to sop up the drips from the extractor fan. He was the man who had successfully organised that piss-up in a brewery, then fallen in. His blood-red eyes stared into mine with a frightening intensity.

'English?' he growled. He was Scottish. All the clues had been there. I nodded. 'Could ye lend me a coupla quid for a cuppa tae?'

'No,' I said. I looked back up to the house. The black girl was wriggling her tongue; for my benefit, I presumed, since exchanging spit with him would surely invite bubonic plague. I smiled. She smiled back. It could have been the beginning of a beautiful friendship, but the dank Braveheart beside me wasn't giving up.

'Go on,' he said.

'No,' I replied.

'Please. Just a few guilder.'

'No.'

'Why not?'

'Because.'

256

'Go on.'

'No.'

'Whaddya want me to do, beg?'

'You *are* begging.'

'Whaddya want me to do, kiss your fuckin' arse?'

'I'd rather you didn't.'

'I hate you, you fucking cunt.'

'Thanks,' I said. I took a deep breath, making sure I was downwind of the decomposing Jock, then mounted the steps. The black girl got off her stool. She opened her door, her inviting smile, ahm, inviting. I rang the doorbell. The black girl frowned.

'Sorry,' I said.

'Fuck you,' she said.

'You fucking cunt,' said Hamish from below.

'Look, I'm sorry. I've no money,' I shouted down to him, and then to her: 'And I think the chances of me getting an erection are few and far between.'

'Fuck you,' she said.

There were footsteps from within.

'Fuck off then,' she spat.

'Look . . .'

'Just fuck off from my door.'

'I'm not at your door . . .'

'Yes, you are, now fuck off.'

'I'm not . . .'

'Do you want me to lick your fucking hole?' the beggar shouted.

Locks were going back. 'Will youse fuck off?' I hissed.

'You fuck off!' the black girl and the tramp shouted together. My hands nervously gripped the switchblade. Too hard. I pressed the switch and the blade shot out, cutting through my jacket pocket and protruding half an inch. I was trying to retrieve it when the door opened and a familiar face looked out.

'Oh,' I said. 'I think I have the wrong house.'

'No, you don't, Starkey, come on in. We've been expecting you.'

He was big and he was Irish and he had once tried to drown me in the back of a car. One of Michael O'Ryan's men. He had a beard now, plus a scowl and a gun. I turned to wish a fond fare-well to my Scottish chum. He was still mouthing off, but the effort of it all seemed to have been too much for him; his head had dropped and he was now aiming urgent curses at the footpath. I used the brief moment of the turn to complete the retraction of the blade without O'Ryan's man seeing. As I turned back I realised that although I had fooled him, the black hooker hadn't missed it. Our eyes met. She opened her mouth; O'Ryan's man grabbed me by a lapel and pulled; she spat, 'Fucker,' as I was dragged through the door.

It slammed behind me.

'Nice area,' I said.

'Fuck up, Starkey,' O'Ryan's man said and prodded me up a short flight of stairs. At the top

258

I was pushed into a lounge, although lounge was probably too grand a word for it. Bare floorboards, a couple of plastic crates, the blonde wife of an international superstar and a second thug, who'd also once tried to drown me. Not just me, of course, the blonde wife of the international superstar as well. I looked at Alice. She didn't look well. Beautiful, but not well. Her eyes were tired and her skin was white where it wasn't blotchy.

'Hi. I came to save you.'

'From what?'

'You pulled a gun.'

'So far so *Fatal Attraction*, Dan.' She smiled. 'You mean this?' She waved the gun at me. 'If you must know I was just asking for something smaller. Something more lady-like.'

She had a point. The gun she was holding looked like it could blow your head off. If she had to have a gun at all, Alice would need one she could keep in her purse, one that looked like a toy, like the Western ladies used to have. One that looked as if the worst it could do was give you a nasty rash if fired from point-blank range. Something stylish.

I sighed. 'What's going on, Alice?' I asked.

'Plenty,' she said.

'Where's Sean?'

'Gone to Cannes.'

'Shit,' I said.

'I understand you have orders to kill him.'

'My wife . . .'

'I know about that. I'm sorry.'

I nodded at the hoods in suits. 'What's with Bleep and Booster?'

'They've changed sides.'

'You mean they've turned Queen's evidence.' Bleep and Booster snorted.

'Not quite. It's a long story, Dan, and it's none of your business.'

'Of course it's my business. My wife is . . .'

'Your wife is dead.' She let it sit for a moment, while my stomach fell away. Then the merest hint of a smile. 'Or at least she should be if these guys are to be believed.' It was, I thought, an astonishing little cruelty. 'How long has it been?' she asked.

It wasn't addressed to me, though I could have told her to the minute. The bigger guy, in a black linen suit with a white T-shirt below, shrugged. 'Don't matter,' he said. 'Michael won't let 'im live. You know what he's like.'

Alice nodded.

'How would you know what he's like?' I asked, though I think I already knew.

She came across the room. She ran a hand down the side of my face. If we'd been somewhere else, and there hadn't been a gun in that hand, it might have been pleasant. 'Oh, Danny,' she purred, 'you're so innocent, aren't you? I saw it in you right from the start. And that first time I mentioned drugs, you were so shocked that some-body could actually get addicted to them.'

'I was only acting,' I said.

'No, you weren't, love. You forget, I know acting. Aren't I married to the best actor in the world?'

'You obviously haven't seen *Light Years from Home*.'

It was done with a ballet deftness, a crack of the hand against my ear, but the hand with the gun so that it was a sharp metallic crack. I reeled across the room. I hugged my hand to my ear. 'I came here to save you,' I said.

'That's really nice of you, Dan, but we really do have to kill you now.'

'That hardly seems fair.'

She smiled. 'I know, but you keep getting in the way, and we can't have that. You've done more than enough damage already. What's that saying? Life's a bitch and then you die?'

'No, I think it's: you're a bitch, and then *you* die.'

When taken in tandem with the switchblade I suddenly produced, then threw in one fluid motion, pinning her gun hand to the bare wall, my response was not only suitably dramatic but it also had a certain style. A *je ne sais quoi*.

If only it had worked like that.

The knife snagged on the hole in my pocket. By the time I'd managed to coax it out of my jacket and flick open the blade, there were three guns pointed at me.

Alice shook her head. I dropped the knife to the floor. 'Poor Dan,' she said, 'all talk, no action.'

261

'That's not what you said in bed,' I replied.

'But it's what I thought.'

'So that third orgasm . . . ?'

'Like the first. Non-existent.'

'So why bother at all?'

'Because I thought you might be worth a ride. Bit of a disappointment, really.'

'But . . .'

She pulled the trigger. There was a bang and something bit into my arm. Putting two and two together is my business. I thought it reasonable to assume that I'd just been shot. I thought about it while I was spun round. I settled on my conclusion as I dropped to my knees.

There was no need to fall, actually. It didn't hurt particularly. But it was one of the rules. When shot, fall, instead of standing there like an eejit. When we were kids we used to play games of commandos and have competitions for who could fall best when shot. I used to win all the time, but this one wouldn't have got more than one out of ten for artistic impression; there was just a dumb slump and a look of surprise.

'Thanks,' I said.

'I didn't mean to shoot you in the arm,' Alice said. She wasn't apologising. She had meant to shoot me in the chest, or in the head. She was a crap shot. But practice makes perfect. She raised the gun again. The two hoods, evidently taken by surprise as much by the sudden gunfire as by her inability to satisfactorily despatch an inanimate object at such close range, stepped wide to either side of me.

'Why are you shooting me at all?' I asked.

'Because you complicate things,' she said. Her finger squeezed the trigger. But not all the way. She was distracted. I followed her eyes to the window. Staring in, drunkenly mesmerised, like he was watching bad TV, was the rancid Scot.

Alice lowered her gun. 'Get rid of him,' she snapped.

The Scot probably didn't hear it, but he lost his grip anyway and dropped back out of sight to the street below. The hood in the black suit turned and hurried down the few steps to the door. He hadn't bothered to relock it, so it was only a few moments before he had it open and was shouting at the beggar.

And then there was a gunshot, and I thought, that's a bit rough on the poor fella.

Except it was the hood who came staggering back into the apartment clutching his belly, and the Scot who came in behind, gun drawn. Behind him came the black hooker in her bikini. In her hand a gun.

Holy fuck, I thought.

'Police! Don't move a fucking muscle!' the Scot screamed.

They didn't.

They moved several.

Alice dived to one side, shooting as she went. The other hood dropped to one knee and fired off several rounds in response to the furious gunfire already being returned from the doorway. I saw blood spurt from the side of his face without any apparent reaction, he just kept shooting. I flattened out. The lack of furniture gave everything an echo, made it twice as loud. I closed my eyes and pressed my face to the wood.

It seemed to last for ten minutes, but it could only have been that many seconds.

When it was over there were low moans and heavy breathing.

I opened my eyes. There was blood on the wood where it had seeped out of my shot arm. There was more blood, a stream of it, on my other side; I followed it back to its source and saw Alice, slumped against the back wall, eyes glazed, breath shallow. Across the room lay the hood who didn't have a black suit; he was face down and there was a pool of blood beneath him; the hood who did have a black suit remained in the doorway, clutching his stomach.

The hooker, who evidently wasn't, stood with her gun stretched out in front of her, shifting its focus from one motionless figure to the other. The Scot had already dropped his weapon back into his disgusting trench-coat pocket. He knelt down beside me. 'You okay, lad?' he said. He was Scottish, but he'd spent at least a week at public school.

I nodded. *Now* my arm was sore. 'You must be bloody desperate for that cup of tea,' I said.

CHAPTER 35

There were dozens of police, both in plain clothes and in uniform. There was a fleet of ambulances. There was the Fire Brigade, just in case. There was TV. There were reporters and bystanders and hookers raising their prices in case anyone got really excited at the sight of dead bodies being removed on wheeled stretchers. There was me, leaning against a car, having my arm examined by a medic and my head examined by an amateur psychiatrist.

'Dan,' said Maurice, 'you have to give this up.'

'How can I?' I looked at him. My head was throbbing. Once again I'd been dancing with death and I was no closer to learning the steps. Maurice's eyes were sympathetic.

'You don't really have any children, do you?' I asked.

He shook his head.

'Ouch!' I said as the medic probed. 'Then you don't understand.'

'Just get in the ambulance.'

I nodded. They'd given me a shot of something and the throb in my head was trying to fight it out with the fuzz of something easing up from the base of my skull. Maurice helped me up, then climbed in behind me. The medic, apparently satisfied that I wasn't going to die on the spot, climbed in beside us but otherwise left us alone. There was a pressure bandage on my arm and a very large hole in my heart.

'She's dead, isn't she?' I said.

Maurice, staring at the floor, nodded for a moment, then glanced up at me. 'Who? Your wife?'

'No, Alice.'

'Not yet, but she will be.' He turned to the medic and said something in Dutch. The medic replied, then gave a little shrug. 'Might last the night, but shouldn't make breakfast,' Maurice said.

I shook my head. There were little stars appearing before my eyes, none of them from familiar constellations. Alice, blood-soaked, head against the wall, fighting for breath. 'Seems a little harsh, if she was just looking for a fix.'

'She was going to kill you.'

'You didn't mobilise the 7th Cavalry just to save me.'

'We did, actually.'

I fixed my eyes on him. Maurice. The Scots tramp. The black hooker.

'We've been watching them for days. The place was bugged, we had pretty much what we needed, it wasn't too much of a sacrifice to go in and save you.'

'I kind of wish you hadn't bothered.'

'You should not give up hope, Dan. Do you not believe in God?'

I stared at the floor. God? If there was a God, he was an Old Testament God, into smiting things and plucking out eyes. But there wasn't. 'I believe we were colonised by visitors from outer space, way back in Stone Age times. I believe that left to our own devices we would have stayed in the caves. That it might have been better fun. Though I suspect that the women would probably have looked more like Mother Teresa than Raquel Welch.' He was staring at me. 'I'm sorry. I should thank you for saving my life. Thank you.'

'It's okay.'

The medic reached across and lifted my hand. He turned it palm up and started to check my pulse.

'Tell me about Alice,' I said. 'Tell me what happened. This isn't all about you trailing me for having horse in my Johnson's Baby Powder, is it?'

Maurice shook his head. 'We've been watching right from the start, Dan. This is an Interpol operation. We had agents on set at *The Brigadier*, we had agents at the party, we had agents at your hotel.'

'Seriously?'

He smiled. He delved into his inside jacket pocket. I could see the handle of his gun in its shoulder holster. He got hold of something, then showed me his closed fist. Slowly he unfurled the fingers. I gulped. It was my wedding ring. 'We were close all the time, Dan.'

'Not close enough to stop me drowning.'

'We would have found a way. It wasn't you. It wasn't even Sean, though he's an unscrupulous scumbag with a bad drugs problem. It was Alice.'

I sighed. Alice. I had already guessed there was more to her than met the eye, though what had met the eye was more than pleasing. The medic let go of my hand, apparently satisfied. He went to make a note on a chart, but Maurice stopped him with a quick wave of his hand.

'Alice used to be an air hostess. You knew that?'

I nodded.

'That's how she started, as a courier, all of the risk and none of the profits, so naturally she wanted to move on. And she did, she did very well. She had a mentor, of course.'

'Michael O'Ryan.'

'Michael O'Ryan. Mentor. Lover. They were an item for several years. She learned the ropes, she learned them well. Then Sean arrived to research his film and she fell for his movie-star charms and ran away with him, taking several million pounds and copious amounts of drugs with her in the process.'

'So O'Ryan wasn't happy.'

'He was furious, and not just because he lost her. Alice, as you know, has a certain way with men. When she left she tried to take his whole operation with her, and nearly succeeded.'

'Those guys that were killed in the house, they were changing sides, right?'

'Thinking about it. They couldn't work out the details, so she pulled a gun on them. That's where you crashed in.'

'I thought she was . . .'

'Like I said, she has a way with men. O'Ryan tried to drown her, remember? He couldn't make his mind up whether he wanted her dead or alive, and now we've made it up for him. What he really wanted to do was teach her a lesson, hurt her, force her back to him. So he decided to kill Sean. There's a certain kind of logic to it, if you accept that he's mad to start with.'

'But demented or not, he must have known there were better ways of killing Sean than me? I mean, I'm crap.'

'Sometimes an amateur is better than a professional. Did you ever see *The Day of the Jackal*?'

'I saw the remake. Bruce Willis.'

'Doesn't matter. For all that sophistication, the professional assassin nearly always gets shot in the end.'

'*I* got shot.'

'Whereas an amateur, say Mark Chapman who shot Lennon, or Hinckley who got Reagan . . . you can't protect against that. You can't predict unpredictability. Even Lee Harvey Oswald got his man and he was . . . stupid.'

'Lee Harvey Oswald was a soldier. He wasn't an amateur. And besides, he didn't shoot Kennedy. At least, not according to Oliver Stone.'

'He was a poor soldier. You ever see pictures

of him, Dan? He looks like a victim of perpetual incest. He was stupid, but he did the job. And he *did do* the job, and he did it alone. You shouldn't believe people like Oliver Stone. He sees a conspiracy beneath every . . . stone.'

'Nevertheless.'

'Nevertheless. I know. Sean is alive.'

'But he'll call it off now Alice is dying. What's the point?'

Maurice shook his head. 'Michael O'Ryan was arrested in Dublin this morning. He's being held in Mountjoy Prison. He has been asked to reveal where your wife and child are being held. But I'm sorry, he has refused. He will not say until Sean O'Toole is dead.'

'But what difference does it make if Alice is dying?'

'Because he doesn't know she's dying, and we can't tell him. We want to get as much information from him about his activities as we can. He's a world player, Dan, not just some provincial hood. Interpol doesn't bother with the little fish, it's the big whales we go after.' He paused, he nodded. 'Okay, so whales aren't fish, Dan. You know what I mean. We know plenty about what he's been up to, but there's plenty more, and if we press hard enough he might give it up. But not if he finds out we killed his girl. See, he still loves her, and telling him that will shut him up for sure.'

'So my family will die so that you can get information about drug trafficking.'

Maurice took a deep breath. 'It's not my decision.'

'So who do I speak to?'

'Dan, there's no point. That's how it works.'

The ambulance came to a halt. There was no move on the medic's part to rush me into ER. He sat and waited.

'So what now?' I asked.

Maurice put a hand back into his jacket. From an inside pocket he produced something wrapped in a handkerchief. Not many men used handkerchiefs any more, but it seemed an inappropriate time to open a discussion on the subject. He placed the object in his lap and carefully unwrapped it.

It was a gun. I pointed this out to him.

'I know,' he said.

'What's it for?'

'Shooting people.'

'I think we should take this conversation to a higher level, Maurice.'

He nodded. 'Okay. It's for you.'

'And why would I want it?'

'Well, you can take it and blow your brains out, because I'm sure you're feeling suicidal. Or you can take it and blow my brains out, because I'm part of the reason you're feeling suicidal. Or third, and this is the option I recommend, you can take it and kill Sean O'Toole.'

'What?'

He nodded at the medic, who gave a slight smile and leant forward; he pushed open the back doors of the ambulance and stepped out. He disappeared

271

around the front of the vehicle. Sunlight flooded in. There was no hospital. There was Amsterdam Centraal. The train station. 'Get on the train. Go to Paris, then Nice, you'll catch up with him in Cannes. Blow his head off.'

'But . . . why?'

'Because a plane would be quicker, but you won't get a gun onboard. You don't get searched on a train.'

'No, I don't understand. Why are you doing this?'

'Because I can.' It wasn't enough. I stared at him until he came up with more. 'Dan, Sean O'Toole is a junkie. He never was the brains behind any of this, in fact I'd be surprised if he even knows about it all. He thinks his films are so important that somebody like the Colonel would go to extreme lengths just to have him killed. Well, he's wrong. He's a bad actor and he's addicted to heroin and about a dozen other drugs. Sooner or later he's going to end up killing himself, so you might as well do it for him and save your wife and child in the process.'

'Jesus. I can't believe I'm hearing this.'

He shrugged. 'Don't get me wrong. As far as we're concerned you lifted the gun off one of O'Ryan's men back in the house. Dan, you don't have to go after him again. It's just an option.'

My head was whirring, and it wasn't just the drugs. I was working out dates and times and whether my wife and child could just conceivably still be alive. I couldn't work it out. *Cannot compute, Will Robinson.* Everything was vague and fugged and all I knew was that a policeman was giving me a gun and telling me to go and kill somebody famous in another country. He was trying to be nice, and that didn't compute either. I gripped the side of the stretcher; pain flexed up my arm. I nodded down at it. 'What about this?' I asked.

'It's just a flesh wound. You've lost some blood. You can go to hospital if you want.'

I shook my head slowly. 'This is very good of you,' I said.

He shrugged again. People heading into the station were peering into the back of the ambulance, trying to see what was wrong. I pushed the gun into my jacket pocket. 'Do you think they're alive, my wife and son?' I asked.

'I don't know. But if they are, I think this is the only chance you have of getting them back. I don't think you can depend on Michael O'Ryan feeling sorry for you.'

He was right, of course.

I had to go back on the chase.

I had to find Sean O'Toole and put a bullet through his heart, and preferably in front of lots of television cameras so that the message could be flashed back to Ireland in an instant and Michael O'Ryan, the Colonel, would see that the job was done and would reveal the location of the ghastly dungeon where my family were slowly being killed.

I stood up. I felt dizzy. I moved carefully down

273

the steps out of the ambulance, but still managed to stumble over the last one. I just managed to keep my feet as I reached solid ground. My arm wasn't really sore at all. The medic's pain-killing shot had, if anything, given me a slight sense of narcotic elation. Maybe Sean O'Toole felt this way all the time. Maybe I should get into heroin. William Burroughs had written many of his novels while addicted to the stuff. He had also shot his first wife in the head. I looked to the station. It was big and imposing and I didn't have a timetable. I had a credit card, but no luggage. My computer was back at the hotel. My clothes, I should get changed, my bill, I didn't . . .

'Dan?'

'What?'

'Get the train, go to sleep, there's nothing more you can do until you get to Cannes.'

He was right. I'd been shot. I needed to rest. I needed to get my head in order. I needed to be perfectly sane before I could do something insane like shooting Sean O'Toole.

Maurice was closing the doors. I nodded up at him. 'Good luck,' he said.

'Thanks.'

I turned and walked towards the train station.

CHAPTER 36

Even though I was intent on killing an international film star, I was not a madman, or at least it was important that I didn't look like one. I was not going to go charging through the streets of Cannes waving my gun and shouting, 'Sean O'Toole! Come out, come out, wherever you are!'

My family were dying, but I had to be cool, calm and collected. Though my head was pounding with the possibilities and my stomach was perpetually hanging around my ankles like trousers in a narrow toilet cubicle, I had to appear normal. I did not need to attract attention. I was a man on a mission. An amateur. Hinckley. Chapman. Maybe even Lee Harvey.

I slept on the train, I read an English newspaper some homesick tourist had left behind. I stayed away from the news section in case there was something about O'Ryan, in case there was a photograph and his eyes caught mine, teasing, gloating eyes made all the more horrific by dotted black and white. I turned to the sports section. Liverpool were doing well again after a ten-year lapse. Bruno was talking about a comeback. I tstudied the lifestyle section and learned how to lose pounds in days by eating whatever the fuck I wanted. Anything to put the time and the miles in. Or kilometres, given the location.

I changed at Paris and bought a baguette. I arrived in Nice with the sun splitting the trees, then took a cab to Cannes. I asked the driver if he could recommend a hotel in Cannes, not too expensive, but not a flea pit either, somewhere with a satellite TV and a mini-bar and maybe south-facing so that it got the sun in the morning or was that north-facing? – I'd never quite been able to work that one out. He looked at me through a haze of cigarette smoke and said, '*Pardon?*'

'You don't speak English?'

'*Pardon?*'

I sighed. He didn't deserve it, but he got it. 'You're just doing it for badness, aren't you? I've read about you French bastards. You just pretend you can't speak English to piss people off. You speak it like a Cockney, you cunt, but you just think you're so fucking superior you expect every-one else to talk fucking French. Okay, granted you won the World Cup but that was only because Ronaldo was pumped full of drugs, and, okay, Napoleon had a certain talent but excuse me if we didn't save your sorry arse in the war, not once but twice, you yellow Vichy bastard.'

So much for cool, calm and collected.

'*Pardon, monsieur? Je ne parle pas anglais.*'

'Up your hole with a big jam roll.'

I wound down the window. It was beautiful weather. I said, 'Just take me to Cannes.'

He shrugged and drove on. He caught my eye in the mirror several times, and halfway there offered me a cigarette. I thanked him and lit up. My hands were shaking, and not just because I didn't usually smoke. I'd shared a Camel with Maurice. I was a real two-a-month man, but only when members of my family were under threat.

I'm a political smoker. I don't inhale. When I was a kid a gang of us rode our bikes to Groomsport with ten Embassy Regal between us. We were eleven years old. We hid up an alley close to the beach and lit up. I smoked mine in twelve seconds, suck in, blow out, suck in, blow out, like it was a race to the finish, and it was, I suppose. And then the minister from our local church came strolling past and caught us on and I didn't touch another one for twenty years. And now another, in a cab in the flaming south of France with my wife and . . .

Stop thinking about them. You'll go mad.
Block them out. Do the job. They'll survive.
No, they won't. It's too late. They're dead.
No, it isn't. Do your best. They can't ask for more.
They can't ask at all, they're dead.
Fuck it.

We were in Cannes. We came down a hill onto the main seafront drag, the Croisette. Traffic was virtually at a standstill. There were thousands of people on the sidewalk. Every twenty yards there was a huge poster advertising a movie. Helicopters buzzed overhead. To my left, beyond the palm trees, was the bay. Dozens of cruisers lay at anchor. Big motherfuckers that could have taken part in the Falklands War were playing host to B-list celebrities for £40,000 a day. I wondered if Sean O'Toole was out there and how I would ever get to him if he was.

My driver was from Nice. If he had any inkling about hotels he didn't let on. He would just drive until told to stop. If I had my way, I wouldn't be staying long enough to need a hotel. If things worked out, the French government would be providing one for me anyway, free of charge, for an extended stay. Twenty or thirty years, maybe, and the chances were there wouldn't be a mini-bar.

I said, 'Just drop me here, Johnny Foreigner,' and he looked at me and smiled and drove on, so I tapped him on the shoulder and pointed at the roadside and pulled at the door handle. The centime dropped. He pulled in. We were in one-way traffic and immediately there came a fusillade of horns from behind. He ignored them. So did I. I fished in my wallet. I'd managed to extract some money on my credit card at a bureau de change when changing trains in Paris. I even gave him a tip.

He said, 'Thanks very much.'

I said, 'Oh.'

He said, 'Many of your criticisms of my country are valid, although I should point out that my father fought for the Resistance. Have a nice day.'

I thanked him and closed the door.

Cannes.

On the other side of the road were the big hotels, the Majestic and the Carlton, where a Coke would set you back six quid, and a Diet Coke just as much, even though all the goodness had been taken out. On the bay side were the extensions to those hotels, semi-permanent marquees erected to feed the 50,000 accredited producers, directors, financiers and journalists who descended each year for the two weeks of deal-making and drinking that constituted Cannes's raison d'être, although not in that order. At the far end of the Croisette there were the blue-carpeted stairs leading up to the Palais des Festivals where all the competition films were shown, and behind it, overlooking the public beach with its tourists and overstacked topless models hoping to get discovered, and getting dis-covered only by the pervs with the video cameras, a series of pavilions dedicated to different countries or companies: there was one for Fox, one for HBO, one for Miramax, a dozen others, then last and least, the British pavilion, a tarted-up caravan with a small marquee added. There was a bar, of course, and I was heading straight for it when a security guy stopped me.

Bouncers, everywhere I go. No dickie, no black suit, but a bouncer all the same.

He was pleasant, but firm: no accreditation, no entry. I asked him where I could get it. He gave me a look that said *first time, yeah*, then pointed me in the right direction. It was only a couple of hundred yards and it only cost me fifty quid and a quick head and shoulders photo from a shark on the promenade. Then into the Palais des Festivals to get the ID. I had an old press card stuck in my wallet. For the *Belfast Evening News*. On the back of it there was my drunken scrawl, the name Margaret, and a phone number. I shuddered. The girl behind the desk was nice and pretty and welcomed me to the festival in perfect English. I smiled and said *bonjour*. I clipped my shiny new plastic ID card into a little blue string necklace they provided and marched back out, part of the most exciting film festival in the world, and only one thing on my mind.

Calm down, act normal, find out where he is.

This time the bouncer let me in. I bought a drink at the bar and started talking to anyone I could, though most of them were busy slabbering on mobile phones. I'd left mine in my hotel in Amsterdam. With my laptop and my clothes. I hadn't washed in days, I was badly stubbled. Perhaps they weren't talking on their mobiles at all, just trying to avoid standing next to me. There was a healthy breeze blowing in off the bay, so I made a point of standing downwind of it. I caught somebody's eye and before he had a chance to look elsewhere I raised my Becks to him and said: 'How're ya doin'? Howse it going so far?'

'Okay,' he said. He was in a white suit and

T-shirt, he'd sandy brown hair and a protruding belly. He also had a hopeful look in his eye. He was in his early thirties, I guessed. He squinted a little as he came across, trying to work out where we'd met, at which one of the myriad parties that crackled along the Croisette every night we'd exchanged names or bodily fluids, but as he came closer his chin dropped a little as he realised he didn't know me from Adam, although Adam would undoubtedly have been wearing cleaner clothes. His eyes drifted down to my ID badge, and mine to his. It was a Cannes mating ritual. He was wearing a little badge on his lapel that said *I Don't Know You Either*. His name was Victor Dalgetty and he ran a small production company in Soho. He'd made two features in the last year and both were being shown at Cannes, but not as part of the competition. It didn't say all of this on his ID, of course. We got talking. I bought him a drink. I didn't give a shit about his views on Cannes, but I thought it might scare him off if I just barged in with *have you seen Sean O'Toole? I'm trying to kill him*.

The film festival was split into two sections, the competition and the market. The competition, though it got all the international press attention, actually meant bugger all to the real world. 'Swedish dramas about incest and Croatian epics on paedophilia!' Victor laughed. 'They're all shit, but they give them all sorts of facking awards here and they think they're great, then they disappear up their own facking arseholes. Gimme *Armageddon* any time!'

For Victor the real reason for coming was the market, where companies like his tried to sell their films to as many international territories as they could, either directly or through a sales agent. He was also trying to raise finance for some other films he was hoping to make in the coming year. 'But of course, you're a reporter, you're not interested in commercial movies that make money, you're here for all the facking arty-farty stuff in competition.'

I shrugged.

'You're Irish,' he stated.

'Northern Irish.'

'Whatever. You'll be here to suck up to that facking Sean O'Toole.'

I shrugged. Mountains, and Mohammed.

'Facking *Brigadier*.'

'Why *facking*?'

'Lotta people's noses outta joint. Cunt like him just walks into competition with his movie 'cause he's a star, others have to make way. They don't like that here. And I don't like it either 'cause he should stick to doing what he does best, making flash bang wallops 'stead of crawling up some intellectual arsehole with crap like that.'

'You've seen it?'

'*Nobody*'s seen it! All I hear is it's in black and white and there's another facking kiss of death at the box office. Tell you this, only two black-and-white movies ever made any money at the facking box office – I mean apart from when they were *all* facking black and white!' He cackled. '*Schindler's List* and that was all the facking Jews crying over spilled milk and the facking new Nazis having a wank over the dead Jews, and facking *Manhattan* and that was only because everyone thought they were going to see *Annie Hall* again and, boy, did they get a facking surprise.'

I tried in vain to think of another black-and-white movie that had made a mint, just to prove him wrong, because he was an annoying bastard, but I couldn't. I sighed and said he had a point and incidentally had he any idea where Sean O'Toole hung out, I'd heard he was in town. I nodded across at the Majestic.

'You jokin'? In there all you get is the cunts on expense accounts and some wannabe producers with daddy's money in their back facking pocket.'

'Out on the boats, then.'

'Same. But, Jesus, people come here t'party, facking superstar or Joe facking Bloggs, doesn't matter, you don't wanna be stuck out on a facking boat. Only one place you're guaranteed to see them all, the facking Cap.'

'The what?'

'Hotel du Cap. You haven't facking heard of it? It's a facking legend. Oh, they're all out there, without a doubt. Half an hour out of town and ten thousand facking quid outta my range.' He clapped a hand on my shoulder. 'Do you wanna come and see one of my movies? They're facking good.'

I took a deep breath. 'What're they . . . ?'

'Kids' films. Animated. They're not Disney, but who the fack is? I hire facking Filipinos to do the animation. Draw like a dream and I pay them facking pennies, then I pull in some sad facking ex-soap star to do the lingo and hey presto I make a facking fortune.' I looked at him. 'At least that's the facking plan,' he added.

He asked me if I wanted a drink, I said yeah. We supped on bottles of Becks for a few moments. He tapped the glass rim against his teeth. It was an annoying sound. He was searching for something to say, and his eyes were searching the crowd for somebody he knew.

'So,' he said, evidently finding nobody, 'you're after Sean O'Toole. I hope you facking crucify him, the cunt.'

I nodded.

CHAPTER 37

The Hotel du Cap lies equidistant between Cannes and Nice at the tip of Cap d'Antibes. It is set in twenty-five acres of ornamental gardens and surrounded by a Mediterranean pine forest. It was built for $130,000 in 1863 by a mixed group of Antibean businessmen and assorted Russian aristocrats with exotic names like the Count de Pletscheyeff and Count Nicholas Stroganoff.

I can read a tourist guide with the best of them.

I sat in the back of a cab and sighed. It didn't make any difference to me if Scott and Zelda had partied there, or Hemingway or Picasso. I didn't care if there was a swimming pool carved out of the blue-pink rocks or that the Eden Roc wing overlooked the Lerins Islands and you could drink English tea on the terrace. I was after O'Toole. I didn't say a word to the driver in case he was undercover. I was getting to think that I was the only person in the world who wasn't undercover. That I was stuck in some weird X-certificate *Truman Show*, that everything I had done thus far had been dumb, and then dumber.

The taxi driver grunted something. I looked

285

forward and there was the hotel, in the distance. Impressive, sure. Fitzgerald had based his Hotel des Etrangers in *Tender Is the Night* on it, and I still didn't give a fuck. I'd a gun and a rough idea of how to use it. *Literature is bunk. Or is that history? And am I?*

There was security at the gate, but they were pretty much for show. It was a hotel, and it welcomed visitors. Things would only get heavy if you couldn't pay your bill. You could just be Joe Bloggs, drive up and ask about a room or a coffee, even if they were both outside your budget. They leant in to check I wasn't obviously barking, and at that moment I wasn't. I was smoking and wearing shades and looking damn cool. I'd left Victor *facking* Dalgetty comatose in his room at the Cannes Palace Hotel; he couldn't handle his drink any better than the concept of black-and-white movies. The last round had finished him off. I'd helped him up in the elevator, then helped myself to his shower and a shave and his shades and his cigarettes and lighter and as much cash as I could take from his wallet without him starving to death, especially after taking his credit cards as well. I wasn't normally a thief, but this wasn't normal. I left him an IOU and signed it Sam Cameron. Then I pulled his trousers and jockeys down round his knees and added *thanks for a great time* to the note.

I paid the taxi driver. I gave him a big tip and he was effusive in his gratitude; I didn't understand a word of it, but the security guys on the door seemed to, they opened up for me and welcomed me in like I was the prodigal son. Dusk had not yet settled on the Cap, or perhaps it had and the brightness of the stars within, rather than those without, was keeping it at bay.

I ignored reception and walked straight into the lounge; Patricia might have said it was eloquently appointed in the French country style, but to me it was just tables and chairs, and the aforementioned stars. If I had taken a bread roll and skimmed it from one table to the next it would have bounced off Martin Scorsese's head and landed on Kate Moss's lap; she would have shooed if off onto Naomi's, and she would have heaved it across the room at The Edge; he would have taken a bite and passed it on to Johnny Depp; Johnny would then have thrown it blindly behind him; it would have shot between Leonardo DiCaprio and Kate Winslet to strike Denzel Washington. Just as well I was all out of bread rolls. I tried not to look impressed. It wasn't hard. I have never been one for awe or autographs, I'd never thought of them as anything special beyond being good at what they did, and my experience with Sean O'Toole proved the point. I stood for a moment, lighting my cigarette – it *was* becoming a habit – and contemplated the room. For every little group of stars, there was a little group of minders: big bastards giving each other hard stares because there was nobody else to look at and you never

ever looked at your employer in case he or she went into a blue funk.

Now there's a phrase.

So they turned their attention on me. I ignored them and swung into action with Plan A. I waved across the lounge at Kate Moss, because it made sense to start with the prettiest and work backwards. She waved back automatically. I hurried across, all smiles and coos. We air kissed. I said: 'Have you seen Sean?'

She frowned. Either she realised she'd never met me or she got a whiff of Victor *facking* Dalgetty's cheap facking aftershave. It had said Calvin on the bottle, but was probably a cheap Filipino copy, like his animation. Calvin and Hobbes. She shook her head and said, 'Nah.'

I moved on. I saw Robert de Niro. I pointed a finger at him and said, 'You lookin' at me?' and laughed and he gave the kind of pained expression that generally precedes a vasectomy. I repeated the Sean question wherever I went but nobody had seen him, or was admitting to it. I returned to reception and said, 'Have you seen Sean O'Toole?'

He was small and swarthy and in his forties. There was a hint of a squint, like he should be wearing glasses but his vanity wouldn't let him. 'I have not seen him this evening, Monsieur Manilow.'

I paused. My brain started to whirr. The first instinct, obviously, was to smack him. I gripped the top of the desk; he didn't look down; if his eyesight had been up to it he might have seen my knuckles whiten in anger. I forced a smile. The whirring stopped at Plan B and I said, 'Can I have my key?'

He smiled and turned, he checked the key rack and then turned back, the smile still in place, although the key obviously wasn't. 'I'm sorry, Monsieur Manilow, you . . .'

'Stolen, give me another.'

'Of course.'

He opened a small safe and removed a key. I thanked him. As he passed it across he said quietly, 'I hope you do not mind me saying, but I think ze nose, it is much improved.'

'You mean, you thought it was big?'

'No . . .' he began, flustered. 'Only now it is . . . smaller.'

'What room is Sean O'Toole in?' I snapped.

''E 'as a junior bachelor suite in our Eden Roc wing, Monsieur Manilow. Very close to your own. Number thirty-seven.'

'Is he in?'

He checked his key rack again. ''Is key is not 'ere, monsieur, he may be . . . but these . . . well, sometimes they forget . . .'

'I didn't forget mine. It was stolen.'

'Of course, monsieur.'

I lifted my key, I nodded, and turned away from the desk. On the way out of reception there was a mirrored column and I paused for a moment to study my reflection. What if his eyesight wasn't that bad and I really did look like Barry Manilow? Or even worse, I was turning into him.

I strolled out of the main building and down towards Eden Roc. If anybody stopped me and asked me for a quick rendition of 'Copacabana' I would kill them, then myself. I swung the key ring in my hand so anyone who was inquisitive would know I was a resident. The Eden Roc wing was situated directly above the rocky coastline. There was a private landing pier with two medium-sized yachts tied up; and even at this late hour there were a few guests splashing about in the water and one rattling past on a jet-ski. There were wooden cabanas close to the shore with sun decks and easy chairs, but few were occupied.

Manilow's bachelor suite was on the third floor. Four doors along was Sean O'Toole's. My hands were shaking. Even for your family, killing is a big thing. I decided on a drink first, just to settle myself. And it was a good thing. As I slipped the key into Manilow's door, Sean O'Toole's opened.

I slipped into Manilow's suite. In the moment I took to check, I saw that it was brightly lit, spacious and there was no indication that an international singing sensation was at home, or even Barry Manilow. There were footsteps outside. I let them pass, then opened the door a fraction. Sean. Shadowed by four of the heaviest heavies this side of heavyville. I cursed, quietly. They were waiting for the elevator.

Slip out and take out as many as I could?

Or bide my time, time my family didn't have?
I cursed again.

Sean was in evening dress. A white suit, black bow tie. He was in Cannes. He was going to a premiere. He would be going up those blue-carpeted steps outside the Palais des Festivals, there would be TV cameras and thousands of screaming fans pressing in on either side.

Just the time to take out a gun and pump him full of lead.

Behind me a nasal twang sounded from the bathroom, 'Is that you, Paulie?'

CHAPTER 38

I closed the apartment door, blocking out my intended victim. Service in the hotel was probably wonderfully fast, but the elevator was tediously slow. I was trapped between a rock and a bouffant hairstyle. The question from the bathroom was repeated, then the door started to open. I nipped smartly across and took hold of the handle and forced it closed again; the surprise of it meant there was little resistance.

'*Paulie*?' the voice came again. I had no way of knowing if Paulie was manservant, bodyguard or the man who provided the flowers that lent a sprightly odour to the suite, or all three, but he certainly wasn't me. From outside the door came the ping of the elevator arriving.

'*Paulie*, are we playing a *game*?'

I didn't reply. I held tight.

'You know I'm stronger than you, Paulie, you can't win.'

And the door began to move inwards. There was nothing I could do about it. All that personal trainer shit was more effective than it appeared. So I gave him a hand and slammed my shoulder into

292

it. There was a crack from behind as it flew back, and suddenly I was looking into the bathroom at a star on the floor holding his broken nose and looking up at me through a handful of blood and tears.

'Who *the hell* are you?' he cried.

'Security,' I said. 'I thought you were an intruder.'

'You stupid *fuck*! You broke my nose! It's my best feature!'

'Jesus,' I said, 'you're in trouble.'

He began to pull himself up. 'I'm going to speak to the *goddamn* manager about this . . .'

Before he could raise himself any further I thumped him on the jaw and he sagged back onto his knees.

'What the hell was that for?' he cried.

'Nothing,' I said, and thumped him again. 'But that was for "I Write the Songs That Make the Whole World Sing".'

If he heard it, there was no indication. He was flat out on the tiles, oozing blood. In time he would recover, and the tabloids would speculate on his expensive rhinoplasty and the fact that it gave added lustre to his voice, thanks to improved breathing. Before I left I cleaned his wallet, but there was little to take. He was too rich to carry money. But there were keys to a red Ferrari. I hesitated. If I took it I would be sticking out like a sore thumb, but I'd be a fucking fast sore thumb. I went to the window. Sean and his bodyguards had emerged from the Eden Roc wing, but instead of turning back up towards the main building they were heading down to the sea. Dressed like that, he wasn't going for a swim. They stepped onto the jetty and walked towards the yacht I had noticed before. A sailor in white saluted, then ushered them on board.

That settled it.

Ferrari time. It was a summer's evening and the roads leading into Cannes would be chocker. The sea was calm and virtually empty. I needed to make up every minute I could.

Before I left I hurried into the bathroom and turned him into the recovery position. He gurgled a little, but he was breathing freely. It was the least I could do. An untimely death would only lead to an explosion in his popularity and I'd do double time for that.

I ignored the elevator and hurried down the stairs. Outside I gave the keys to a bellboy and he hurried away. I retained my shades and my silence. There was no need to explain or justify, he knew bizarre behaviour went with the territory. The kid, not more than seventeen, came roaring back. I gave him two hundred francs and climbed in. Then I kangarooed the mean machine up the path towards the entrance. I checked the mirror to see if the bellboy was smirking, because the tip could easily be reclaimed, but he remained gravel-faced.

For several hundred yards I continued to drive

like Stevie Wonder. I lost one wing mirror to a gate post and managed to inflict a long scrape along the right-hand side thanks to a protruding rock, but by the time I pulled out onto the open road I had mastered the beast. Not bad for a Ford Fiesta jock.

I was cruising, until I hit the traffic.

It would have been quicker to swim. I got as far as the top end of the Croisette then was turned away by the gendarmes; they'd declared gridlock and nobody else was getting through. I didn't protest, or shoot them. I found a backstreet and parked. I left the keys in the ignition. Happy birthday, somebody.

There was a gun in my pocket and one thought in my mind. I stopped at the Petit Carlton, a pub version of the larger seafront hotel and the focus of most British drinking activity in Cannes. It was full to overflowing, as were the drinkers. They crowded out onto the pavement and the road. I slipped through them into the pub so that I could peruse the dailies, the freebie trade newspapers that kept everyone up to date on the deals that were being made and what was being shown, where and when; they sat unread on a table squashed into the corner. It only took a moment to check. If Sean was attending a competition film at the Palais des Festivals, then he was attending his own.

It shouldn't have surprised me.

While my world had been falling apart, while

people had been dying and getting thumped and dealing drugs and floating face down in pools, Sean had been working away, completing his film. Even though I was virtually certain that several of the cans of film I'd liberated from Paralog had ended up in a canal, he had evidently still been able to claw from the police what was left of his masterpiece and complete his post production in record time, and now he was ready for his moment of triumph.

I checked my watch. The movie had started. His fans, and there were many, would have screamed for him as he entered, and I intended to give them an additional reason to scream as he left.

They were forty-five minutes into the film already. The guide listed it as a three-hour epic. And after that there would be time for the standing ovations and the press conference; then, and only then, would he appear back on the Palais steps to acknowledge his fans and then leave.

I had three drinks, two beers and a Smirnoff, just to settle me. I was thinking about a fourth for good luck when I saw Victor *facking* Dalgetty weaving through the crowd outside. I didn't know whether he'd kiss me or kill me, so I ducked out the side entrance before he saw me. I snuggled the gun in my pocket and started to walk. I'd had my last drink, perhaps for ever.

It was a fifteen-minute walk to the steps of the Palais des Festivals. The road remained gridlocked. Tens of thousands of film fans were jammed on the sidewalks and pressed between the stationary cars; equally many stood penned back from the Palais steps by crash barriers. The whole scene was depicted on a giant video screen which dominated the front of the building. From time to time the focus of the screen would change from the Palais exit to the steps, and from there to the huge white stretch limo waiting at their foot. A double line of crash barriers had been set up around it and stretched for several hundred yards, allowing the vehicle to cut not only through the crowd, but also through the gridlock. If he wanted to, Sean could make a swift exit. But I knew him well enough to be sure that he would linger to milk the adulation. They wouldn't have seen the film, they didn't know if it was a classic or a piece of shit. All they were interested in was that he was a star, and just as they wouldn't have been able to guess from his demeanour that his wife was dead, neither would they be able to judge how his movie had been received.

I eased into the crowd. I spent the best part of forty minutes working my way forward. An inch, a foot at a time; the nearer I got to the front, to the limo, the tighter it became. I was drenched with sweat. I stepped on toes. I kicked the backs of heels and looked away. I oozed, I eased, I pushed, I blew alcohol and farted ill wind. But I got there, because I had to. I would not be moved. My hands gripped the crash barriers. Just a few yards separated me from the limo. There would not be enough space for me to lever my body over the barrier when he appeared; I would be lucky to get enough room to remove the gun from my pocket and start shooting. There was excited jaw-jaw to my left and right and behind, and I understood none of it; maybe it was French, maybe it was English, nothing was getting through.

My brain was gridlocked.

Time stood still, or seemed to.

My wedding day.

Little Stevie.

Walks in the park and laughs.

Elmo in Grouchland at the cinema.

There was moisture on my face, but it wasn't sweat.

I had to kill in their name.

He was not an innocent man, neither was he the worst in the world.

But he would die, because it was the only chance they had.

Some time later a roar went up. I glanced at the video screen and saw Sean O'Toole emerge.

Camera flashes and screams filled the air. His face seemed to be sixty feet high, and the smile that filled it did not seem to be one of disappointment.

I eased my hand into my jacket. He was coming down the steps. For once his guards were giving him a little space. It was contrary to the rules of security, but Sean was making his own rules. This was his moment. One of them, anyway. And perhaps his final one.

My hand closed around the gun. My finger caressed the trigger.

As Sean drew closer the roar around me grew in volume and pitch. The crowd pressed forward, edging towards hysteria. The security guards were pointlessly scanning the sea of faces for trouble: too many camera flashes, too many waving hands, too many manic faces.

And then he was but a car length away.

I removed the gun, kept it tight to my chest.

He stopped, raised a hand, smiled, waved.

The moment.

Do and die.

I raised the gun.

I aimed, I fired.

I did not drop the gun until six bullets had exited the barrel.

I did not drop the gun until I saw blood explode first on his arm, then on his chest; once, twice, three times.

I did not drop the gun until I saw him fall behind the car.

I did not drop the gun until my job was done.

CHAPTER 39

There is a silence of relief which comes with being locked in a cell after carrying out a heinous but necessary crime. It is not a real silence, because there are always phones ringing and footsteps on stairs and the cries of other prisoners, and there is also the memory of greater noise: of people screaming and sirens wailing and the thump-thump sound of fists into face; but it is still a kind of silence, a calm satisfaction that comes with having completed your task. That you have done everything you can, that you no longer have any control over what others might do.

Hours.

I was brought water, and peered at quite a lot through a peephole.

The gendarme with the water said nothing, but did not seem especially unfriendly. Perhaps he was not French.

I said, 'Has it been on TV? Are there reporters outside?' He put down the plastic bottle of Evian, raised his eyebrows a fraction and left.

But of course there were. It was a stupid question.

Sean O'Toole was dead. Film star. Cannes. Murder on the Croisette. Any moment now the door would re-open and Hercule Poirot would stroll in.

Somewhere, somewhere else.

Mouse was a reporter, it would have come in over the wires moments after I'd killed Sean O'Toole; if he was at home, they'd phone him, but he wouldn't be at home; he wouldn't just have left it to the police, he would be out with them, and if not, he'd be out there by himself, searching, following leads; he would not go home until he found my family.

The Colonel, sitting in his bare cell, would be told, and he would think a while, then he would demand proof. They would show him a TV and he would know it was true because there would be nothing else but Sean O'Toole. *That's showbiz.* Hastily compiled obituaries and clips of his finest big screen moments. And then there would be pictures of me, from TV cameras and handicams and use-once-and-throw-away tourist cameras, pictures of me dragged and beaten by the mob and then rescued by the police. Grave-voiced commentators would refer to me as the man *suspected* of killing Sean O'Toole, when it was all too bloody obvious that I had done it.

I was an assassin.

Does France have the death penalty?

I couldn't remember. Probably not.

But does it still have Devil's Island? Was I destined

for some Papillon-like existence, dressed in rags and endlessly trying to escape? More likely I would get an agent, sign a book deal and sell the movie rights for many millions of dollars. That was the way it worked. Nanny child-killers and cancer-stricken bank tellers did it, so would I. My money problems would be over, once I had served my time, much reduced because of mitigating circumstances. We could spend the rest of our lives on a sunny island somewhere.

We.

I hammered on the door. 'I need to know about my wife! I need to know about my son! In the name of Christ tell me what's going on!'

I thumped and kicked and slapped and cried and cracked my head against it.

Nothing.

Heartless.

Cruel.

I lay on the bed and buried my face in the pillow. It smelled of detergent.

After an eternity the door clanked open again. I stayed face down. The voice said, 'Dan?' and it was Irish with a twinge of America and I turned and looked at Sean O'Toole smiling in. 'How're ya doin'?' he asked.

I swung my legs off the bed. 'I'm asleep. You're a ghost.'

'No, you're awake and I'm a critically acclaimed director. If we spin this out long enough they might even give me a posthumous Palme d'Or.'

302

I said, 'What the fuck are you talking about?'

He stepped into the cell, and then to one side as Maurice, my taxi-driving Interpol agent, entered behind him.

I put my head in my hands. 'I don't believe this,' I said.

Maurice crossed to the bed. I thought for a moment he was reaching out to shake my hand, but instead he passed me a mobile phone. 'It's Belfast. The Colonel has given the location.'

I sat up straight, I held the warm plastic to my ear. 'Hello?' I said.

'Mr Starkey?' came the response, slightly out of breath, with the sound of a roaring car engine and a siren nearly drowning him out. 'This is Inspector . . .'

'Give me the fucking thing,' came a voice from his background, and then there was a burst of static and then: 'Dan? Is that you?'

'Mouse?'

'Listen, we're getting there as fast as we can.'

I looked from Sean to Maurice, I said: 'Where?'

'Ormeau Baths.'

'I don't under—'

'It's an art gallery now. The Colonel says there's a basement below, that's where they are.'

'Does he know if they're . . . ?'

'No, all he gave us was the loca—'

I lost the signal. I looked up desperately. Maurice took the phone back and punched a number. I said to Sean, 'You look well.'

303

He smiled warmly. 'Considering you shot me six times, I suppose I do. But then blanks don't generally do you much harm, although you'll agree those blood squibs are quite effective. Give you a bit of a sore tummy if you swallow too much . . .'

'Have you got it?' I snapped. Maurice shook his head.

'Once it was explained to me,' Sean continued, 'I had to go along. Well, I'd no choice really, they caught me with a carload of stuff . . . but I would have done it anyway. Put you in a terrible position . . . if it's any help, I would have done exactly the same, I'd have shot me. Of course I wouldn't have done it over that bitch, she got what she deserved, been going through my bank account like . . . well y'know . . . too romantic, that's me, cost me a fucking fortune . . .'

'Got it!' Maurice said.

I took the phone back from him. I looked him in the eye and said, 'Thanks,' and he knew it was for more than just getting me the line. 'Mouse?' I said.

'Dan, welcome back. We're there. We're going in now. In through the door, lots of pretty pictures, the staff have just seen us, look at their faces, we must look like the 7th Cavalry coming through . . .'

'You are, Mouse.'

'No, *you* are, Dan. Where's the basement? Where's the fucking basement? This is where most people would say it's going to be okay, but I'm not going to lie to you, son. Do you want me to stop this now? See what the score is, phone you back?'

'No, I want to stay with it.'

'Okay, mate.'

There were footsteps, dozens of them. Heavy breathing, a door being hammered.

'What's happening, Mouse? Mouse, what's happening?'

'Sorry . . . sorry, they're just trying to get in . . . okay, okay, there's boys with axes going to break it down . . . sorry, stand back . . .'

There was the sound of sharp metal on dank wood. Then metal on metal, then a loud crash and more footsteps.

Then voices – but not Mouse's: 'Where are those torches?'

'That fucking smell . . .'

'Get it up here for Jesus . . .'

I sighed. Sean looked away. Maurice put an arm round me and I shrugged it off.

'Okay, Dan, we're going in . . . Jesus, dark and . . . where? Okay . . . must be . . . watch where you're fucking walking . . .'

There was a muffled, distant, 'Over here!' Then answering shouts and a flurry of footsteps and Mouse's laboured breathing . . .

'Mouse?'

There was no direct response, just urgent removed voices. 'Doctor! Where the fuck . . .'

'Mouse?'

'I need space, I need fucking space!'

305

'The boy! Check the boy!'

'Mouse!'

'Dan, I think she's alive. I think she's alive.'

'Mouse!'

Just heavy breathing.

'Mouse!'

'She's alive, oh God, she's alive.'

'Mouse . . .'

'Dan . . .'

'My son . . .'

A pause. 'What can I say, Dan?'

Little Stevie had been dead for two days. My wife had clasped him to her for all of that time, aware that he was dead, but unable to let go. It wasn't the hunger, it was the cold. Hypothermia. He was only a toddler. He was just learning to talk in sentences and he loved Winnie the Pooh.

CHAPTER 40

The festival had been over for a week.

Sean had been tipped to pick up the top awards, but his fake assassination and the perception of it as a tawdry publicity stunt to boost *The Brigadier*'s chances persuaded Martin Scorsese and the rest of the judges to bestow their favours on a Latvian soccer drama and a Taiwanese adaptation of an obscure Finnish love poem instead. But the press loved it, especially the French film critics; they were already hailing him as a post-modernist genius.

Sean was on top of the world. Fox had made a lucrative offer not only to distribute his black-and-white art film in the States, but also to throw their weight and money behind an Oscar campaign. Nor was he particularly tearful over Alice's death; he wasn't even sure if they had been married at all; no certificate had surfaced and he had no memory of the actual event, just her word for it. There was a photograph of them in a Las Vegas chapel with a priest dressed as Groucho Marx, but what did that prove but that they were just heroin addicts deeply in lust?

By the end of his stay there was another girl on his arm, and they were already talking about marriage, although not until after the Oscars. If he was still addicted, there was no indication, but then there never really had been. An orgy at a party and a needle in his arm. So what? You take your kicks where you can, I've just never had any inclination to try either, apart from the former.

Sean paid for an apartment for me, told me to stay as long as I wanted. He didn't have to. Maurice disappeared and never really told me anything, beyond the fact that he'd exerted a little pressure on Sean to cooperate; once convinced, Sean had gone for it in a big way, suggesting the fake blood squibs himself. He'd spotted me at the Hotel du Cap, but hadn't let on. It had been an exhilarating experience for him and he was already talking about making a film based on it. A film about a film about a film.

I ate in hotel cafés, facing the beach. The prices had come down now that the film junkies had departed for their next festival, this time in Venice; there was a preordained annual circuit, like Formula One, only faster.

One day, walking along the beach, I saw a familiar figure coming towards me.

'*Bonjour*,' I said.

'*Bon appetit*,' said Mouse.

'Funny bumping into you here.'

He nodded. He was wearing a Hawaiian shirt and flip-flops.

'Walking?' I asked.

He nodded again, and we began to stroll across the sand. The sea was rough. There was a storm a-comin'.

'When are you coming home, Dan?'

I shrugged.

'Patricia needs you.'

'How is she?'

'Still in hospital. She's getting better. But one phone call, Dan, it's not enough.'

'I know.'

I kicked at the sand. 'You hear that about people who haven't eaten for a long time, they gobble everything down, then they're as sick as dogs. Was she like that?'

'Dan.'

'It's what I hear.'

'Come home now. She won't let them bury Little Stevie until you come home.'

'Why?'

'Because he's your son, Dan.'

I shook my head. 'No, he's not.'

'Dan.'

'She had an affair. He wasn't mine.'

'Dan.'

'He had ginger hair. Did you ever look at him? He looked nothing like me.'

'Dan, don't do this.'

'I like it here. It's sunny. Let Tony do it. He's the dad. He can hold the coffin. Little white ones, aren't they? They're always little white ones. Like

309

shoe boxes. I bought him shoes. Do you know that? I bought him shoes once, and they had Winnie the Pooh on the side. He said, "I love these so much," and he wouldn't wear them. They're too small for him now, Mouse. They're too small.'

I looked at Mouse, and there were tears rolling down his cheeks. It might just have been the sand, blowing up. There was a lot of sand.